This book is dedicated to the scared inner child inside us all.

SHADOW'S DEADLINE

SHADOW ISLAND SERIES: BOOK THREE

MARY STONE

LORI RHODES

DESCRIPTION

When death has a deadline...

The late Sheriff Alden Wallace has barely been laid to rest when another body is found on Shadow Island. Once again, former FBI agent turned interim sheriff Rebecca West's vacation plans will have to wait.

This time, the victim is the son of one of Shadow Island's privileged elite. Found gruesomely posed at a picnic table in the park—suffocated, choked, and shot, with a cryptic note shoved in his pants—his death is as personal as it is disturbing.

And he's the first one on the killer's list.

When a second young man is murdered in a similar fashion, the questions and the stakes increase. Who had so much rage against these men? A girl they treated poorly? Or were the murders somehow connected to the secretive and exclusive organization of rich men no one on the island wants to talk about?

The deeper Rebecca digs, the more certain she is the Yacht Club is involved in the spate of crimes on the island...and the late Sheriff Wallace may have been covering for them. The club members will stop at nothing to keep their secrets. But Rebecca is determined to expose them, regardless of the cost.

From the provocative beginning to the edge-of-your-seat conclusion, Shadow's Deadline—the third book in the Shadow Island Series by Mary Stone and Lori Rhodes—will remind you to choose your friends wisely.

1
———

Bryson Gilroy hunched over next to a longleaf pine tree, using its trunk to stabilize himself. He took a few deep breaths, hoping to keep his stomach contents down. He wasn't drunk. Not exactly. Not anymore. But a massive hangover was in his very near future.

Swiping beads of sweat from his temple, Bryson stood and continued his walk of shame.

Couldn't the bastards have taken me all the way home?

Some "club" they were. He didn't feel special at all.

Though the humidity was like a weight pressing on his chest, at least it wasn't boiling hot, since the sun hadn't yet risen. Storm clouds lay thick and heavy over the ocean, creeping toward land and cooling the air a few merciful degrees.

It wouldn't last, he knew.

The mounting barometric pressure did nothing to help his growing hangover. With a shudder, he took another swig from the beer bottle he'd somehow managed not to drop.

Hair of the dog, right? Isn't that what Coach used to say?

Bryson gritted his teeth as his mind conjured up an image of the man who'd ruined his life.

"Don't think about him."

He needed to get home so he could collapse on his bed. After zigzagging across the beach, he'd headed for the park, a shortcut. Time was of the essence. Who knew how much longer his stomach could hold onto its contents? Plus, he didn't want to be seen by anyone in his current condition, and the sun would be rising soon.

"One foot in front of the other."

He ran his hand through his hair, the oily residue of his gel melting in the humidity. Wiping his hand down his long-sleeved, button-down pink shirt, half of which was untucked, he longed to feel clean again. Maybe he'd take a shower before crawling into bed. The idea of hot water streaming down his neck and shoulders was almost enough to get him to walk faster.

Almost.

It had been another night of doing what everyone had come to expect of him. Partying, drinking, networking, and banging. Unconsciously, he scratched at his crotch where remnants of his sexual encounter had dried and taken hold.

Yeah, I need a shower.

Bryson took another swig of beer as he tried to forget the face of the girl he'd taken into a cabin on the lower level of the yacht. He actually cared about her. Gabriella. In truth, he was devastated to see her come aboard. And so, he'd snuck her off to a seldomly used room so the other men wouldn't mess with her.

It hadn't worked.

One of the "boys" had come bursting into the cabin, telling Bryson to join him in the hall. After assuring Gabriella he'd be right back, he had. It wasn't like he had a choice, after all…

"You gonna do her or what?"

Bryson hated this creep most of all. Almost. Hal was what everyone called him. Bryson didn't know his full name and didn't want to.

"Uh, yeah. Of course." Bryson did his best to seem cocky. In truth, he wanted to cry, scream, punch something.

This was Gabriella*. The girl he'd liked for years. The girl who was way too good for him, even now.*

"Then do it." Hal pressed Bryson into the wall, holding him by the throat. "Or I will."

He would, Bryson knew. He couldn't let that happen.

Bryson swallowed against the pressure still on his neck. "I will."

The hand dropped away. "Make it a good show. Not just missionary either. Doggy. Sixty-nine. Your last show was less than stellar."

So Bryson had.

Humiliated and disgusted with himself, he stumbled through the park.

His tears had mingled with Gabriella's as he'd climaxed. It should have been different with her. Special. But once again, his happiness had been stolen, controlled by someone else.

Bryson's life was not his own.

Had it ever been?

Yes. But that was before. The day his coach took a *special* interest in him, life as Bryson knew it had ended. And he'd barely been sixteen.

He paused to take a long pull on the bottle in his hand. Funny how the drinking couldn't wash away the memories of all those encounters. Or the drugs. Temporary relief at best.

If he was honest with himself, or anyone for that matter, he knew he needed help. Real help. But asking for it was out of the question. His high and mighty father would never allow it.

Weak. That's what he'd say. And the man would want to know *why.* And that was a secret Bryson would just as soon take to his grave.

He sighed as his shoulders sank.

What's my life even worth?

It was that bastard's fault. The perv who couldn't keep it in his pants. The way he'd place an arm on Bryson's shoulder after a game and let it linger there. The way his fingers brushed against his skin.

His stomach turned, and he had no idea if it was from the memories of Coach or his drinking binge.

It's Coach.

All those extra special practices when Bryson had to stay longer than everyone else. As soon as his last teammate left, that man would do unspeakable things no shower could ever cleanse.

He shook his head and regretted it immediately as the trees listed from side to side. He'd entered the park as a shortcut to his home, or rather, his father's home with his new wife. What was she? Ten years older than Bryson?

She could be my damn sister!

Again, he shook his head and was angry for forgetting the state of his alcohol-soaked brain. At this early hour, he was the only one on this trail, so he was alone with the scars of his past and present.

Realizing he was actually on a trail, Bryson paused and looked around. The tall shagbark hickories and rosebushes blocked his view, and his heavy eyelids didn't help.

Wiping his hand over his face, he checked the bottle in his hand. Half full. He could grab another when he got home before hopping into the shower. His privates were starting to itch, and he pondered if he'd contracted an STD.

No, he knew he'd been Gabriella's first. He hated himself for that. Maybe they could've had something. Bryson chuckled a mirthless laugh. His father would say she was below his social standing, and that would be the end of that.

His mind was awash with self-disgust. And Bryson's memories, both old and recent, refused to abate in this self-inflicted, weakened state.

Coach watching him in the locker room. Coming up behind him. Pinning him against his locker, pressing the full length of himself against him. Into...

He broke into a light jog until his inebriated brain sent the message that it couldn't handle all the bouncing. Nope. He could never tell dear old dad what happened that day, or the others that followed. Somehow, it would turn into his fault.

Not strong enough. I was asking for it. Queer.

It wasn't Bryson's choice to live with his father and step-mom. He supposed most people would envy the various creature comforts, complete with an ever-present waitstaff. But that was only because they had no idea what a prison it was. The price his soul paid by staying there. He had no independence. No freedom. No sense of self. The on-site caretakers might as well have been prison guards.

Everything was orchestrated by his father and the others to maintain control. Except for one thing.

Bryson had begun drinking and using after he'd been repeatedly violated by his coach. And guess who'd provided the illicit drugs and drink? Yep, Coach himself. The man had been intent on screwing Bryson in every possible way.

The only thing that freed him from the perv's clutches was graduation day. It should have been a day of celebration. But he'd traded one prison for another when the tassel was moved to the other side of his mortarboard.

The night before graduation, his father had dropped the bomb. Bryson's "behavior" had proven he couldn't be trusted to go off to college. He would live under his father's roof and be given a position at his father's company while one of the assistants monitored his progress in obtaining an online degree. If he refused, he'd be cut off financially...forever.

At that point, nothing mattered except for the next pill.

And doing whatever the bastards told him to do.

Oh sure, Bryson had a title at his dad's company, but the salary was basically a glorified allowance.

Trying to be optimistic, Bryson had rationalized that the job might bring him closer to his father. A way to connect. But then dear ole Dad had killed that pipe dream by refusing to let him do any meaningful work. It was a slap in the face. Once again, the great Albert Gilroy had made it clear that he had no respect for his only son. The stares from his coworkers and the whispered insults were more salt in a wound that ran soul-deep.

Could he blame them?

He spit to free himself of the bile rising in his throat. Everyone always told him how lucky he was, but they had no idea. The booze, drugs, and girls never made him feel any better. Worse, actually. It was all an act. A house of cards.

"Bry...son."

What the hell was that? It's official. I'm losing it...

"Bry...son."

Bryson whirled to his left, trying to locate the source of the whisper. Adrenaline punched through his system, fight warring with flight enough to tangle his legs. He nearly tripped over his own feet but managed to stay upright.

Coach? Shit. It can't be. Can it?

Steeling all his nerves, he willed his tired eyes to search the surrounding trees. There was nothing on the trail or in the woods. He picked up his pace, careful not to upset his intoxicated mind.

"Bry...son."

The whisper came from the right this time. Or had he just

gotten turned around? Was he going back the way he'd come?

"Bry...son."

He whirled around and stumbled over a tree stump in his path.

Where the hell did that come from? Jesus, get control of yourself.

He grunted with frustration, wondering how he'd gotten so far off course. He'd come this way countless times, and he'd never passed that stump before.

Chicken. Baby.

"Bry...son."

As he swiveled, his brain sloshed against the inside of his skull. Had he seen something move in the trees? In the predawn shadows, he couldn't make anything out.

Reorienting himself toward the direction of home, he stumbled toward the path, lurching over the soft, sandy soil.

He walked into a couple of branches before getting back on the open trail. With a few scratches on his face, he finally began to make some headway.

"Bry...son."

This time the whisper was closer.

His face pressed against his locker. The scent of stale sweat.

Raising his beer bottle into the air like a club, Bryson charged toward his tormentor hiding in the trees, ready to fight. Bursting through the tree line, he did his best warrior impersonation. "Come on out, you fucking coward!"

There was movement on the ground, and then an explosion.

White wings flashed and swirled around Bryson's spinning head. Orange beaks and feet streaked his vision, flying wildly away. The flock of seagulls assaulted Bryson's senses, and he winced from the pain their cries caused. He'd interrupted their breakfast, and they were enraged, exacting their revenge as they flew away.

As their angry rant diminished, Bryson realized his right arm was wet. His rolled-up sleeve was soaked, drenched in lukewarm beer that was dripping off his elbow.

"Just perfect. Story of my damn li—"

A plastic bag slid over Bryson's head, wrapping and twisting around his face and neck, cinching tight. He filled his lungs to scream but only managed to suck the bag into his gaping mouth.

Swinging wildly, Bryson lashed out with the empty beer bottle, smashing it against something. The grip slackened on the bag, and Bryson wrenched himself free.

Sprinting away with his only weapon, he fumbled with the bag around his neck using his free hand. His exhalation reeked of beer and clouded his vision. But the inhalation was worse. He was suffocating, sucking in the moist plastic bag and not much oxygen. And no matter how hard he tried, he couldn't get the bag off. It was knotted around his neck.

Through the fog, he could make out a figure. A head, arms, shoulders. Approaching. Unwavering.

His lungs screamed for air, desperate to expand. He dug his fingers up under the front of the bag and sucked in what little air was available with a strange, high-pitched whistle. He could feel his pulse pounding in his ears. Running blind and out of breath, he tripped and crashed to the ground, only throwing his hands out at the last second.

The bottle he'd been carrying shattered on a rock. Pain tore into his palm. Unable to clearly see, he pushed to his feet. His heart raced as his lungs futilely gasped for even a mouthful of air.

With both hands free, Bryson clawed at the strings wrapped tightly around his neck. A desperate fire burned in his lungs as if he'd been underwater for too long as the plastic, once again, was suctioned up his nose and into his mouth.

He tried biting through it, but then he was yanked backward by the collar of his shirt.

The plastic pressed tighter against his face, further blurring his vision and choking off the last remnants of oxygen. Tumbling back, Bryson slammed into something hard. Stars danced in his vision from the impact of his head against what had to be one of the many trees in the park.

A shadow fell over him. His assailant. As he tried to sit up, thick leathery hands came down around his neck, crushing Bryson's larynx. He was pressed against rough bark. He needed to get his coach's hands off him.

Stop touching me!

Bryson clawed at the gloved hands, but his arms betrayed him, growing weaker from the effort. They were tingling. He could barely feel them.

"Bry...son."

A face pressed against his.

Not Coach.

Heat radiated off his attacker's forehead as he pressed it hard against Bryson's.

Bryson's pleas for mercy dwindled to whimpers and then became unspoken altogether as darkness overcame him.

I'm sorry, Gabriella.

He was sorry for all the others too. All the girls he'd forced into the spider's web.

Bryson's arms fell limp at his sides, his distorted features became lax and still behind his mask, and the world faded away with each thud of his heart...until that was gone too.

2

Shadow Island Interim Sheriff Rebecca West drummed her fingers on the steering wheel of the cruiser while she waited for Senior Deputy Hoyt Frost to join her. She still couldn't believe it.

Another dead body on this peaceful little island?

Found on the day the island's previous sheriff was laid to rest?

In fact, she'd only been at the oceanside post-funeral get-together a few minutes when they'd received the call.

Unbelievable.

Worse, she hadn't even gotten a taste of Meg Darby's famous peach cobbler.

Heaving out a long breath, Rebecca yanked her inner drama queen back into the far corner of her being. Not eating cobbler was certainly not worse than a dead body, but dammit…

Another case so soon after the last was as unexpected as it was unwelcome.

But here she was, waiting for her lead deputy to change into his uniform so they could head to Sand Dollar Park to investigate. When Hoyt folded his long legs into the SUV, he was still buttoning his shirt.

"Couldn't find a telephone booth to change in, Clark Kent?"

The corners of Hoyt's mouth turned up, deep wrinkles furrowing paths around his dark blue eyes and mouth. "Haven't seen a phone booth since," he frowned, "hell, I don't know. Had to make do in the back seat of my truck."

Rebecca glanced down at her trusty khakis and navy polo shirt and was glad that she'd gone home after the burial to change out of her dress. Since she was only supposed to have worked one case after the late sheriff had knocked on her door begging for help, she didn't have a uniform. Only a cobbled-together duty belt given to her by Deputy Frost's wife.

Speaking of Angie...

"Your lovely wife okay with you having to leave so quickly?"

Hoyt adjusted himself so he could tuck in his shirttail. "Yeah, she was fine, but Boomer was not."

Rebecca smiled at the thought of the long-haired collie. "Pouting?"

"Full force." Hoyt buckled his seat belt. "Those puppy eyes should be illegal."

Thrusting the transmission into drive, Rebecca took off. She wasn't only driving because Hoyt had to change. He was barely back on duty after an emergency appendectomy a couple of weeks back. She'd taken a bullet to the vest during their last case, and it'd left quite the bruise, but she was in less pain than her deputy.

Her duty belt wasn't the only thing that was cobbled together. The sheriff's department staff was too.

She was serving as the interim sheriff to a group of exactly four deputies. Hoyt, the most senior, still wasn't allowed to drive per doctor's orders. Darian Hudson, the youngest of the group, was supposed to be on paternity leave, cuddling his new baby girl. Like Hoyt, he'd come back after the death of his sheriff. Trent Locke...ugh.

Rebecca growled low in her throat just thinking of him. If she wasn't so desperate for coverage, she'd use her interim powers to take him and his badge to the street.

That left Greg Abner, a sixty-one-year-old mostly retired deputy, to fill out their ranks. He was only supposed to work part-time, but since Rebecca had been on the island, he'd been pulling many more hours than that.

"Oh...you're going to need to drop me back home since Angie needed my car."

"I'm sorry about this, Frost." She jerked her head in the direction of the gathering on the beach behind them. "I would've liked to hear more stories about Sheriff Wallace. And I hated to pull you away."

"It appears we're never gonna catch a break with all the crap going on around here. That means we'll be working together a long time."

She felt his gaze on the side of her face, clearly checking for her reaction. She offered a noncommittal "um" in response.

"Anyway, I have plenty of time to chew your ear off about Alden. And I think it's time you start calling me Hoyt. 'Kay, Boss?"

"I'll call you Hoyt if you'll stop calling me *Boss*."

"Chain of command, I'm afraid. Not gonna happen." Hoyt's smirk was so wide she could see it in her peripheral vision.

"Can you tell me what dispatch said? What are we walking into here?"

"I don't know much. Melody said a witness is waiting for

us at the park. Stated they *think*, emphasis on think, that they found a dead body at a picnic table."

A dead body was never good news. But on the heels of finally laying the late Sheriff Alden Wallace to rest, it was almost too much to bear.

Rebecca's stomach growled, and she briefly pondered if the person at the picnic table had died of starvation like she was sure to. To no fault of the witness, the interim sheriff and her senior deputy had been called away before either of them could try the homemade cobbler and barbecue being served at the wake.

Hoyt slumped in the passenger seat, gazing idly out the window, apparently unaware of her hunger pangs. Clearly, he was mourning. Having to delay burying the man so they could catch a kidnapper and stop a child sex trafficking ring had taken its toll on the whole sheriff's department. But they'd saved three little girls and busted up the ring…for how long, she didn't know. There was always another scumbag to replace the ones they took down.

Rebecca had been relaxing at the makeshift beach wake they'd held for Wallace. She was especially enjoying spending time with Boomer.

Maybe once I settle down, I can get a dog. Of course, I'm never home long enough. Not very fair to a loyal companion.

Refocusing on the task at hand, Rebecca pondered how calm Deputy Frost had been when he'd relayed the message about the corpse just a few minutes ago. Perhaps she needed to give him more credit than she had been.

She made a mental note to not only get the witness's full statement but also their shoe prints and contact information. Hoyt's deep sigh drew her back to the present.

"You okay?"

"I just can't believe this shit." Hoyt sat more upright, his hand moving to his healing side with the movement. "Can't even put Wallace to rest, and we've got this to deal with. What the hell has happened to my idyllic home?"

"Ya know, I was just thinking the same thing. I remember Shadow Island being a sleepy little town where nothing much happened."

The Yacht Club popped into Rebecca's mind. The secretive organization of rich, elite men. Had they been operating here back when she was just a little girl playing on the beach?

She sighed. The beach.

Now the members would party on their yachts and make pit stops along the beach to pick up girls and drugs. And by girls, sadly, it was literally *girls*, not young women. Teenagers. So far, every local she'd spoken to knew something about it, but not much. Just the rumors they'd heard from other locals over the years.

All except one young woman who'd left town following the death of her best friend and her own subsequent assault. She had been to a few Yacht Club parties and knew faces and names. At least, she had said as much in the brief conversation Rebecca had been able to have with her. Once.

Serenity McCreedy had never come back in after giving her victim statement. Her father had said she needed to get away to heal and asked they respect her need for privacy. Rebecca wasn't sure how much of that she believed, but she also wasn't going to hound a barely legal teenage girl to get her to talk about one of the scariest moments of her life.

Especially when the Virginia Commonwealth's Attorney didn't need her testimony, since Rebecca had gotten a full confession and three officers had witnessed Stacy McCreedy's assault, which was the name on her birth certificate.

"We were a quiet little island. Alden handled most of the calls by himself, even. Of course, we'd still run the domestics, the property disputes, the kids caught stealing bikes, and typical tourist bullshit. But mostly, that was it. Nice and boring, just the way I like my job. And home every night twenty minutes after the end of my shift." Hoyt threw a mischievous grin at her. "Hell, sometimes Alden would even finish up my paperwork so I could leave on time."

Rebecca's head bumped into the Explorer's headrest with the force of her snort. "Lemme just stop you there. You're going to do your own paperwork tonight, Deputy Frost."

It was good to laugh and joke. It was what cops did to relieve the tension caused by their job. But part of her wondered if there really had been so few crimes. Or was it possible that Sheriff Alden Wallace had hidden most of it? Had the previous sheriff turned a blind eye, and the steady misdeeds over the last few weeks were the real norm? That was a terrifying thought.

Only a few days ago, they'd stopped three little girls from being sold after getting kidnapped. Had that happened here before without any reports being filed? The idea turned Rebecca's stomach.

"Everything changes, even us. If things really are changing here, I'm glad you're the one in charge of taking care of it."

Rebecca glanced over at Hoyt, but he was focused outside his window. Was he goading her again?

"What makes you think I'm sticking around?"

"Well, you did rent that house for three months. I think we can win you over before that runs out."

Rebecca groaned just thinking of the little Sand Dollar Shores cottage she'd barely spent any time in since her arrival on the island. It was the home her parents rented each year when she was little. Rebecca had chosen it to steep in the memories of her mom and dad and to just relax a little.

She snorted again. "I rented a *vacation* house. So I could take a *vacation*. Not so I could go back to work. I wanted to sit back and drink craft beer, get sunburned, eat some fish, and read some books. Then, and only then, did I plan to think about what I'd do next."

"Still trying to figure out what you wanna be when you grow up?"

She flipped him the bird. "Funny."

Why did he even want her to be sheriff? Most men his age would refuse to work for a younger person, especially a woman nearly twenty years his junior.

Her father had been sixty-one when he was brutally murdered, only a few years older than Hoyt now. She briefly wondered what her dad would be doing if he hadn't been killed. Would he be on Shadow Island? This was the time of year they'd always vacationed. She'd still be with the FBI but would have joined them unless she was stuck on a case. Which meant she wouldn't be acting sheriff now.

Deciding to get this out in the open, Rebecca cleared her throat to get Hoyt's attention. "Why do you keep insisting I take on the role permanently?"

Hoyt turned to face her as much as his seat belt would allow. "Because I don't want to stand in Alden's shadow." His blunt response mirrored his expression, one as serious as any she'd seen from him.

"Oh."

"Alden was my best friend. A great guy. A great cop. And politically savvy. I was at his side for most of that. If I became sheriff, I'd always be compared to him. And always come up short. At my core, I'm a deputy. Not a leader. To be sheriff, you need to be both. That's not me. It's you." He opened the glove box. "Besides, you're the one who signed the paperwork when Alden died."

Turning into the park's entrance, Rebecca put the Explorer in park before throwing her hands up in frustration. "I was the only deputy not on leave. Someone had to sign it!"

Hoyt held his hands out in an open shrug. "Round here, we'd say that was God's plan. So just accept it, *Sheriff* West." He opened the door and slammed it shut, as if that settled the matter.

Rebecca was going to be sheriff whether she wanted the role or not.

She'd parked in the small lot, not wanting to disturb any potential evidence in an effort to get closer to where the caller had said they *thought* they'd seen a dead body. Until the scene could be investigated, Rebecca couldn't be sure how wide any evidence might be scattered.

She slid out of the Explorer, her shoes sinking into the sandy soil. Sighing, she reached for the bag she'd recently begun storing behind her seat.

Tossing it on the floorboard, she unzipped it, and pulled out a pair of coveralls and old sneakers. Dropping the sneakers, she stepped out of her work shoes into the coveralls and wiggled her foot into the first sneaker. Repeating the process, she was covered and ready to work. She tossed her shoes into the back seat where they wouldn't get ruined and hoisted her bag onto the driver's seat.

She pulled out her modified utility belt. The sheriff's office didn't have one small enough to fit her, so two of the deputies' wives had thoughtfully made one for her. It worked just fine, for now. If she was honest, she was growing rather attached to it.

Shrugging the coveralls into place over her shoulders, Rebecca zipped them up and walked around the SUV to meet her deputy while settling her belt into place.

Hoyt glanced over at her and grinned, transforming his stern expression into a charming one. "Are those hand-me-downs from your big brother?" He nodded at her outfit, lips pressed together in a clear effort not to laugh as she rolled up the too-long sleeves. She'd already taken a pair of scissors to the legs so she wouldn't trip on them.

Rebecca lifted an eyebrow at her senior deputy but ignored how much her outfit was amusing him. "One of the good things about living close to so many bases in D.C. is all the secondhand gear you can get." She held her hand out to him and waggled her fingers.

Hoyt passed over the crime scene camera they kept in the cruiser and shrugged. "Why are they shiny?"

"Waterproofing. It seems wherever I go on this island, I encounter something *wet*." She let the word hang in the air, and Hoyt smiled.

Rebecca approached a ghostly pale man in red basketball shorts and a tie-dyed t-shirt who stood at the edge of the lot. She lifted her badge and introduced herself.

"I'm Sheriff West. Are you the citizen who called 911?"

The man nodded, his lips so deplete of blood flow, they were blue. "I'm Jeff Calhoun." His dog tugged at his leash, and Mr. Calhoun leaned down to pet the miniature schnauzer. The dog rolled onto his back for more. Straightening back up, the witness looked from Rebecca to Hoyt and back. "I was just out walking Moose and wanted to refill my water bottle." He held it up and shook it, indicating the task had gone unfulfilled. "We both get pretty thirsty in this heat."

Rebecca was pleased Hoyt was recording the statement in his notepad. "What happened?"

"I knew there was a drinking fountain by the smaller picnic area, and so we headed that way." Mr. Calhoun shuddered and inhaled an uneven breath.

"I know this can be upsetting. You're doing a great job. Please tell me what you saw."

"Thanks, yeah. Okay, so when we came into the clearing, I

noticed someone sitting oddly at the picnic table. But I wasn't even sure it was real because there was a bag streaked with red over the head. It almost seemed like a Halloween stunt." He shook his head before sighing. Moose tugged at his leash again.

"What happened next?"

"I was going to move closer to inspect, but then Moose started whimpering. He backed away like he was scared. And I, I looked again at the table and...oh god—" Mr. Calhoun slapped a hand over his mouth and turned away.

Rebecca placed a hand on his back and patted gently. "I'm sorry. Are you okay?"

Their witness nodded, straightened, and wiped his arm across his mouth. "Sor-sorry. That's basically it. Moose was freaking out, so we hightailed it away from there. I called 911, and she told me to wait until you got here."

"Thank you for that. I know reliving that wasn't easy." Rebecca removed a business card from her breast pocket and handed it to Mr. Calhoun. "If you need someone to speak with, to help you deal with what you've seen, call the number on that card, the medical center."

Mr. Calhoun glanced at the card before shoving it into the pocket of his shorts. The schnauzer was officially done and made it clear he had better places to be. Rebecca bent and petted the dog's uncropped black and gray ears, giving one a slight tug. She wanted to put the man and his companion at ease. Kneeling next to the dog was less threatening.

"I just have a few more questions before you go. Can you tell me if you noticed anyone suspicious in the area while you were walking this little cutie?"

He shook his head. "No, no one." He smiled down at Moose before shifting his gaze to her.

Rebecca ran through the rest of her questions with the

same result. Nothing had seemed unusual or out of the ordinary until he'd stumbled upon the body.

"We'll need to get an imprint of your shoe for exclusion purposes." Rebecca gestured to one of the CSI techs who'd just pulled in. She recognized him as one of the attendants of the funeral. Lance Something-or-other. No wonder he'd gotten there so quickly.

"Oh, uh, sure. Can we make it fast? I don't want Moose to get overheated."

Standing, she extended her hand and shook Mr. Calhoun's. "We appreciate your time and will work as quickly as possible." She nodded at the CSI tech, who nodded his agreement. "Thank you for reporting this and waiting around to speak with me. Please don't hesitate to call that number if you need it."

Hoyt handed him another card. "Call if you think of anything."

Once Mr. Calhoun's shoe print had been obtained, he made his escape. He moved to the far side of the small parking lot, with Moose leading the way, and disappeared down the road from which they'd come in.

Rebecca exchanged a look with Hoyt. "No time like the present. Guess we should see what freaked out Mr. Calhoun so much he almost lost his lunch."

They walked in the direction the witness had indicated and were soon gobbled up by the trees. It was at least ten degrees cooler in the shade. She almost missed the narrow trail that veered off from the one they'd been following.

"Sign's down." Hoyt indicated the *Picnic Area* sign hidden behind a bush.

When they stepped into the small clearing, they both stopped to survey the scene.

Propped up at a cement picnic table was a man in a pink dress shirt. He was seated in an unnatural position, his head lolled over his right shoulder. It was impossible to ID the vic because his head was completely encased in a blood-splattered plastic bag.

"I guess that's technically a *red* bag." Rebecca sighed. "Frost, tape off the perimeter, then call the M.E. Coordinate with the crime scene techs too. I have a bad feeling about this."

3

"Good thing we put booties on." Hoyt's gallows humor briefly lightened the mood. Then, keeping an eye on where he was putting his feet, he stepped onto the gravel bed where the picnic table sat. "Okay...yeah, we definitely have a real vic and not some Halloween prank."

Rebecca snapped pictures, beginning with the front of the body. As if he were simply enjoying a picnic, he sat with both of his arms resting on the table, apparently propping him up. His arms twisted outward in what would have been a painful position...if he were alive. His chest leaned forward, and his legs were akimbo. Rebecca pondered if rigor had helped hold the man in place.

Her gut told her he'd been posed.

She made mental notes of all the questions she'd have for the M.E., starting with the estimated time of death. Based on what she understood about rigor mortis, this man would have been dead for hours based on current rigidity. How had he been there all day without a single other person noticing him?

The bagged head tilted to his right. If the vic had been

alive, she'd have thought he was deep in thought. He appeared to be male, medium build, undetermined age, though she guessed he was young, considering the lack of wrinkles, wear, and age spots on his hands.

"Manicured fingernails on the unidentified male, but the skin is dirty and scraped. Right palm appears to be cut. We'll need to ask the M.E. about possible defensive wounds."

As she recited information, Hoyt jotted everything in his notes.

A notepad was another item she'd need to add to her belt.

Kneeling, Rebecca avoided touching the body as she inspected it under the table. The front of his khaki pants was dirty and scuffed, and they were bunched around the knees. His leather boat shoes were in even rougher shape.

Was the victim killed here or elsewhere? Were the pants bunched because the body had been staged here? Had he been dragged?

From her distance just across the table, glimpses of the anguished face peered through the blood-splattered bag encasing the victim's head and neck. A single, clean hole punctured the front of the bag at the forehead.

Rebecca snapped additional photos of the ground, table, and surrounding area before moving to the victim's right side. One could never tell what piece of evidence would break a case, so she worked to document even the most innocuous detail. She paused to study the head from the new angle. "Can you tell what kind of bag is over his head?"

Hoyt was on the opposite side of the body. He crouched and leaned closer. "Not sure. Almost looks like one of those nicer bags you can get at a shoe store or something. Except this bag is transparent and appears to be even thicker. And I don't see a logo on it anywhere." He peered over the victim's tilted head. "Man, the bag is really snug around the neck. Almost cutting in with the drawstrings pulled tight, though I don't see any dried blood." He lifted his eyes from the neck area. "Okay, correction. I see plenty of blood *inside* the bag. Just none where the bag is cinched."

Rebecca inspected the neck too. Bruising on both sides along with raised welts. "So far, we have a GSW to the head, possible asphyxiation, and evident strangulation. My instincts are screaming this was personal."

Sizing up the victim from this angle, it was apparent that the cuffed sleeve on the arm closest to her was discolored, and when Rebecca leaned in close to determine what it could be, she inhaled a faint hint of...beer? It was difficult to tell over the growing aroma of blood and death, but she thought so. She narrated all her findings to Hoyt before continuing behind the corpse.

The back of the coral pink shirt was dirty and scuffed. "Back of the shirt is much dirtier than the front. Scratches in the fabric indicate possible contact with something rough."

There was little blood on the concrete pad, but Rebecca trod carefully. Although she was wearing booties on her shoes, she didn't want to crush any evidence not immediately apparent to the naked eye.

"These might be drag marks." She indicated two lines marring the area, disappointed that they didn't extend farther. "The marks aren't long enough to serve as arrows pointing us in the right direction, but the killer may have gotten tired of carrying the body and put him down more than once. We'll need to get CSI to flag this whole area and see if they can find an origination point." The camera whirred as Rebecca snapped multiple photos.

She added more questions to her list of mental theories. Was there more than one killer? Was that why he'd been suffocated and shot? But if there were more than one killer, it'd be unlikely the victim was dragged, which was what appeared to have happened. So was the killer—*singular*—

somehow infirmed or frail? Possibly old? Possibly a woman? Though that felt like a stretch, for some reason.

If the body had been staged…why? To send a message? Out of remorse? To show up the sheriff's department? Or maybe to humiliate the victim in some way?

On closer inspection, the victim's braided belt was scratched and coated in sandy soil, especially along the back bottom edge. Leaves and detritus clung to the scraped fabric and gathered inside his cuffed sleeves, indicating he'd been dragged the usual way, by his legs.

"There's no exit wound I can see. Bailey can tell us more about the bullet when she does the autopsy."

"Did I hear my name?"

Rebecca smiled at the approaching medical examiner. "Wow. I thought it'd take you longer to get here. Does my deputy need to write you a retroactive speeding ticket?"

Dr. Bailey Flynn chuckled. "Do you want me to turn around and go home? Say no more." She pretended to turn back toward the parking lot before spinning back around with a wink. "I ran by the Community Health Center after the funeral to see a few old friends, so I hadn't even left the island when I got the call."

Rebecca took in Bailey's black dress. "I'm glad you did."

Bailey stopped short of the taped-off area to finish assembling her protective gear. As she approached the victim, she snapped on her nitrile gloves.

She peered at the face distorted by the plastic. "Do we have an ID on the vic yet?"

Rebecca gestured to the bloodied bag. "Nope. We can't get a clear look at him through all the blood and brain matter, and I didn't want to touch him yet to check for a license."

Bailey stepped around the concrete pad, taking Hoyt's spot next to the man's left side. "Okay, I overheard bits of what you were saying when I arrived. I can confirm a GSW to the forehead." Leaning closer, she recited her observations. "Bruising indicates signs of strangulation. And this bag," she waved her hand, "indicates asphyxiation. Too little blood on the head wound for the gunshot to be the cause of death."

Proud of herself for being right, Rebecca nodded. "That's what I thought too. The gunshot was just to make sure the victim was well and truly dead."

"Mission accomplished." Bailey continued to move around the body. "I'm afraid any grand unveiling will have to wait until he's on the table. I called one of my assistants to bring the wagon from the mainland so we can transport the body."

"Much appreciated. I…" Rebecca paused when Bailey frowned. "What?"

"This might be a suicide bag."

Rebecca shivered. She'd heard of those but had never seen one up close and personal. "How do you know?"

"See how thick the plastic is and the tight connection around the neck? Some bags have Velcro, but others are similar to this." She walked a full circle around the body before going on. "Obviously, the tubing that would introduce a fatal gas into the bag is gone."

Rebecca studied the plastic. "But if a person wanted to suffocate someone, a plastic this thick would sure help."

"It sure would, and the strings would have made it very difficult to remove." She pointed to a section of exposed neck. "See the scratch marks? Looks like he did try to free himself. Oxygen deprivation would have set in quickly, especially since he most likely would have been breathing much faster than usual."

An image of this man clawing at the bag flashed through Rebecca's mind. "That's terrible."

"It sure is."

The M.E. nodded and continued to study the corpse until

a physically fit, thirty-something woman pushing a gurney with a body bag emerged through the trees. "Here she is now. Sheriff West, this is Margo Witt, one of my assistants. Sharp as a tack and gunning for my job."

"Ha. Maybe after you become Chief M.E. for all the Commonwealth. Until then, I'm at your service." She mock bowed, and her auburn ponytail swung down by her freckled face.

With one hand on the victim's shoulder, Bailey tipped him back and forth. The body didn't unfold. Each joint was locked into place. "He's in full rigor. I'll know more later, but the rough guess on time of death is eight to twelve hours ago. Livor mortis will give us additional clues when I get him on the table."

Rebecca pulled off her gloves and wiped her sweaty palms on her pants. "It's bothering me that this man sat here all day without anyone noticing."

Bailey glanced around. "It is strange, but of course, it's not out in the open right here."

"True, and the picnic sign was down." The surrounding trees suddenly seemed foreboding. "I could use an ID pronto."

Bailey shot her a thumbs-up. "Will do." She reached for the body bag. "This is going to be tricky."

Rebecca grimaced. Playing Tetris with a body in full rigor wasn't something she ever wanted to do. "We'll leave that to you then." Ready to escape, Rebecca gestured to the woods. "Since it appears he was dragged to this location, we need to locate the actual crime scene." She gave the M.E. a little salute. "Talk to you soon."

Bailey blew a stray strand of black hair from her face. "I'm sure you will."

"Hey, Sheriff." Lance, the crime scene tech, waved as Rebecca emerged back onto the main path. His entire body was cloaked in protective gear, with only a circle of pale face visible from where the hood covered most of his head. Aviator-inspired glasses perched on the bridge of his nose. "I got something you'll want to see."

Hoyt joined her, and they walked to where the technician squatted next to an evidence marker. Rebecca recognized the indention in the ground for what it was. A footprint.

Lance traced the outline of the imprint with his finger. "I'll make a cast but thought you might want to photograph it first for your case file."

Rebecca snapped a few images. "Looks like it might belong to a man." Lance nodded his agreement. "Find any blood or indicators that our vic was killed in the park?"

He shook his head. "We're working our way out from the scene." He gave a small shrug and nodded toward the picnic table. "Seems like overkill, eh? You thinking jilted lover?"

Out of nowhere, a mental picture popped into Rebecca's mind, and she recalled a time she'd believed she'd found the love of her life. Calvin Steel. He was a data analyst with the Bureau and insisted she stop investigating her parents' death. He'd maintained her quest was no different than some people's obsession with Bigfoot. She couldn't be with someone who didn't support or respect her. Or believe in Bigfoot. That was the real scale tipper.

A childhood memory pushed thoughts of Calvin to the side.

Blood on tiles slowly spilling away from a gashed wrist.

Half-closed, dead eyes...

The mental picture was replaced by another, but it wasn't of her parents this time. Now, a thirteen-year-old girl lay dead in a bathroom stall of her middle school. Rebecca never found out why she'd cut her wrists. Or why the girl chose to kill herself at school instead of at home.

Even though Rebecca had been the one to find the body,

the police had convinced her parents not to give her any information about the situation. They said she was too young to process it. That it was "better this way," so she could forget about it and move on.

Instead, being kept in the dark had propelled her down a path to join the FBI, so she could always get answers. As much as she had loved her parents, they'd been overly protective in some regards.

"Sheriff?"

Rebecca blinked and stepped back into the present. "Yes?"

The crime scene tech looked concerned. "You okay?"

She forced a smile. "Of course. Sorry. I was sorting through all the things we still need to do."

Lance returned the smile. "Seems like it never ends."

Rebecca wiped at a bead of sweat trickling down her temple. "Nope. Frost taped off what we think is the dump site, but we need to comb through the park to see if the victim was killed here or brought from another location."

Lance sighed and rested his forearms on his knees. "I was afraid you were going to say that." He looked at the open woods around them. "I'll need to call in some backup to help out. Otherwise, we'll be here all night. My bosses don't like all the overtime we've been getting recently."

Rebecca nodded. She completely understood that. A large part of the sheriff's department's overtime had been spent scouring the island recently too. "Do what you need to do. If need be, I'll talk to your boss."

"Mighty nice of you, ma'am."

"Let's get back to the cruiser so I can get some of this detail down."

Hoyt stood and stretched out his back before following. When they emerged from the woods, he stopped. "There's another paved parking lot about a quarter mile that way. A trailhead there." He pointed to the northeast. "There are a few small businesses around there. We should check them too. Maybe we'll find someone who saw something."

Rebecca mulled that over. "Bailey estimated the time of death at eight to twelve hours ago. Any of those businesses open at five in the morning?"

Hoyt pursed his lips. "Not likely, but they might have security cameras. Looking at footage worked out so well on the last case. We may as well try to use it for this one too."

Her deputy was a quick study. Maybe staying on as sheriff wouldn't be so bad with her current team...except Locke.

A loud engine interrupted Rebecca's thoughts. Since forensics was actively tagging the crime scene and Bailey and her assistant were still with the corpse, Rebecca wondered who would be arriving. Everyone who should be here was accounted for.

She turned as a shiny black Cadillac skidded to a halt next to the cruiser. As the driver's-side door flung open and an angry man emerged, Rebecca silently cursed.

What hell was descending on her now?

4

———

Beside Rebecca, Hoyt sighed and rolled his shoulders, as if getting ready for a fight. "Well, hell."

Rebecca took a step closer, lowering her voice. "Who is it?"

Hoyt ignored her question and headed toward the Caddy, his arms in the air, waving to get the new arrivals' attention.

The angry-looking man stomped their way, the tail of his tailored business suit flying behind him like a cape.

Then the passenger door opened, and a second man emerged, half the age of the first. Maybe early thirties.

"Is it true?" the first man screamed from twenty yards away.

The guy who'd ridden shotgun yelled after him. "Mr. Gilroy...sir. Let's go somewhere else to talk."

Gilroy? Where had Rebecca heard that name before?

"Don't tell me what to do!" Gilroy's face was mottled with emotion, spit exiting his mouth along with his words. "Now you tell me." He narrowed in on Hoyt. "Is that Bryson?"

The younger guy picked up speed and was now jogging in their direction. His equally tailored suit provided no indication that he was carrying a weapon, but Rebecca kept an eye on him.

A glance at Bailey indicated the body was already wrapped up. They just needed to finish zipping the body bag closed.

Hurry, she mentally projected at the M.E. Because, without introduction, she knew this man was indeed the victim's father. They were built exactly the same, with similar brown hair. His green eyes blazed.

Shit. Shit. Shit.

Putting her body between the men and the crime scene, Rebecca approached just as the sharp-dressed man stuck a finger in Hoyt's face. "You better tell me the truth, you little son of a—"

Enough was enough.

"Mr. Gilroy." She stuck out a hand. "I'm Sheriff West. I'm happy to answer your questions, but here isn't the place or time."

He ignored her hand, his face growing redder as his mouth worked to find a sentence. Before he could, the second man spoke up. "Why wasn't my client notified that his son was killed? This is a violation of his rights. He has a right to see his son's body."

How did they know the victim's identity? Hell, even she didn't know.

She couldn't risk the crime scene becoming contaminated. But they seemed to know more about the victim than she did at the moment, so...

"What makes you think the victim is your son?"

Both men ignored her. Gilroy was now on a tirade, spouting everything he would do to Hoyt if he didn't get his way.

To his credit, her deputy simply stood with his arms held wide, blocking them from getting closer to the trail.

Rebecca didn't like being ignored, nor would she tolerate her deputy being disrespected. It was time to assert herself. She pitched her voice lower and squared her shoulders, projecting from her diaphragm, as she'd been trained to do. "Excuse me. I need to know what you're doing here. I cannot have my crime scene contaminated."

Both men stopped bickering and turned to stare at her.

"Do you know who my client is?" The skinny lawyer personified shock and indignation as he gaped at her. Rebecca stifled a chuckle as she contemplated the man's physique. Deputy Frost possessed a wiry frame, but this man made Hoyt look stout.

Gilroy began to sputter. "I'm here because I want to see my son. Now let me pass!"

"Your son?" Rebecca glanced over her shoulder and then back at the two well-dressed men. "Can you tell me how you know the identity of my victim when—"

"Your victim? And just who exactly are you?" Globs of spit flew from his mouth as he emphasized the last word.

"I'm the sheriff." Rebecca stepped between Hoyt and Gilroy, moving him by simply invading his space until he had to fall back. She needed to preserve her crime scene and find out why this man thought he knew the victim. He didn't retreat as much as she'd hoped, apparently too confused or shocked to do anything for a moment.

"Sheriff? Wallace was sheriff around here. Where is he? Bring him to me so we can get this straightened out." Gilroy was trying to order her around like a show dog.

"Sheriff Alden Wallace died in the line of duty and was actually buried today. We've just come from his grave. And I would like to know why you think the body found in this park is your son, Mr. Gilroy."

Rebecca stared him in the eye, watching every move he made.

She could feel the heat of Hoyt's body behind her, not stepping any closer but not backing down either. "Especially since there's been no positive ID."

That statement seemed to stump them both, and Gilroy looked at his lawyer. The attorney rolled his shoulders. "Why not let my client see his son? Then he can identify the body right now."

Rebecca gritted her teeth but kept her tone neutral. "If Mr. Gilroy's son is our victim, I cannot allow you to see him right now. First, we don't know if this is your son, as I said. But if it is…" She faced Gilroy squarely, giving him a sincere look of sympathy. "Some images never leave our minds. Don't make this the last time you see your son's face. Let us transport him back to the morgue and get him cleaned up, then you can see him." She softened her tone even more. "I understand the wait will be agonizing, but you'll appreciate it more every day moving forward."

For a moment, the pain won out, and Gilroy ducked his head, spinning away from her. His hands moved up to cover his face.

"Our medical examiner will take very good care of him. Meanwhile, I'd appreciate it if you could answer some questions. When the M.E. is ready for you, you can identify the body properly. This way, we can maintain the crime scene and have a better chance at catching whoever did this."

"See that you do." Gilroy spun back around, enraged. He shook his finger in her face like she was a naughty child. "Because if you don't, I'll find someone who will."

5

A t almost ten that night, Rebecca massaged her temples, fighting off the headache the new case had caused. Bailey Flynn had confirmed that Bryson Gilroy was, in fact, the body posed at the park picnic table. The ID had come, no thanks to his father.

For a man who'd been hell-bent on seeing his son at the scene, he apparently couldn't be bothered to visit the morgue. But thanks to Bryson's run-ins with the law over the years, his fingerprints were on file.

Once the victim was identified, the case had kicked into high gear. Rebecca attempted to contact some of Bryson's snobby friends first. Not a single one of them had been helpful, if they'd deigned to speak to her at all.

She was still waiting to hear about a warrant for the boy's phone, financial records, and living quarters. While combing through a victim's family and friends could be tedious, often valuable clues to the killer's identity were buried in the details.

Bryson resided with his father and stepmother, Annika Gilroy, Albert Gilroy's second wife. The senior Gilroy had a place on the beach in the exclusive Sandcastle Court area only a quarter mile or so from the park. He worked as a lobbyist in D.C. and came down whenever it suited him. His son and second wife lived on the island year-round.

She was still awaiting the crime scene report. The techs, working more overtime, had promised to call the office with any findings.

It was way past dinnertime, and her grumbling stomach echoed through the mostly empty office. Locke was on night shifts now, but he wasn't in the station. Melody Jenkins, the night shift receptionist, worked dispatch. She read in between calls, so the office was silent except for Rebecca's playlist streaming from her phone while she slumped over her desk with a paper cup of coffee and a stir stick to chew on.

Rebecca had churned up Bryson's past. He'd been the captain of his private high school's lacrosse team. His grades had been good until a few months into his sophomore year, which was also the same time he'd begun to accumulate "warnings" for underage drinking and public intoxication, as well as several speeding tickets. But no real consequences seemed to follow his actions. It was difficult to know if there were any underlying issues or if the kid had just stopped caring.

One surprising detail was that someone of Bryson's social class had not gone on to college. Rebecca speculated that the senior Gilroy could have more than compensated a university to accept his son, despite his lackluster GPA. Instead, after graduation, Bryson had gone to work for his father's lobbying business. She couldn't fathom how an eighteen-year-old fresh out of school with zero experience could have survived in those shark-infested waters. But he had for two years.

Bryson's social media presence was fairly active, typical

for someone his age. He had both real and spoof accounts on several platforms. Lots of sexist memes you might expect from a rich kid and a lot of pictures of him partying. She'd ascertained that some of his social media "friends" included a few locals, but none she knew. Perhaps one of her deputies, or even Viviane, might recognize some of the names and faces.

While Bryson was apparently coasting through life, Albert Gilroy had been hard at work. Lobbyists typically remained low-key, but outside of the D.C. Beltway, Albert was quite active in other pursuits. His name and face were linked to a myriad of businesses. But her digging had not revealed what he did for any of those companies.

The ringing of Rebecca's phone paused her music, and she glanced down at the screen. It was Hoyt.

"Did you miss work so much you're eager to come back in?"

"Just the opposite, Boss. After you dropped me off, I got word from my neighbor that a pipe broke in his kitchen. Just got back and cleaned up, then realized you're probably still stuck at the station." He paused. "You are, aren't you?"

Rebecca stretched the muscles in her neck. "Yep, but not for long. Do you need anything?"

"Have you eaten dinner yet?"

Rebecca perked up at that. "No. I'll just grab a sandwich."

"Angie is still used to cooking for two extra hungry boys. There's too much for both of us. You wanna come join us?"

She glanced at the time. "At ten o'clock?"

"Broke pipe, remember? We're just about ready to sit down."

Rebecca's stomach voted yes. She tossed her stir stick into the trash. How could she argue if someone else was cooking?

She stared at her computer screen and the smarmy smile of Albert Gilroy. He might be an asshole, but he and his family deserved justice. Perhaps Hoyt could identify some of Bryson's friends from his social media or provide any unofficial dirt on the family.

The details of the murder screamed it was personal. She needed to know everything about the family she could get her hands on. Plus, it was a home-cooked meal, and she wouldn't have to eat alone.

"Do you have any good beer?"

❄

"I CANNOT BELIEVE you invited Rebecca to dinner tonight without talking to me about it first!" Angie stewed, running around the kitchen and straightening all the things that didn't matter.

Hoyt stood at the stove, rolling asparagus around in the skillet. He exchanged a glance with Boomer, his ancient collie. From her soft bed, the dog gave him a *you screwed up again, asshole* look before curling back into a tight ball.

Angie breezed by him and ran into the front room to pick up a stray cup off the coffee table. While there, she spotted Hoyt's boots and tossed them into the big bin at the front door. Then she ran to the bin and pulled the boots out, setting them beside the door on their own instead. When that was done, she stared at the cup in her hand, as if wondering how it had gotten there.

Yup, she'd worked herself into a tizzy. Hoyt giggled on the inside just watching her. "We've got plenty of food, and she lives all alone in a rental house. It's the neighborly thing to do."

Angie huffed at the cup before turning a glare at her husband.

Hoyt quickly went back to stirring the vegetables. He knew better than to interrupt one of her tizzies.

"We're not neighbors, though!"

Surprised at her attitude, he turned to search her face. "Honey...this is a small town. Everyone's our neighbor here. Why don't you want to be neighborly to West? Is it because she's new?"

Angie froze, her jaw falling open, then she flung her hands up in frustration. "You're looking at this all wrong. Of course, we should have her over for dinner. But not last minute."

Storming to the sink, she dropped the cup in with a clatter and opened the oven door, making Hoyt dance back so as not to get burned.

"She's your new boss, and this is the first time she's coming over. The house is a disaster. My hair is a mess. I need to change my clothes. And all I made for dinner was chicken, some veggies, and mac and cheese." Angie grabbed the fork and poked the chicken breasts before turning the casserole dish. "I could have made a roast, or Momma's lasagna or—"

"It's your famous crispy ranch chicken!" Hoyt stared wide-eyed at his wife, dumbfounded at how she was demeaning her excellent cooking. "And this isn't the boxed crap. This is your baked five-cheese macaroni. It's my favorite meal."

Angie paused in her fretting and looked up at him. The anxiety drained from her face. Then, rising on her tiptoes, she kissed him. "You are such a dear. A dear, sweet, loving man I am blessed to be married to." She kissed him again.

Hoyt started to lean into the kiss, heedless of the heat by his shins, when a car door slammed in the driveway.

"She's here!" Angie jumped back, kicking the oven door closed with her heel as she spun and ran for the bedroom. "Stall her. I need to get changed."

Understanding dawned as Hoyt walked to the front of the

house. Just as the first knock sounded, he swung the door open.

West stood on his doorstep still wearing the same khakis and polo from before.

"Hey, come on in. Dinner's almost ready." He stepped back and let her in, then closed the door. "Angie's just freshening up real quick. She made her world-renowned crispy chicken tonight, so I hope you're hungry."

Inhaling, West smiled. "Smells delicious." She glanced down at the row of shoes and the bin of sandals. "Would you like me to take my shoes off?"

"Um…"

Hoyt was caught off guard, not sure how to answer. Angie hated when people tracked sand into the house, but she'd also rebuked him for treating this like having a friend over. West saved him from having to decide.

"I probably should." She slipped her shoes off.

Her expression indicated she was only doing it to be polite, but he appreciated it.

Holding her hand up, she showed Hoyt a bottle of wine. "Looks like I brought the wrong kind. I don't think you drink this with poultry. It's pretty basic." She passed him the bottle, and he read the label.

"Rosé, huh? I'm not much of a wine man, myself, but if I do drink it, I like muscadine pretty good."

West grimaced. "I've never had it myself, though I hear it's all right. I didn't want to show up empty-handed." She tapped her short nails on the bottle. "This one is pretty sweet from what I know of it, so maybe it's like muscadine?"

Hoyt headed to the kitchen. "I reckon we're about to find out."

"Thank you again for inviting me over."

Hoyt nodded toward the dining room just off the kitchen. "Have a seat. You can relax while I get things finished." He set the wine on the table and then went back to the pan on the stove as Boomer trotted over to greet their guest.

What a day.

It'd begun with the burial of his dear friend. He'd been celebrating the life of Alden Wallace at the beach, surrounded by people who loved the man. Then, before grass could grow on his boss's grave, a dead body had surfaced at the park.

At the scene, it was fairly clear the death had been overkill. Personal. West had theorized as much.

What the hell is happening on this island?

Who had this much rage toward a twenty-year-old kid? A girl he'd treated poorly? Or was it somehow connected to the Yacht Club?

Life had been peaceful on Shadow Island until his new boss had smacked the hornet's nest. Had her unofficial war on that group caused all this?

Hoyt shook off the question. No, none of this was her fault. Besides, he was at home and needed to relax. Grabbing hot pads out of the drawer, he tossed them on the table.

"Anything I can help with?" West offered, spreading out the pads he'd just tossed.

"Nah, take a load off. You want something to drink?" He checked the asparagus, saw it was done, and set a lid on top before turning off the heat. It was his only contribution to the meal, so he didn't want to mess it up. "I can open the wine, or I have that beer."

"Whatever you're having is fine."

The legs of one of the chairs scraped on the floor as West pulled it out. Releasing a relieved sigh, she settled onto the thick cushions. Boomer curled up at her feet.

Hoyt grabbed two beers out of the fridge and returned to the table with her drink and the skillet.

"So what kept you at the office so late?" He set the food out and slid the can over to her before sitting down.

"Just checking out the victim and his family." She cracked open her can and then leaned forward on the table, careful to keep her elbows off it, he saw. "Anything you can tell me about the family? Or who might want one of them dead?"

That was just like West, jumping straight to the point. "Albert Gilroy is a lobbyist in D.C. I doubt he has many friends." Hoyt shook his head. "Except I can't see any reason to kill his son. The boy might've had some minor brushes with the law, but never for things where he hurt someone, far as I know."

"And the dad?"

"That man would just as soon sue you as shake your hand. You met his lawyer today. I don't think he goes anywhere without him."

"Speaking of the attorney, do you know his name? The guy was so keyed up, he never identified himself."

"That's Steven Campbell. I was surprised when he didn't shove his name and credentials down your throat. He tends to puff up a bit like a rooster, but he's mostly harmless. Albert's a different story, though." He shook his head. Memories came into focus the more he pondered the man.

"Come to think of it, most folks Albert Gilroy shakes hands with have been sued at one point or another. Anyone who's had a business dealing with him. Even the real estate agent who sold him his house. And the county, too, for some zoning issue. Rich man trying to make more money by taking it from people who don't have any to give. No one in town will do business with him now. He even has to get outside contractors to mow his lawn."

"So not really a pillar of the community, then?"

"More like a cesspool. A drain on the community. Bad as

he is, though, I reckon he still loved his son. It's a damn shame when a parent outlives their child."

West turned the can in her hands. "It is."

Hoyt cursed himself, remembering that West had lost both her parents more than four years ago. Given her manners, he suspected her parents were good people who'd raised her right.

Your life isn't the same after you lose a parent either. Let alone both.

"I have to say, though, Albert was never around very much. His wife and kid lived here all year long, but Albert treated his visits like a vacation. Only he didn't spend that time with his son. I've heard from folks that when Bryson was younger, there were a handful of nannies, caretakers, staff, and people like that to watch over him. Once he was a teenager, his behavior became more erratic. He'd cruise around in that convertible his dad bought the minute he got his license. The kid got more than a few speeding tickets in that. Gave him a few myself."

Hoyt ran his thumb over his jaw, wishing he had something stronger than beer. There was something about seeing the body of someone you watched grow up. Made you rethink every interaction you ever had with them.

Thank God his face had mostly been obscured by the bag. Still, the reality of what Bryson had experienced in his final moments had been plain to see.

"One time when I pulled him over, he was cocky as hell. But what seventeen-year-old boy in a souped-up car isn't? He asked if I knew who his dad was, and if I knew the connections he personally had. Told him I did, and if he wanted, he could use those connections to beat the ticket, but I was still writing him up for speeding. He paid his ticket, and that was that."

West barely waited for him to finish his sentence before leaning over the table. "And did he have connections?"

Hoyt knew where this line of questioning was going and got right to the point. "Rumors had him running with the Yacht Club people. Just like his dad did. I've caught glimpses of him on more than a few party boats out on the water, but that's about it." He rubbed his jaw again and leaned back from the table. "Wallace always took care of those reports, though."

It felt disloyal to say that about his friend to the man's replacement, but Hoyt didn't think Alden would mind. Too much. He'd always said if there were someone else that could take down those bastards, he'd wish them all the luck in the world. That recollection led Hoyt to another realization.

"Near as I can figure it, and I've given this a lot of thought over the last few weeks, Alden had some deal with the Yacht Club. I'm not sure if it was anything bad, but I do know we weren't ever really bothered by them. Any crimes linked to them were small, petty things. I can't see Alden turning a blind eye to anything big."

The bedroom door swung shut, and Angie walked out, cutting their conversation short. Her light brown hair was freshly brushed. She'd put on one of her favorite dresses, he noted, and was even wearing a few pieces of jewelry.

"Rebecca, I'm so glad you could make it to dinner. It's nothing fancy, but I hope it'll fill you up."

Hoyt stood, smiling at his wife, while West rose to meet her hostess, holding out the bottle she'd brought. Boomer groaned and plodded back over to her bed.

"Anything homemade is better than what I could've cobbled together for a meal. I'm honestly not a big fan of cooking, but especially with an electric stove. My place in D.C. had gas. I've already burned every grilled cheese sandwich I've tried to make, thanks to not controlling the temperature better."

Angie chuckled. "It can be tricky. I've never known anything but electric, so I'm sure you'll pick it up given time." She bustled to the oven. "Sit yourself down and let me get dinner on the table before I'm the one who burns the meal." She handed Hoyt the oven mitts. "If you want a few pointers, I'd be happy to teach you."

Hoyt could tell that she was trying to keep any censor out of her voice, and he loved her for it. Kids these days just weren't taught the basics anymore.

West's cheeks turned pink. "I know how to cook, but it's difficult when the oven doesn't act the way I'm used to. And, well, my last year in D.C. got pretty, um, complicated, and I lived out of hotels for a while. One of the things I was looking forward to when I rented the house was cooking nice meals. No longer having to survive on takeout. Maybe even grill."

"Well, you don't have to worry about that tonight." Angie set the casserole dish on the table while Hoyt placed the chicken.

West's eyes widened as she took in the cheesy noodles and perfectly breaded chicken breasts. "Between the heavy workload and my ongoing battle with the electric oven, I haven't succeeded in making anything nearly as delicious as all of this smells." Her eyes darted between the dishes. They settled on the skillet of asparagus as Hoyt lifted the lid.

She was practically drooling, the poor kid.

Angie winked at him. The simple gesture was her way of telling him that he'd done the right thing by inviting West over. She smiled at their guest. "Don't stand on ceremony, dear. Dig in. There's plenty."

West apparently didn't need to be told twice. And, after

helping herself to a heaping portion of vegetables, she used the serving fork to spear a crispy chicken breast.

Hoyt picked up the serving spoon, scooped up a big helping of cheesy noodles, and plopped it onto her plate, earning him a grateful smile.

It had been madness almost every day since the woman across his dining room table had signed the paperwork to help Sheriff Wallace track down a missing girl. Only a couple weeks later, she was now attempting to fill his shoes.

If she stayed.

If she didn't suffer the same fate as Wallace.

The hairs stood on Hoyt's arms at the thought. His new boss had poked a bear. There was no doubt she was great at her job, but at what cost? Would her desire to learn more about the Yacht Club and its members cost them much-needed tourist dollars?

Or worse?

What had Alden been doing for the group? Hoyt refused to believe his friend had been a dirty cop. But he couldn't ignore how much was being unearthed by West's investigations.

Each case since Wallace's death had him second-guessing everything. Was it just criminals thinking they could get away with their crimes now that a new, untried interim sheriff was in charge? Or had this always been going on, and his old friend had kept it hidden? Even from his senior deputy?

Hoyt wasn't sure he wanted to find out.

6

Rebecca walked into the sheriff's department juggling a box of doughnuts and a large to-go carafe of coffee. For once, Viviane wasn't sitting at the receptionist's desk. No one was. That was strange enough, but as Rebecca balanced her packages to use her key fob to get through the little half door, whispers coming from around the corner ceased as it opened.

Viviane, Darian, and Hoyt all looked up from where they were huddled around Hoyt's desk.

Oh yeah, they were talking about me.

Viviane's expression gave it away. Rebecca shrugged it off.

"I brought in doughnuts and coffee if anyone wants them."

Rebecca set the box and bag on the table next to the coffee maker before choosing her favorite raspberry-filled treat. "I know we have coffee on hand, but Alden told me this was the good stuff. I figured I'd pick some up while I was there."

No one moved. They all continued to stare at her silently.

Rebecca took a bite of her doughnut and poured herself a cup of coffee from the carafe. Still, no one moved, but they did look uncomfortable.

"No one likes doughnuts?" She scanned their faces. "Or was your conversation just so intense you want me to leave so you can get back to it? Perfectly fine eating all these myself."

That got them moving.

Darian hurried over, flipped open the lid, and selected a maple bar for himself. "Does this mean you're sticking around, ma'am?" Crumbs fell from his mouth onto his shirt, and he brushed them aside.

Rebecca gazed at her pastry. "Are doughnuts seen as some sort of sign of commitment in these parts?"

"As far as I'm concerned, doughnuts are always a sign of commitment." He licked glaze off his thumb. "If you're trying to win me over by feeding me, I'm totally okay with that, by the way. Anything that will help me stay awake when Mallory summons me in the middle of the night." He grinned broadly, his pale brown eyes sparkling.

Hoyt boomed out a laugh. "I love my boys, but I do not miss those midnight feedings. People say you get used to it, but you don't. You just have to get through it and enjoy every minute with your baby while she's still your baby."

"That's the plan. And having a boss willing to stuff me with sugar will help with that." Darian shoved a huge chunk of the doughnut into his mouth.

Viviane walked over and peered into the box. Rebecca made a bet with herself about which one she would choose. She was pleased when Viviane selected the chocolate sprinkle and took a big bite. She'd guessed right.

Now that the others had made their selection, Hoyt joined them, pouring himself a cup of the excellent coffee but not taking one of the sweets.

"We weren't gossiping or anything." Viviane looked at the men. "Okay, maybe it was gossip, but it was nothing bad. We were just talking and realized you've barely had a day off since you started."

Well, Rebecca had been forced to take a few days of leave after discharging her weapon, but other than that, she'd been at the station every day since.

She reached for a second doughnut. Was that really what that was all about? "Well, no, I haven't. But it's not like there's been an opportunity."

Viviane frowned and looked even more guilty than before.

Darian waggled the maple bar at her. "I'm back on full-time duty, so there's no reason you can't take a few days off. I can man the fort for a bit on my own."

It was sweet that they cared so much about Rebecca's well-being. When was the last time someone had worried about her at all?

Hoyt raised his hands in surrender. "Hey, I'm just looking out for the new kid. If you're going to do this job, then you need to take care of yourself. You can't do that if you spend all your time at work. And I happen to know that you're the one who writes the schedules."

Rebecca took a sip of her coffee, thinking it all through. They weren't wrong. She could use a couple of hours to unwind. But taking any time off was out of the question right now. They had a case to solve. Once again, Rebecca questioned the late sheriff's management style.

Had everyone just taken time off when they were tired? They were already a skeleton crew. Who did that leave available?

"Tell you what." She shook her doughnut at Darian, mirroring his mock scolding from earlier. "Once we get this case put to bed, I'll take some time off if the workload allows."

"Can we get that in writing?"

Rebecca smiled without responding.

Hoyt and Viviane exchanged glances and nodded.

The senior deputy finally took a pastry without even looking. "In blood?" he joked.

Darian took a step forward, any hint of amusement wiped from his face. "But you are sticking around, right, ma'am?" He nodded toward the vacant sheriff's office. "You didn't really answer when we asked. And I'd like to know if the person I'm following is in it for the long haul or is a short-timer."

Rebecca sighed. "Honestly, I don't even know how that would work. I haven't looked up how long an interim sheriff can hold office. I assume there's an election of some kind, but I don't know when that would be. And I'm no good at politics either. Not to mention, I'm not a familiar name around town."

"You are now." Viviane's smile was as bright as ever. "Everyone was talking about you after the funeral, especially after you and Hoyt left so quickly. But I don't know about the rest of the legal stuff either."

"See? I may not even have a choice about sticking around. I might get *voted off the island*." Rebecca grinned at her own joke, but none of them apparently shared her amusement at the *Survivor* reference. "Look, that's a problem for another day. Let's deal with today's problem. I don't know how you guys have done it in the past, but I'd like to start the day with a morning briefing when there's something to be discussed."

They nodded and sat or leaned on the desks and chairs around her, apparently comfortable doing it right then and there.

After recounting yesterday's events, Rebecca got down to business.

"There are indications the victim's body was sporadically dragged to the picnic table. That would seem to lend itself to the theory that his corpse was staged. One question we need to answer is why."

Hoyt had moved over to the whiteboard by his desk and began transferring the information to the board.

Viviane frowned. "Had he really been suffocated, choked, *and* shot?"

Before Rebecca could respond, Darian scrunched up his face. "I know he had a reputation as a ladies' man, but damn, did they really have to go all Rasputin on him?"

She refused to smile. Although Rebecca understood, as much as anyone, that gallows humor kept a cop sane. "We're not sure why the killer, or killers, went to such extremes, but the working theory right now is that this was personal. Deeply personal. Can any of you think of a reason why someone would hold that much resentment toward this young man?"

Everyone shook their heads.

"Darian, you said he was a ladies' man?"

The deputy nodded, keeping direct eye contact with her.

Rebecca always appreciated that. "Then could it be a jilted lover? A betrayed spouse?"

Darian lifted one shoulder. "Not any I know about. Far as I know, the boy ran with the party crowd. Didn't really have much to do with the locals. And most of the kids around here avoided him. Or at least, they didn't want their parents to know if they were with him."

"And why do you think that is?"

Darian glanced at Hoyt, his eyes pleading with the senior deputy to jump in. Hoyt shook his head. Looking back at Rebecca, Darian gave her the one-shoulder shrug again.

"Can't say for sure, ma'am, but it might have to do with his dad being so quick to sue anyone who upsets him."

"Yeah, I met the father yesterday. I'm pretty sure he's already threatened to sue us too. For now, I'm writing the threats off as grief, though he didn't even bother to go to the morgue to identify his son."

Rebecca paused to scrutinize her assembled staff.

"It appears he has better sources than we do." She let that hang in the air. "Someone leaked information to Mr. Gilroy. None of us knew who the vic was, and dispatch didn't even have a name. I can't rule out that the killer anonymously provided a tip to Albert Gilroy. But information is getting around, and it's a bad look, folks."

All heads nodded in agreement.

There was a long pause.

"I cannot stress this enough…we need to keep tight lips on this. Don't tell anyone any more than you have to in order to get answers. Neither confirm nor deny anything. Do not answer questions, even if it's from his family or their lawyer. If anyone gives you trouble, send them to me, and I'll deal with them."

Rebecca looked around at the three faces, all of whom she hoped she could trust. They all nodded.

"To be clear, we do not yet know the motive or have any suspects. So that's what we'll be focusing on today."

"Anything from the medical examiner yet?" Viviane asked. Her dark brown eyes twinkled with curiosity and what Rebecca assumed had to be pleasure from being part of this meeting.

Rebecca needed every brain she could get right now, and Viviane was sharp as hell. As long as the 911 line stayed quiet, she'd be happy to have her sit in any time.

"Not yet, but hopefully soon."

Darian raised a finger. "What about the victim's parents? Anything from them aside from the run-in at the park?"

Rebecca frowned, irritation stirring in her gut. "No. The attorney answered when I called yesterday, letting me know that the Gilroys wouldn't be available until this afternoon."

Viviane crossed her arms over her ample chest. "Seriously?"

"Yep. After that call, I did a search on the victim and called a couple of his friends. My goal was to establish where he'd been in the days and hours leading up to his death."

"Learn anything?"

She shook her head at Hoyt's question. "Very little. I have a list of other friends and ex-girlfriends in the case folder. Those are pulled from social media, so it's not exhaustive."

Darian lifted a finger again. "I can work on making those connections."

Rebecca smiled at the young deputy. "I was actually going to ask you to do that. Maybe you'll have more luck since you're a local and closer to their ages." She handed him two lists of names. "Here are the people who refused to talk. And there's also a list of girls he may have dated, at least based on a few of his social media posts. Try to connect with as many as you can and lean hard into your status as a local to get as much information on our victim and his family as possible."

"On it."

She took a sip of her coffee. "Viviane, can you follow up on the status of the warrants I requested last night?"

"Absolutely."

"Hoyt, can you—"

Rebecca's phone buzzed. She pulled it out of her pocket and checked the notification. It was a call from the medical examiner's office.

"Hopefully, this will give us more information." She showed the caller ID to her deputies. "While I'm dealing with this, Hoyt, see what else you can pull up on our victim. We need to know why he was in that park. We also need to know where his car is currently located."

"Yes, Boss."

She was about to accept the call when something else occurred to her, and she turned back to the group. "If this has anything to do with the Yacht Club, I want to know about it immediately."

She got silence in return.

"The Yacht Club is not the Bogeyman. They are flesh-and-blood people, and we can arrest them the same as anyone else. Privilege does not make anyone immune to consequences, not in my jurisdiction."

"Yes, ma'am." Hoyt tipped his hat to her with a smile.

Rebecca finally answered the call. "Rebecca West speaking."

"Hi, Sheriff West." Bailey Flynn's voice was as chipper as ever. "You've won a prize."

Coming from a medical examiner, the sentence was cryptic as hell. "Do I even want to know what it is?"

Bailey laughed. "I'm not sure, but you'll have to come here and see it for yourself."

7

The drive to Coastal Ridge Hospital took about half an hour, so it was almost eleven when Rebecca walked in. Like last time, Bailey was waiting for her in the hallway.

"Did you think I was going to get lost?" Rebecca teased. "Or lose my nerve and run away?"

"Neither." Bailey took a sip from a bright pink travel mug. "I just needed some more coffee and figured I'd wait for you here. I like to get out of my office when I can and stretch my legs."

Rebecca nodded in sympathy. "I understand. I feel like I nearly live in the office now."

Bailey led the way to the back. "That's not healthy."

"I know." Rebecca laughed. "That's why I decided to take a vacation."

"That's a good idea. When do you leave?"

Rebecca suppressed a full laugh. "June twelfth." Bailey's confused expression was expected. "The reason I came to Shadow Island in the first place was to take the summer off after leaving the FBI, where I put in too many hours and burned myself out." That was partially true, anyway. "Then I got roped into helping the local sheriff's department. And now here we are."

Bailey's laugh was part groan. "Honey, you suck at vacations."

"Tell me about it." Everyone else was lecturing her, so the medical examiner might as well too.

She sobered when they strode into the autopsy room. Bryson Gilroy was on full display on the table. A small, white sheet was draped over his groin, but the rest of him was uncovered. Completely. His torso was cracked open, his body cavity exposed. Rebecca glanced down at the man's liver sitting in a bowl on a scale next to the table.

"What did you find?"

Bailey gestured to a table of protective clothing. "Gear up, and I'll walk you through it."

A few minutes later, Bailey began. "To start us off," she indicated the victim's bloodshot eyes and the marks on his neck, "he died of strangulation."

That was a surprise. "Not asphyxiation from the bag?"

"He would have if the killer hadn't been so impatient. Petechiae in the victim's eyes confirmed that he was struggling to breathe when he died. There's also a fracture of the hyoid bone, and tiny hemorrhages along the skin of the victim's scalp and neck. Ligature abrasions follow a predictable pattern of horizontal circumscription about the neck. A blood fluidity test will confirm my initial findings, but we'll have to wait for pathology reports on that. And you can see where he clawed at the bag in an attempt to free himself."

"He was awake and aware when this happened to him?" Rebecca bent over to examine the man's fingertips.

Bailey nodded. "Definitely alive. I can't be certain how

'aware' he was. All of that was before he was shot in the head, as indicated by the unusually small amount of blood loss I would expect postmortem after such an injury. The circulatory system had stopped, but gravity will cause unclotted blood to flow. If you look closely at the entry point of the bullet, you can see the bits of plastic from the bag in the wound."

Rebecca moved up to his head and looked where Bailey had directed. She'd already noticed the hole in Bryson's forehead. It was hard to miss.

"No stippling?" Rebecca asked, turning to the medical examiner.

Bailey nodded, pointing to the plastic bag that had been set aside. "There was, just not on his flesh. It was on the bag. There's also no exit wound, so the bullet is still in there. We'll fish that out later so you can get ballistics on it."

"Must have been small caliber."

"Probably. I've already sent his clothes off to forensics. Since he had some dirt on his knees and back, I had them test to see if there was any blood there as well. I've also asked them to run gunpowder residue tests on the shirt. On their own, each one of these was a fatal attack. Whoever killed this man really wanted him dead. And even more disconcerting, the killer wanted to watch it happen."

Rebecca stopped examining the body to look up at Bailey. She doubted she'd have said that without solid proof. "What makes you say that?"

"Other than the fact that the perpetrator used a fairly transparent bag, so the victim's face was on display, we also found traces of body oil, saliva, and skin on the outside of the bag. Although the material was never punctured, the victim's fingernails indicate he clawed at the bag. We'll test what we found for DNA and compare it against the victim. But since the bag was never punctured, the saliva couldn't belong to the victim."

Rebecca's heart picked up speed. "I'd love that sort of solid evidence."

Bailey grinned. "I thought you would." She checked her notes. "We found a few smeared prints on the outside of the bag, all on the left side, all belonging to Bryson Gilroy. That would lead to the conclusion that he used his left hand to try to remove the bag."

Bailey moved to Gilroy's right side. She lifted his arm and pointed at the palm. "As you know, the victim had cuts to only his right palm. Since his right shirt sleeve smelled of beer, my preliminary report states that he may have been carrying a beer bottle, or the perpetrator was. The puncturing nature of the wounds to his palm and the trace amounts of beer found on his skin lead me to surmise the cuts are from a broken bottle and not defensive wounds."

The M.E. mimed lashing out at someone with a weapon in a slashing motion. "If the attacker held a broken bottle in his hand, he would most likely slash to do the most damage. He wouldn't poke at the victim in such a way that he'd be stabbed by the glass."

Rebecca bit back a laugh. "Sorry. If you ever get tired of all this gore, you should take up acting."

"And how do you know I don't have the starring role at the Coastal Ridge Playhouse?" Bailey winked before continuing her assessment. "We found Bryson's left-hand fingerprints on the bag. We also found one set of glove prints. So the killer was wearing gloves."

Killer. Singular.

"Just one killer then?"

"Without another set of prints, there's no indication there was more than the one. But I can't confirm that at this point."

Rebecca made a mental note to circle back with CSI to

see if they'd found more than just the one footprint at the scene.

Bailey continued her narration. "Considering the saliva on the outside of the bag, I believe the killer pressed his face to the victim's."

A shiver crawled its way up Rebecca's spine. "So this was personal. I know strangulations by nature are a more personal crime, but since there were three forms of attack, I didn't want to assume." As brutal as this murder had been, Rebecca reasoned that if this were a personal matter, then the perpetrator should have no reason to continue killing now that the target of his wrath was dead. "Is there anything else you can tell me?"

Bailey gestured at the gunshot wound, and Rebecca turned back to it. "I can tell you that the perpetrator was likely right-handed, based on the angle of trajectory."

Rebecca nodded. That aligned with her own observations.

"You know," Bailey pulled off her gloves, "I'm not used to people coming in and actually looking at the things I'm pointing out to them."

Rebecca smiled. "This isn't my first rodeo. I've seen plenty of dead bodies, autopsied or not." She gestured at the corpse laid out before her. "When it comes to murder, this is where I'll get the best answers."

Bailey blew on her knuckles. "Aw, shucks. I do try."

It was so comfortable being with this medical examiner. How a woman who spent her days around death could retain so much enthusiasm was a question Rebecca would have to ponder later.

"Can I ask you something?"

Bailey nodded and pulled on a fresh pair of gloves. "Of course."

"My nonscientific opinion is that this was our killer's first murder. Let's ask ourselves why he'd choose to asphyxiate the victim and then change his mind midway through. Did he change his mind when he was in the act because he enjoyed it?"

The M.E. raised her eyebrows. "Or because he was impatient?"

Rebecca's excitement in her theory grew. "Exactly. An experienced killer would know how long it took to suffocate someone, I'd imagine. And I can't get past the clear bag. Seeing the changes a body goes through as it screams to take in oxygen isn't for the faint of heart."

Bailey bounced up on her toes. "So did the perpetrator not know what he was going to see? The reality of taking a life."

Rebecca found herself mimicking the doctor. "Did it upset him so much he decided to choke the victim instead?"

Bailey stopped bouncing and sank back onto her heels. "You know there's no science to this theory, right?"

Rebecca shrugged. "Chalk it up to an educated assumption."

"Well," Bailey winked, "I hope you don't make an ass out of you and me in doing so."

God, the medical examiner was funny. "I hope not, too, but thanks for talking it through with me."

"You're always welcome." The M.E. turned a page in her folder. "Back to the science of things. I will say, the rest of the findings didn't surprise me for a young man his age. He had a high blood alcohol level, traces of narcotics, and a few other drugs in his system. Those tests are still running, but I can tell you that his liver is enlarged and fatty."

Rebecca thought through the possibilities. "Alcoholism?"

"Could be. Again, we'll have to wait on the tests to confirm." She checked her notes again. "He recently had sex.

I found some dried vaginal discharge in Bryson's pubic hair and a few drops of blood. I'm having the lab run the DNA, but unless the female who left that on our victim is in the system, her DNA won't do you much good."

Hell, yeah. A person of interest. If they could find her.

"Still, it's good to have. I'd like to ask her some questions, assuming we learn her identity."

"Two more things, and then I'll let you go. First, Bryson had his phone on him when he was killed. It was stuck down into an internal pocket of his pants. I took the liberty of sending it over to Cyber. They know to contact you as soon as they learn anything."

"Wow. That's good news. And second?"

Bailey picked up a plastic evidence bag and held it in front of Rebecca.

"What's that?"

"A note. We found it shoved down his pants."

Rebecca grimaced. "Seriously?"

"Yeah. Not inside his underwear, though. It was tucked in by his waistband."

The note in the bag was short and to the point.

Not so exclusive after all.

"Damn."

❄

"This is Deputy Frost speaking. How may I help you?" Hoyt didn't even bother to look away from the screen as he answered the phone. Given the time, he was pretty sure he knew who it was. His hunch proved correct when West responded.

"I'm finished with the M.E."

"Learn anything interesting?"

He put the phone on speaker as she related all the basic information he'd expected. Suffocation. Enlarged liver.

When West got to "vaginal fluid," he perked up.

"Could this be a jilted lover situation?"

"Maybe, maybe not. Bailey's running DNA, but unless we get a hit, we'll be out of luck going down that particular path. Hold on a second…" A car door slammed, and an engine turned over. A click was followed by the tell-tale echo of her phone transferring to the vehicle's speaker system. "Get this, it looks like the perp might have pressed his face up against the bag to watch Bryson suffer. Bailey pulled some saliva that couldn't be the victim's."

Across the desk, Darian raised his eyebrows. "That's sick."

Hoyt agreed. "Any fingerprints?"

"Just the victim's, but she did find one set of glove prints."

He scratched his nose. "So only one killer?"

Hoyt could almost hear her shrug. "Maybe. Bailey and I tossed some theories around, and it's basically what I was afraid of. We've likely got an inexperienced killer who wanted to get up close and personal with his victim. This has all the markers of being a deeply personal grudge against Bryson Gilroy. However, I'm not ruling out other possibilities yet. It could be more than one killer, with each having their preferred method of attack, or it could be a brand-new serial killer with his first-ever kill who hasn't decided on his signature kill yet…"

Hoyt grimaced. "You know, Boss, I'm really hoping that it's just FBI paranoia kicking in there, and this is a simple crime of passion."

West laughed, though it was tinged with bitterness. "You and me both."

Darian frowned and rolled his chair closer. "You and me three."

The sheriff plowed on, unphased. "But here's what we

know. Bryson Gilroy was nearly suffocated. Before he could slowly die from lack of oxygen, the killer compressed his throat so tightly that he was strangled to death. Once he was dead, our killer dragged him to the picnic table, staged his body, and then shot the corpse in the forehead. Whether this case goes serial or not, we've got one sick individual."

"Wonderful. Any more good news?" Hoyt's disdain was evident.

"What we don't know is if the killer is a man or a woman. Since the body was dragged and not carried, that might point to a female killer. Also, with three very personal methods of killing, we can't rule out a woman who was scorned and snapped, especially considering the vaginal fluid. The important thing here is that we don't get tunnel vision. Everything is on the table until it's not. Understood?"

"Copy that, Boss." Hoyt appreciated her methodical way of working through all the leads. While Alden Wallace had been a dear friend, perhaps Rebecca West might just turn out to be a better mentor.

"Were either one of you able to come up with a reason someone would want our victim dead?"

"Nothing stands out." Darian leaned in so he could be heard. "Not yet. I'm tracking down his friends at the moment. Bryson didn't appear to have a girlfriend or any female friends."

"Well, he slept with someone shortly before he died."

Darian lifted a finger. "Could be a hooker or," he lifted a second, "a one-night stand." A third finger went up. "Friends with benefits."

"Okay, okay, I get it. I'm going to swing by the Gilroy house on my way back since it's close to the time the attorney said the parents would be available. Maybe they'll let me into his room without a fight. Darian, keep after the names on the lists I gave you. And Hoyt, see if you can find out where Bryson was the night he died and keep searching for his car. There can't be that many sitting abandoned on the island. Maybe the local businesses' security footage will give us some answers."

Viviane approached and handed a memo to Hoyt. He silently read it as Viviane hurried back to her desk to answer another incoming call.

"Forensics is on the other line. They've got something they think is urgent."

A horn honked in the background. "Go ahead and answer them. You can catch me up when I get back."

Rebecca cut the call, and Hoyt swapped over, keeping it on speaker. "Deputy Frost here. What can I do for you?"

"Deputy Frost, this is Lance Davis. We concluded our search of the park and wanted to update you."

Hoyt took a deep breath. "Good news, I hope?"

"I couldn't say. Just news."

"Okay, what do you have for me?"

"Remember that footprint we found at the scene?"

"Yup."

"We found an area where similar prints were left. It appears there was a scuffle because the impressions aren't distinct. We took casts out of an abundance of caution, and I'll upload them to the case file. But we only recovered the one clear footprint."

"Any from the victim?"

"We did find a few prints, but they take an unusual path. Like someone who was intoxicated."

"That tracks with the rest of our evidence." Hoyt pressed his lips together, remembering the sheriff's admonition about not saying too much. "Any gloves or other evidence? You didn't find his car abandoned somewhere, did you?"

"No, sorry. But maybe this will be helpful. The footprints we cast that looked like they were part of a scuffle were all roughly the same size as the clear one we found. And there are small portions of the tread that match."

Hoyt ran the sentences back through his head. "Does that mean what I think it means?"

"If you think it means that there's only one attacker, then yes."

8

Rebecca pulled up to where the gleaming, white stucco mansions with floor-to-ceiling glass windows rubbed elbows with each other, fighting for the most coveted view of the Atlantic. She turned into the truncated driveway that was the hallmark of mansions on postage-stamp lots. Privacy was a luxury not even the elite could claim among beachfront properties.

Albert Gilroy's home was a massive building on stilts. The bottom, or what would have been the first floor, was set up with several garages, outdoor seating areas, an extravagant outdoor kitchen with brickwork grills and ovens, and several staircases leading up to different levels of the house.

The grand stairs were wide with elegantly curved railings and balusters that gleamed in the sun. But the staircase only led to a decorative frame on what was essentially a vast wraparound, screened-in porch. Though "screened-in porch" didn't do it justice. It was essentially a giant den, complete with entertainment centers, luxury furniture, and even a wet bar, as far as she could tell. It was a good thing they could afford top-notch security systems. Otherwise, their precious possessions would be stolen from under their noses.

Finally reaching the door, Rebecca rang the bell. She didn't hear a thing from inside and wondered if the doorbell was broken.

Yeah, right. I'm sure nothing here is allowed to be out of order. The door swung open, and a middle-aged woman wearing a sharply tailored navy suit appraised her from over a pair of horn-rimmed glasses.

"Yes?" The woman huffed in annoyance, her gray helmet of hair barely moving. After taking in the sheriff's entirety, she did nothing to hide her disdain. She moved to fill the opening the door had created as her hand lightly trailed over a ruby necklace.

Rebecca flashed her own jewelry. Holding her badge at eye level, she smiled at the other woman. "I'm Sheriff West, here to speak with Bryson Gilroy's parents."

The woman glanced over her shoulder before sighing. "Come in." She moved aside and held the door open as Rebecca stepped into the mansion. As soon as she could, she shut the door and locked it. Before Rebecca could even take in her surroundings, the woman spun on her heel and strode away. "Follow me."

The house was immaculate. White walls and floors with highly polished wood trim around every window. There was even a giant round pane of glass above every cluster of windows. Natural sunlight poured over everything, and it was nearly blinding.

It was an open floor plan with no hallways. The rooms simply opened into a new space, and each one had a different type of flooring. Tile floors gave way to pale hardwood. Rebecca and the woman finally stopped in an area with cream couches and a giant rug that was at least an inch and a half thick and spanned the entire room.

"Wait here."

Once again, the woman spun on her heel and left.

As rude as that was, Rebecca wasn't about to stop her. This gave her a chance to snoop around uncensored. She'd been given access to the house, after all. Taking a quick lap around the room revealed nothing. It didn't even have any personal touches.

The home might as well have been a picture in a magazine. Sometimes the absence of items told a story of its own. On the walls hung paintings, not photographs. The tables were empty except for a few tastefully placed...Rebecca poked a crystal object and wondered if it was supposed to be a piece of art or a paperweight. Maybe it was both.

"Can I help you?"

Halting her poking, Rebecca turned to face the new arrival. A young woman stood just inside the room. She wore a tight sports bra and matching short-shorts, her hair pulled back into a smooth ponytail, clearly just having come from a workout.

"I'm waiting for Albert and Annika Gilroy." She looked over the woman's shoulder, checking to see if anyone else was coming.

"I'm Annika Gilroy. And you are?" Despite the polite words, her tone turned icy.

This woman was Gilroy's *wife*? Rebecca had known there was an age gap but staring at the reality of their disparity was shocking, nonetheless. He had to be at least twenty years her senior, if not thirty.

Realizing rudeness wouldn't open any doors, Rebecca offered a sympathetic smile. "I'm Sheriff West. I'm sorry for your loss. I was told you and Mr. Gilroy would be available to speak to me. Is now a good time?"

A bit of the iciness faded. "Actually, it isn't. Albert isn't here."

Rebecca gritted her teeth. "Do you know where he is?"

"Yes."

Seconds ticked by. When it was clear the woman wasn't going to expand on her answer, Rebecca changed the subject. "Do you know if Bryson's mother is on her way?"

Mrs. Gilroy lifted an eyebrow. "How should I know?" When Rebecca said nothing, she sighed. "As you're probably aware, that evil woman moved back to Michigan after the divorce and wants little to do with my husband or her son. They've not spoken in years. She's not well, and she's battling drug addiction. Only recently, she got out after spending six months in rehab, which my husband kindly bankrolled. But even after everything Albert's done for her, she acts like she wants to be left alone. We respect her wishes." Mrs. Gilroy flicked her hand to the side, indicating the well-dressed woman who had let Rebecca in.

She had, somehow, stealthily reappeared.

"My maid can get you her contact information. Is that all you needed?"

Maid? That woman's outfit cost more than my truck! How can she be the maid? With her ability to go unnoticed, she should consider a career in the CIA.

The maid nodded and disappeared to retrieve the information for her mistress.

"Since you're his stepmother and lived with him, could you answer a few questions for me?"

Mrs. Gilroy paused, clearly uncomfortable. "Maybe I should call my husband's attorney first."

"That is, of course, your right. But it's a simple victim statement. We're trying to figure out where your stepson was in the days and hours leading up to his death. Did he happen to tell you where he was going? Do you know who he was with?"

"Bryson and I were never really close." Mrs. Gilroy finally

relented and settled onto one of the couches. She motioned for Rebecca to sit. "I'm afraid I won't be much help. His father and I have only been married two years, so it's not like I watched him grow up or anything. He was an adult who didn't need a mother figure. So I don't know where he went that night or who he was with. And before you ask, the last time I saw him was Sunday evening around seven. I didn't see him at all on Monday."

Rebecca made a note of it.

"Did he have a girlfriend or multiple girls he was dating?"

"Bryson?" She scoffed. "No. I may not have known him well, but he definitely didn't have a girlfriend."

"Forgive me for asking, but how can you be so certain? As you say, you two weren't close."

Mrs. Gilroy lowered her voice to barely a whisper. "Because the apple doesn't fall far from the tree. The Gilroy men can't keep it in their pants, if you'll forgive me for being crass. Monogamy isn't a relationship style they adhere to."

Rebecca blinked while she processed this information and deliberately misread the woman's meaning. "Did he not like girls? Was his preference boys?"

The stepmom's laughter echoed off the tile and glass of the cavernous room. "Oh my god. No, no, no. Albert would kill him. Even if he did swing that way, he'd never be permitted to act on it." Mrs. Gilroy's eyebrows knitted together, deep in thought. "I'm sure I heard him mention a girl or two to Albert, but not in any serious way. More of a male bragging kind of thing. Ya know?"

Rebecca nodded. As she scribbled notes, she continued firing questions, unsure how much longer the youthful wife would tolerate the conversation. "Did Bryson like to visit Sand Dollar Park?"

"I couldn't say for sure," she eyed Rebecca as she continued writing in her notepad, "so don't quote me. But I think I'm the only one in the family who ventures down there. I like to jog the trails. It's very cathartic."

"Are you aware of anyone harassing or threatening your stepson?"

"That's probably a better question for Albert's lawyer. I can have Janet retrieve his name and contact info if you'd like."

"Thank you, but that won't be necessary. I've met the man."

"Ahh, yes. I think he spends more time with Albert than I do. If Bryson was in any kind of danger, he'd have told Mr. Campbell."

None of this was helpful. "Can you tell me what kind of car he drives?" She already knew but wanted to ask questions that were easy to answer.

Mrs. Gilroy brightened. "Oh, that's easy. His beach car is a silver Jeep CJ-7 Custom SUV."

A beach car. He had a beach car. As opposed to what? A pavement car?

Rebecca made a note. "Is his Jeep still here?"

"I'm not sure. I'll have the staff check." She leaned over and pressed a button on the side table.

"Yes, ma'am?" It was the well-dressed maid again.

"Can you have someone check to see if the Jeep is in the garage, please?"

Rebecca was pleasantly surprised to hear the woman speak politely with her staff. After seeing how her husband acted, it was a wonder the couple got along. Or maybe Mrs. Gilroy was polite to make up for her husband's shortcomings.

"It's not, ma'am. I haven't seen it since Monday. If it helps, Mr. Bryson was to be picked up by one of his friends Monday just after noon. They were going out to lunch in Coastal Ridge."

"Thank you, Janet."

Before the maid could turn away, Rebecca raised a hand. "Janet."

Annoyance flicked on the older woman's face. "Yes?"

"I'm trying to catch the person responsible for Bryson's death. We need to talk to anyone who was with him over the past forty-eight to seventy-two hours. Do you know who picked him up on Monday?"

"He didn't end up being picked up, ma'am."

"No?"

"No. I heard Mr. Bryson mumble something about his plans changing, but he still left the house."

Rebecca grasped for questions. "Do you know if he still went to lunch?"

"I'm sorry. I don't."

Rebecca flipped the page in her notepad and kept writing feverishly. "Thank you, Janet. I may have more questions for you later, if Mrs. Gilroy doesn't mind?"

"That's fine."

Rebecca wanted to seize the opportunity with the second Mrs. Gilroy. She felt the sands slipping through the hourglass of patience with Bryson's stepmom. "Was your husband home Monday night?" She worded her question carefully, hoping not to invoke the threat of the lawyer.

"Albert was with me all day, actually. One of our rare times together. We left Monday, before Bryson woke, and got home late. We didn't see him all day. I don't think they spoke on the phone either. Albert is struggling with that now." Mrs. Gilroy shrugged. "I wish I could be more helpful, but Bryson was a grown man living his own life. He didn't need to check in with us, and he came and went as he pleased, so we sometimes wouldn't see each other for days, even though we lived in the same house."

A family that lived together but was so busy running off

to social engagements and meetings that they didn't even see each other for days. *What kind of life is that?* Rebecca would give nearly anything to have one more night of sitting down to dinner with her parents or even one more phone call with them. But, then again, maybe that was a pain Albert Gilroy was about to come to grips with.

After peppering Annika Gilroy with more questions, Rebecca still learned very little. Albert and his second wife had gone onto the mainland on Monday. While Albert attended a meeting, Mrs. Gilroy had done some retail therapy. Then her husband had joined her, and they'd traveled to the eastern coast, where they'd attended a function at a country club.

Although the visit with the stepmom had been a bust, Rebecca knew every trail was worth following. And knowing more about this family and its secrets might just help them catch a killer.

"Are you certain you don't have any idea where Bryson was in the days before his death?"

Mrs. Gilroy perked up like she'd just remembered something. "You can always check his calendar. It's in his room."

Hallelujah.

"That would be perfect."

Mrs. Gilroy stood and led her to another room, where she pushed a button on a wall. Rebecca waited to hear the maid's voice again but was greeted by the ding of an elevator. The wall in front of them slid open, and the metal doors behind it retracted as well. Mrs. Gilroy stepped in, and Rebecca followed.

The elevator was silent and fast, with the doors opening again a few seconds later.

She's young and fit but takes an elevator to go up one floor in her own house? Rich people confuse me. The more Rebecca learned, the less she understood.

This floor had a few touches of family. The vast halls were lined with pictures of a younger Albert Gilroy, along with a few shots of another woman Rebecca assumed was his previous wife. Little Bryson looked like an ordinary kid. Wearing a lacrosse jersey, playing on a beach, and posing with his father. Then, standing beside his dad holding a fishing pole, a young teenage Bryson beamed at the camera, on the deck of what appeared to be a yacht.

Down the wall a bit more was a more mature teen version of Bryson, once again standing on a boat with his father and several other older men in the background. That version of Bryson was the most serious of any of the photos.

"Did Bryson have any hobbies?"

Mrs. Gilroy stopped walking. "He and his father both have a thing for boats. I never really understood why. They're boring to me. They ride out and then just go in circles around the islands all night. It's like a traveling poker night for the boys. And it's always just the boys. They never invite me..."

Rebecca guessed her hostess's thoughts. "Why do you think that was?"

"As I mentioned downstairs, Albert isn't faithful. I assume I wasn't invited because there were other women on the boat."

"I'm sorry, but you seem so calm about that. Don't you care that he cheats on you?"

Her overinflated lips turned up at the corners. "We have an understanding, Sheriff. Our marriage is much like other marriages up in our circle. I'm arm candy for Albert when he needs me to be. When he doesn't...well, my time is my own. And I want for nothing." She swept her arm around as if to say the house made up for a philandering husband.

Rebecca couldn't imagine such a life. "You were saying about the boat parties?"

"Right. I know why *Albert* was interested. I suppose Bryson was for the same reasons, though he seemed far less enthusiastic about going than his father. They used to go out together nearly every night. More recently, it was mostly just Bryson."

"He went out alone?"

"No, he and his father are...*were* part of some group. The members all go out together." Mrs. Gilroy tucked a lock of escaping hair behind her ear. "They don't even have a name for it. They just call it the Yacht Club."

9

Climbing into her cruiser after locking the evidence bags in the trunk, Rebecca hoped the items she'd collected would provide new information. She'd been given Bryson's calendar with his contacts, his laptop, and the spare keys to his Jeep. Now the techs could comb through it for evidence.

Bryson's room, like nearly every other room in the house, had expansive windows but also had an exterior door that opened onto a second wraparound porch. From that porch, the park where Bryson had been killed was clearly visible. He had cut through the park on a few occasions. Janet had offered that detail when she'd returned with the contact information for his birth mother.

Learning that Bryson may have been walking home changed things. Why hadn't he taken his vehicle when he'd left with it? Did he walk because he'd been drinking? Types like Bryson generally thought they were above the law when it came to everything, including driving under the influence. But where was the Jeep now?

Had Bryson been alone? Or had a companion abandoned him when the attack occurred?

Rebecca growled, her frustration mounting. As was often the situation early in a case, there were far more questions than answers. But she would never give up. If her years of searching for her parents' killers had proven anything, it was that Rebecca West was relentless in her pursuit of justice.

As the wooded area loomed in the distance, Rebecca decided it was time to revisit Sand Dollar Park.

Pulling into the small lot, she parked the cruiser by a trailhead marker. Various signs pointed to a jogging trail, a picnic area, and the beach. Rebecca, Frost, and the crime scene techs had already canvassed the picnic area. The crime scene tape was down, which meant forensics was done processing the scene.

Tucking a few evidence bags and nitrile gloves into her pocket, Rebecca grabbed the camera from her glove box, thinking about the evidence in the case and what it might mean.

What if the park had been Bryson's destination all along? The killer could have used a ruse to lure him here. If Bryson was inebriated, had he even planned to enter the park? Where was Bryson killed? If it wasn't here, why bring his body here?

Like a beacon calling Rebecca into action, the sign pointing to the trail loomed before her. Goading her. According to the marker, the trail was a loop, which ran to the park's northern border and came out on the beach on both sides. Rebecca guessed the northern arc would be closer to Bryson's house.

Working a theory that Bryson was attacked inside the park, she decided to head in the direction of the victim's home. Exploring every theory helped stave off tunnel vision. Or so she hoped.

Methodically checking the trees along the trail for any indication of a struggle or attack, she walked the loop. Her stomach growled and reminded her that she hadn't eaten anything since the doughnuts that morning. Nor had she had anything to drink since she'd finished the coffee in her cruiser. It was shaping up to be another day of fast food and indigestion.

At least the trail wasn't long, and much of the path was paved.

Rebecca had already been methodically walking for close to an hour when she heard a rhythmic *thump-thump* noise growing louder. Pausing, she looked up, checking all around her. The pounding noise settled into the steady drone of someone running. Not wanting to scare anyone, Rebecca walked out of the trees and into plain sight. She waited on the path for the runner to reach her.

Before a person came into view, a beagle appeared, its white-tipped tail curled forward. A woman dressed in black-and-white leggings and a baggy, royal blue shirt darted around the curve. Her eyes jumped to Rebecca, and her pace faltered before smoothing out again. Rebecca pulled her badge off her belt and held it up.

The jogger slowed down. Fishing behind a shock of dirty-blond hair to remove one earbud, she stopped in front of Rebecca and wiped her forehead. She patted her leg, and the dog moved to her side and waited.

"Sorry to interrupt your run, but could you answer a few questions? I promise not to take long."

The woman peered at her badge, and Rebecca held it closer, smiling and waiting patiently while her ID was confirmed.

"Can you walk with me? I'm at the end of my workout and need to get going. I'll cramp up if I stand still for too long." The woman clicked some buttons on her fitness watch.

"Sure, and as I said, I'll make this quick. I'm just wondering if you jog here often and how well you know the park." Rebecca had to walk quickly to keep up with the woman and her dog.

The woman wasn't short of breath, despite her workout, and Rebecca was jealous.

"I jog here most days, but usually early in the morning. I try to work out before work. It's usually quiet and empty, so I can get a good run in…undisturbed."

The pointed comment signaled the runner's impatience, but Rebecca had a job to do. "Did you happen to see anything out of the ordinary Monday morning?"

"Nope." She shook her head. "But there was some broken glass on the trail. That could have hurt someone pretty seriously. The sheriff's office needs to step it up and take care of things like that."

Was she really suggesting the sheriff should be on litter patrol?

"Do you remember where the broken glass was?"

"Do I look like the kind of person who would leave broken glass out like that? Besides, my dog was going nuts, so I did what any decent person would and put it in one of my doggy waste bags and tossed it in the trash. I kicked any of the little shards off the trail so they wouldn't hurt any animals."

Rebecca inwardly cringed, knowing some of their most important evidence might now be in the landfill. Shit. She increased her pace to move alongside the jogger. "I'd appreciate it if you could show me which trash can it was and where you saw the glass originally."

Annoyance oozed from the runner's sweaty pores. "I'm sorry. I don't have time. I'm meeting a friend for an early dinner and need to get cleaned up. But I can tell you it's the trash can at the trailhead by the parking lot." She also offered directions to the approximate spot she'd found the shards of glass. "I remember there was an unusually tall Japanese plum yew next to the bottle. It was over ten feet, which is why I remember it. Hope that helps."

Rebecca pulled out her phone and found the picture she'd saved of Bryson's driver's license photo. "Have you ever seen this man in the park or on the trails?"

After only a second of looking, the woman shook her head. "Never seen him. Is he someone I should keep an eye out for?"

Knowing where that line of thinking was heading, Rebecca was already shaking her head. "No, ma'am. He was attacked here the other day, and we're just trying to piece together a timeline."

"Attacked? Oh, no."

"You haven't heard about it? It's been all over the news."

"No. I've been working long hours for a client. This is my first day off in weeks. Besides, I don't watch the news. It gives me wrinkles." She took a sip from an insulated water bottle.

After Rebecca collected her name, Lindsey May, and contact information, she thanked her and let her leave.

As soon as Lindsey was dismissed, she picked up her pace, leaving Rebecca in her dust.

Rebecca jogged in the other direction, wanting to get to the trash can pronto.

Please let it be full. Please let it be full. Or, as an even better alternative, maybe the CSI team already removed the contents.

When the parking lot and brown, slatted bin came into view, Rebecca sprinted the final distance. She removed the top with its swinging lid and peered inside.

A candy bar wrapper and one empty plastic water bottle were the only "inhabitants." The trash had definitely been emptied since Monday morning.

Undeterred, Rebecca followed the path back to where

May had said she'd seen the broken glass, searching for an unusually tall Japanese plum yew.

After her unplanned afternoon run, it was nice walking through the shade. The trees were sparse, so it was easy to look through them, and they barely slowed the wind. Which begged another question.

If Bryson was attacked here, how had someone snuck up on him? Or had he seen the attacker coming?

Even standing in the trees, she could see at least twenty feet in every direction.

Bailey had said Bryson's blood alcohol levels were elevated. He was a white male who'd likely never had to worry about his safety. Why would he pay attention to his surroundings, even when inebriated? He likely had no concern that he might become someone's victim.

As someone who'd had personal safety drilled into her head every day since before she'd reached puberty, that concept was foreign to Rebecca. Situational awareness was crucial. She'd learned this as a young girl, long before Quantico reinforced it. If Bryson had been worried, would he have taken this secluded trail?

Just because the victim was free of concern didn't mean someone didn't hold a personal grudge against him. The numerous methods of attacks and their highly personal nature all pointed to this being a person who had issues with Bryson. But who?

When she came upon a Japanese plum yew that appeared to be at least eleven feet tall, Rebecca stopped and conducted a closer inspection.

Glints of light reflected near the trail's edge, and Rebecca bent over to investigate. Like May had said, tiny bits of broken glass rested in the sandy soil. Some of the glass had not yet settled into the sand, but she'd need to be careful.

Rebecca kneeled low to the ground and donned a pair of

nitrile gloves. After snapping several photos of the area, she opened an evidence bag and carefully deposited the tiny specks of glass into the bag. One piece, roughly the size of a fingernail, had a discoloration on two edges. The camera whirred as she documented it, even using the macro zoom to capture all the detail.

Gently lifting each piece of glass, she noticed some type of reddish-brown substance in the sand as well.

Blood?

Rebecca snapped a few more pictures, then sat back on her heels. She glanced at the area around her. Some rose-bushes, the hickories with their shaggy bark, and some scattered weeds. A flash of silver caught her eye, and she turned to inspect it more closely. A gum wrapper. Again, she photographed it and placed it in a separate evidence bag.

She had no way of knowing which pieces of evidence mattered and which were everyday trash, but everything was important until proven otherwise.

Having scooted closer to the wrapper, Rebecca's perspective on the scene changed. The light came through the trees at a different angle, and she was seeing her surroundings through fresh eyes.

A large chunk of bark, about five inches long and three inches wide, rested not more than two feet from where she knelt. Finding bark on the ground near these trees wasn't unusual. Finding only one piece that appeared broken could be.

Again, Rebecca snapped multiple photos. She moved closer to the bark and reached to bag it. A small tangle of short brown hair was twisted into the wood. Lifting the bark by the edges, she gently placed it into an evidence bag after photographing it. Quickly getting to her feet but careful where she stepped, she moved to the closest hickory. There on the tree, directly at eye level, a large chunk of bark was missing.

Rebecca radioed for the forensic team to return. She'd maybe found the point of attack.

10

S truggling to keep the box of paperwork and files balanced, Rebecca stepped out of her office, locked it, and headed for the front door. It was well past dinnertime, and she'd just gotten back from the crime scene.

Although the pieces of glass might simply be trash, her instincts told her they held meaning. The bark with hair matching the color of the victim's and the trace amounts of what could be blood were the first real breaks they'd had. Everything she'd collected, plus anything the CSI techs had found, had gone to the lab. They wouldn't get the results back until tomorrow at the earliest.

The victim's spare car keys and calendar rested on her desk in their evidence bags. But her focus was initially on the young man's laptop.

His online presence was unsurprising for someone his age. So far, she'd found public accounts and ghost accounts. *Vaulty* was installed on his hard drive, so she'd emailed Coastal Ridge's cyber experts to let them know she'd be needing their assistance.

She'd assembled a file for every face she'd been able to put a name to. If relevant, she'd conduct a background search. There were many names and files to go through, but nothing was jumping out at her. She couldn't concentrate on such an empty stomach.

The only way she was going to get any work done was to pack it up for the night and head home.

Maybe, if she got lucky, she could throw together an easy dinner with some of the items she'd picked up at the grocery store. She needed to use them before they spoiled. Dinner with the Frosts the night before had whetted her appetite for another good home-cooked meal and some semblance of normalcy. Even if she spent her evening tediously sorting through the box she'd packed up.

Paper versions of the files she'd first received from Wallace when she'd started poking into the Yacht Club were also in her daunting stack of "homework." And since they were all closed cases, it was perfectly reasonable for her to take them to her home office to familiarize herself with them.

She couldn't shake the idea that Bryson's murder was somehow connected to the world's most poorly named criminal organization.

Couldn't they have at least called themselves something cool, like the Pirates? Or would that be too on the nose? Still, it would fit the locale reasonably well.

Rebecca thought about the staggering number of pirate ships buried under the ocean, sinking into the sand beneath the waves, and hoped these modern-day pirates would soon walk the plank.

"That's a creepy grin. What are you thinking about, Boss?"

"A giant plate of spaghetti slathered in parmesan and topped with freshly sliced basil. Garlic bread, slightly toasty on the edges, covered in full-fat mozzarella, dripping with butter. Meatballs the size of my fist." Rebecca licked her lips, selling the lie.

Hoyt laughed.

"You were making that creepy face while thinking about dinner?" He pulled his papers off the printer and walked toward her.

"You didn't let me finish. I was also thinking about what I would do to anyone who stood in the way of me getting that meal." Propping the box on the desk, she readjusted her ponytail and winked. "I need to bring you up to speed on a few items. I'm starving, so I'll make it quick."

"Shoot."

"First, Bailey found a note stuffed in the back of our victim's pants." Hoyt's disgust was evident. "Not inside his underwear, if that's what has your face all scrunched up."

"What kind of note? 'If lost, please return me to my rich daddy'?"

She chuckled. "Nope. It said, 'Not so exclusive after all.'"

Understanding opened Hoyt's eyes wide. "Oh."

"Not hard to figure out what that's in reference to. Someone has a personal hatred for the Yacht Club." She held up a hand. "I'll tell you more about that in a minute but get this...I managed to get Bryson's laptop, personal calendar, and his spare set of keys from his stepmom. Then I stopped by the park and spoke to a woman who jogs there regularly."

"No wonder you're hungry."

She flipped through the pages of her notepad. "Lindsey May. Know her?"

Hoyt scrunched his eyebrows. "Not right off."

"She'd seen a broken bottle while running Tuesday morning. Unfortunately, she picked up the pieces on the trail and threw them away." She held up her hand in a stop motion. "And before you ask, the garbage bin was emptied."

"Crap. But the stuff from the kid's house is useful, right?"

"Hope so. He used *Vaulty*, so I'm sure we don't have access to everything."

Her senior deputy's blank stare amused her.

"Deputy Frost," she teased, "you need to familiarize yourself with modern technology."

He shrugged. "Did you learn anything else? I need to tell you what forensics said."

"Right. I did. In addition to the broken glass, I found tiny drops of what looked like blood. I dropped it at the lab so they could put a rush on it. It sure would be nice if it was our killer's blood. But even if it's only Bryson's, it still helps tell a story. The last thing I found at the park was a chunk of bark with hair twisted into it. The same color hair as our vic. That's also at the lab for analysis."

"Wow. It seems like you don't even need us, Boss."

She shot him a *don't go there* look. "Uh-huh. What did forensics say?"

"In addition to the footprint they showed us when we were there, they also found some partial prints. Portions of the tread are the same as the first. And the other incomplete prints were roughly the same size. But Lance, that's the guy in forensics, said the person who left the partials might have been shuffling his feet. The biggest takeaway was that, because of the lack of other prints found, forensics is leaning toward the theory that there was only one person who attacked Bryson."

Rebecca closed her eyes as she contemplated this new information.

"I'm starving, but I think my hunger will need to wait a bit longer. Can you please tell me everything you know about the Yacht Club? Everything screams that group is mixed up in this somehow."

"Why do you think that?"

"Because Bryson's stepmother spoke of how Bryson and

her husband went out on boat parties with a group that was cleverly named…" She raised her eyebrows.

Hoyt cursed. "Are you kidding me? She called this group the Yacht Club."

"Bingo." She gave him a hard look, the kind she gave hardened criminals. "Tell me everything you know about this club."

Hoyt sighed, and his shoulders went slack. For entirely too long, he didn't say anything.

"Hoyt?"

He held up a hand. "How much do you already know?"

"Pretend I know nothing."

He popped his neck before starting. "The Yacht Club docks at the Seaview Marina owned by Lewis Longmire. That's based on hearsay, mind you. I do know that most people can't afford to dock there, and the few who can afford it have been turned away for no reason. No matter how big their yachts are. Not only are they picky about who they let dock there, but they're also picky about who they employ."

He swallowed and shifted on his feet, wringing the papers he still had in his hands.

"And?" She crossed her arms.

"I don't know any of this for certain. We've never known —at least *I've* never known—anyone we could confirm as a member of the club. Sometimes I've seen a face I recognize on one of the boats. After all, the marina is a private business, and we've never been called out there for anything. Not even for a trespass or a drunk-and-disorderly."

"And?"

He held his hands out in a pleading gesture. "I wish I knew more. I really do. But I don't. Wallace insisted on handling all that himself. I'm not sure what else I can tell you. Do you want me to tell you about the rumors? How they're running coke from South America? Guns for terrorists?

Rhino horns out of Ethiopia? How Bob at the bakery simply has to be a member because he always has fresh, raw honey for his biscuits, and the only way to get that through customs is by smuggling? There's too much gossip about them and not enough facts. Always has been."

Rebecca studied him in silence for another minute. He remained quiet but didn't drop his head this time. She judged he was telling the truth.

"Then it looks like I need to drop in and have a little chat with Mr. Longmire at some point. See if he knows our victim or where he might have been the night he was murdered. We still haven't figured out where he was or who he was with." She uncrossed her arms, ready to collect her box. "Which reminds me, were you able to find any video footage of the park?"

Hoyt looked down at the twisted and crushed papers in his hands. "None of the businesses had any, but there's a bank with an ATM in the right position. I asked them, but they insisted on a warrant." He straightened out the papers, showing them to her. "I filled out the paperwork and should hear back from a judge soon."

"Even if you get it tonight, you won't be able to serve it until tomorrow. No point in you waiting around. You're already past your shift. Go home."

Rebecca scooped up her box of paperwork. Invigorated by the discoveries, she wanted to get out of the station and have some time alone to think.

Carrying her evening's entertainment, she walked out of the bullpen and into the lobby. Using her back, she pushed open the glass front door. She'd nearly made it out when the door hit something solid and she stumbled, dropping the box on the ground.

A few of the folders sprang open and papers went flying. Cursing her luck, Rebecca knelt and started grabbing at the pieces before they got blown away by the breeze. When most were safely in her hands, she turned to look at what she'd stumbled into.

Albert Gilroy loomed over her, his glare slicing through the air between them. Steven Campbell, the Gilroy corporate lawyer, bent down and grabbed a few pieces of paper before she could stop him. He scanned them. With a scowl, he turned the top sheet around so Gilroy could see.

Speak of the devil, and he will come. Along with his attorney.

Once everything was collected, Rebecca rose, hitched the box on her hip, and reached out for the papers the lawyer was holding.

The lawyer sneered, the wrinkles etched around his nose and mouth revealing this was an everyday look for him. "You should be careful where you put your nose. You wouldn't want to stir up a hornet's nest. That would be more than you can handle. Digging into an urban legend based on the mafia isn't the best use of your time when a grieving father stands before you, awaiting answers."

Urban legend? Mafia? What a load of bullshit.

Anger rose in Rebecca like a heat wave up her spine. She was getting damn sick and tired of people telling her how to do her job when no one else was stepping up to take the position. Snatching the papers from his hand, she quickly looked them over, then forced herself to relax.

"What makes you think a three-year-old drug deal case has anything to do with Bryson's murder? Are you acknowledging they have something in common?"

Gilroy turned his glare on his lawyer, who took a step back. He might be a bigwig in the boardroom while dealing with contract law, but he was digging a hole for them when it came to criminal cases.

"I came by to see what kind of headway you've made into my son's murder investigation. But clearly, you're just grasping at straws, if this is where your investigation is heading." Gilroy waved his hand dismissively at her box of paperwork. "If you're not up to the task of being sheriff, perhaps you should step down and let someone *more qualified* take over."

Rebecca knew that tone. "When you say *more qualified*, do you mean someone with a penis?" Trying to remind herself that this sleazy scumbag was still the father of a victim, she swallowed the rest of the retort. "Again, what makes you think an old drug case has anything to do with your son's case?"

Gilroy's lips pressed into a thin line. "I don't."

"Mr. Gilroy, is there something you'd like to tell me about your son? Did he know this drug dealer? These are just some old case files I need to go over as part of my administrative duties. But if you think I should check them over for links to your son, I will happily do so."

Gilroy looked like he'd eaten a whole lemon, which pleased the petty part of Rebecca's heart. While she might not have the best poker face, Rebecca was exceptionally skilled at making up lies on the spot. It often got her the best information, as it had just now.

This drug dealer was, in fact, linked to Bryson, Albert, or the Yacht Club. And that was not a connection he wanted her to make. She could sniff out a liar a mile away, and these two might as well have been screaming that there was a connection. They didn't need to, though, as their silence and sideways glances said it all.

"With a single phone call, I can have your position yanked out from under you." Gilroy gave his jowls a good workout as he shook his head at her. "I'll send you back to whatever meaningless job you had before you managed to worm your way into the sheriff's office. Then I'll get someone competent to take over this case."

Rebecca chuckled. "Don't threaten me with a good time."

Gilroy scowled, his jaw clenching.

She let out a long breath. "Mr. Gilroy, I assure you the Shadow Island Sheriff's Department is doing everything in its power to find out who killed your son. And as soon as I have any information I can share with you, I will let you know. If you have information on the case you would like to share with me to speed this investigation along, I would be more than happy to head back inside and take your statement. So far, no one is willing to talk to us about your son. Do you know why that could be, Mr. Gilroy?"

Gilroy's face turned a frightening shade of red as he screamed, "I'm not here to do your job for you. Just find out who murdered my boy and stop concerning yourself with things that aren't important!"

"That's precisely what I'm trying to do, sir. But you're in my way." Rebecca looked pointedly at his feet, where he was blocking her path. "Now please step back and let me do my job."

❄

REBECCA FLIPPED another page as she munched on celery and hummus, a jar of olives at her elbow. By the time she'd gotten home, she was too tired to even turn the stove eye on. Instead, she'd prayed the items in the fridge would keep another day and settled down with easy-to-eat snacks.

What pushed her along, even into the late evening hours, was the need to catch this guy and find out what he knew about the Yacht Club. Was he a former member himself? A business associate who'd gotten burned in a deal? Someone from a different organization trying to take them down in some turf war type of scenario?

How did the unsub know Bryson Gilroy was a member?

Or was he just guessing? Was he targeting the son to get to the father?

That last idea was where Rebecca placed her bet. The way Gilroy had approached her twice now—without a hint of pain or loss, only anger—made her suspicious. He wasn't reacting the way a father would after losing a son. It was more like a businessman reacting to the loss of an asset or key employee. He hadn't even been home the morning after. Not to spend time with his wife, sit in his son's room, or drink himself into oblivion. Nothing.

She wondered if there was a grief support group on the island. If there was, she could recommend it to Albert Gilroy so he could learn how to at least pretend to grieve for his son.

While she knew that everyone grieved differently, this felt off. And his new wife had not spoken highly of the man. He'd openly cheated and rarely spent time with family. The only time father and son seemed to spend together had been on yachts belonging to Yacht Club members, at least according to Mrs. Gilroy.

Luckily, digging into the Yacht Club lined up with her investigation of Bryson's death. She'd pulled the records of every person she'd been able to identify as a friend or contact of the victim's. And, according to the lawyer, that was precisely where they did not want her looking.

"Too bad."

Everything she'd read so far had proven that theory correct. Various small, petty charges on a wide assortment of people, local and out-of-towners, but they were all loosely affiliated as far as she could tell.

Jim bailed out John, John testified for Joe, Joe had an alibi for Jack, and Jack owned the car Jim was driving when he was caught. On and on, the web spun larger and larger.

Small, insignificant interactions that only made sense when you looked at the big picture.

Hell, maybe there were even some Jills and Janes to take into consideration.

But the missing thread Rebecca couldn't find on paper was a connection to anyone in power. Neither Gilroy showed up in her files. Nor did Campbell. More than likely, she would have to start a new search centered on the senior Gilroy to find where those connections began. Until then, she only had Bryson's pictures to go on.

Of course, she had another name to focus on, one that did come up in the connections she'd already managed to assemble. Seaview Marina.

A few of the names she'd pulled had been employed by the marina at the time of their encounters with the police. If Hoyt was being transparent, and he'd said some of the information was pure gossip, then there was a reason they'd been given employment at such an exclusive business. Albert Gilroy owned a yacht, but there was no mention of where it was docked.

Rebecca wasn't going to try getting a warrant to dig into his finances since the case would be long cold before his lawyers let that happen. It didn't matter. Her investigation into Bryson's murder gave her plenty of reason to go down to the marina to check it out herself.

There was one other lead she needed to follow up on. Bailey had sent over the preliminary autopsy report that evening, which included information on the bullet she'd fished out of Bryson's brain. It was listed as a .22. Not a standard caliber for gangsters, hitmen, or assassins. People who knew how to kill usually used a 9 mm at the least. Another sign that the killer wasn't experienced?

She made a mental note to look into local businesses that sold that ammo. A .22 was generally a smaller pistol, sometimes used for home protection and often sold to women who preferred a weapon with a softer kick. They still hadn't been able to rule out a jilted lover and a crime of passion.

Rebecca glanced up at the clock. Nearly midnight.

With regret, she stacked the folders with her notes so she could tuck them away and out of sight. She needed to get some sleep if she planned to march into the Yacht Club headquarters in the morning.

11

I t was hours before sunrise, but I found myself walking along the beach anyway. The darkness and I had become, if not friends, then at least well-acquainted. I'd given up on sleep what felt like a lifetime ago.

It was a different life then.

The waves slithered onto the beach to pull at the sand greedily, washing it and anything caught in its path away. To be pulled down into the abyss, into the darkest darkness, never to be seen again. I hated the ocean.

My therapist said that was unreasonable. That I may as well hate the sun and the moon. For that unhelpful piece of advice, I'd fired her. Because I did hate the sun and the moon. Not as much as the ocean, but I did. I hated everything now.

Once, I had been a person who loved. Who cherished. Who worked and laughed and lived my life. But that had been before. Now all I knew was hatred.

Was it unreasonable? Of course it was. I knew that. Logically speaking, it made no sense. But emotions rarely did. If they did, maybe everything wouldn't hurt so much. Perhaps I could have stopped all of this from happening.

Neither did the world. It made no sense. It was just pain and misery as we revolved around the damn sun while the dumbass moon circled us. At the same time, the ocean pulled us into oblivion and destroyed everything good.

All while protecting the bad.

The waves tapped gently at the sides of the boats. I could hear it. That's how I knew where I was in the dark. It's not like I was paying any attention to where I walked. The beach had led me here. Again.

I clenched my fists as I listened to the soft *lap-lap-lapping* of the boats rocking gently on the little waves. To anyone else, this would be a lullaby.

My hatred seethed.

I wanted to make it stop. It had to stop.

I moved carefully through the shadows. At least the moon was covered by clouds tonight. It couldn't paint the ocean in those silver shimmers to camouflage the horror stories it both created and contained. It couldn't light my path.

It wasn't until I was halfway through the parking lot that I realized it was nearly full. I'd been moving between cars without even noticing. My body was on autopilot, moving of its own volition as my heart filled with rage.

Why are there so many cars in the parking lot in the middle of the night?

This could be my lucky break. I walked to the door of my destination and jerked the handle. It didn't move. It was locked up tight.

My lips twisted as I caught on. They weren't here. Those fancy boys with their fancy toys. They'd left behind their shiny cars and slipped away on their boats. To head out onto that damn ocean to perform their deeds in the dark, where no one could see them or hold them accountable.

I looked around. Surely there would be a tank of gas or propane, something. Anything I could use to destroy their fancy toys and let them know that once they took their eyes off something they loved, it could be stolen without warning. That was a fact of life on this miserable planet, and these cocky little bastards were going to learn it.

Tracing the building all the way around, I found nothing. Nothing! The gates to the docks were locked and too tall for me to climb over.

It isn't fair! Why do they get all the luck? Why do they get to protect what matters to them after they took so much from me?

I grabbed my hair, ripping it out. The jolt of pain cleared my mind, and I stopped stamping around in circles. Reaching into my pocket, I pulled out my phone. I didn't need to look at the screen anymore. My fingers flew in a familiar pattern, and I held it up to my ear.

Closing my eyes, I ignored the taunting *lap-lap-lapping*, as well as the slithering, and focused on what truly mattered. My heart slowed. It was all I had left of the good that had once been mine. I listened as tears ran down my face.

Soft words filled my ear, and I opened my eyes. I was still standing next to the building by the gate to the dock. The ocean was loud, overwhelming the girl's voice. But still, I heard it.

Turning my head, I caught the noise of waves again. Followed by a braying laugh.

Rage coursed through my veins as a male voice interrupted my focus. Were those rich little bastards coming back? If so, I could show them what it was like to lose everything. Bryson Gilroy hadn't understood at first. But I'd taught him. As I'd squeezed the life from his body, I'd seen in his eyes that he finally knew how precious breath could be. I'd just had to take it away to get him to understand.

I followed the voices to the flickering light on the other side of the dune, beyond the tall grasses. Hunching over, I climbed up the sand, careful not to be spotted. My rage intensified as the voices crescendoed. I made my way through the bushy tufts of grass so I could finally see into the light.

A small bonfire crackled near the edge of the beach. It looked semipermanent, with pavers ringing the fire and a stack of split firewood off to the side. There were even wooden folding chairs and tables where four people sat, drinking and laughing. Two cocky guys with two teen girls. A bottle passed between them, and a speaker on one of the tables played a raunchy hip-hop song.

I knew they hadn't lugged all those items down here or chopped all that wood. Just look at their thin arms and shoulders. No, they'd paid someone to do it for them.

These pampered little shits couldn't even do something as simple as hang out on the beach without flaunting their wealth. All the money in the world—money that could do so much good in the right hands—and these brats paid someone else to do their dirty work, keeping their hands clean while they sat back and enjoyed themselves.

Their frivolity carried into the cool night, overwhelming the soft sounds of the ocean. I slid my hand over the butt of my gun. I'd holstered it to my leg for easy access. I'd learned my lesson. Life came at you hard and fast, determined to take everything you loved and leave you with nothing but pain and misery.

But I was fighting back.

I hated them and their carefree faces, deceiving young girls like that. Through the red fog of rage, their insipid smiles, donkey-like laughs, and clumsiness when passing the fifth seared into my consciousness like a branding iron. The stupid-sounding one had to lurch forward to catch the bottle. When he sat back up, his face was close to the fire.

I knew that face. I'd seen it before. That guy had worked with Hell's newest resident, Bryson Gilroy.

Remembering the last time I'd seen Bryson's face, I smiled for the first time today. *His eyes bulged. And even through the plastic—coated with his breath and spittle—his pleading eyes turned red. As red as his face as he struggled for air, begging for me to stop.*

I hadn't stopped. I would never stop. Not until I choked the life out of every single one of them.

My heart raced, almost convincing me I could find happiness again. But I had to get rid of them first. My fingers wrapped around the gun at my side, and I nearly pulled it, ready to charge over the hill and destroy the joy written across the smug face of Donkey Laugh.

"No. Stop it!" one of the girls shouted.

I froze.

"Guys, come on. I have to get up for work in the morning. If I'm late again, my boss will write me up. I need to go home." The girl next to Donkey Laugh was pleading with him as he urged her to drink more.

The punk leaned in, trying to make a trade. For a kiss, she could stop drinking, and he'd take her home. But the girl wasn't falling for it.

She was a good kid.

Blond and probably a sophomore in high school. The other one, the quiet one, seemed even younger. Like so many other girls on the island, they were in simple beach clothes, nothing fancy, nothing showy. Just local girls out enjoying the night air. Innocent. They both seemed to be.

What were they doing out here with these wolves? Both guys were much too old. But these pampered buffoons could only trick the young and naïve ones into spending any time with them. That's who these punks preyed on, simple girls from hardworking families.

They didn't know. Didn't know what they'd stumbled

into. What these bastards did when they weren't smiling and acting all charming.

But I knew.

And I was going to put a stop to them. Soon.

I watched for a few more minutes to make sure the blond girl wasn't falling for any of their lines. She'd be okay tonight and take the other one with her. Turning away, I headed back the way I'd come.

As for the two Lotharios? I'd let them live another day.

Besides, I needed another bag.

12

B lood on the counter.
   No.
Blood on the stall.
No.
Blood on her hands.
No.
Blood on the pillow.
No.

Daddy was laughing, telling her about the funny thing he'd just read in his book that was only funny to history buffs. He was smiling at everyone. It was good to see Daddy happy.

Blood dripped from his head, staining his lawn chair as he turned back to his book, still talking to her.

A disturbance caused Rebecca to turn toward the dune blocking her view of Sand Dollar Shores, her "vacation" rental for the summer.

Why don't you know my name, Rebecca? I know yours. We went to school together. Why don't you know my name?

Dead eyes stared at her as blood spread out from her pubescent form, staining her clothes and shoes. It ran in tiny rivulets, following the grout of the floor tiles, and dripped onto the sand beneath her. The wet sand crumbled and fell away. More blood dripped, and the sand fell faster, the dune eroding beneath the tiles, tumbling toward where Rebecca sat on her beach towel, a plastic bucket and shovel next to her. A golden retriever puppy ran past and disappeared into the trunk of a car.

No. This can't be real.

"And she thinks that just because she caught the people who paid to have her parents killed that everything will be okay." Daddy laughed, and she turned toward him again.

What?

Daddy sat in his lounge chair with a pillow tucked behind his head. Mom sat with her back against the cupboards next to him. Both hands were limp on the floor, palms up and curled with the languor of death. Her dead eyes stared into the clear summer sky as glistening drops of blood dripped from her fingertips.

"I said, she thinks that just because she caught the people who paid to have her parents killed, that everything will be okay. That everything is solved. But she never found out who gave those men the money to hire the killer. Or why they did it."

Daddy turned his dead eyes to her, and she could see the bright blue sky through the hole in his head.

"Do you really think we were the first people to be killed by them? Or the last?" Daddy laughed, his dead eyes wobbling in their sockets.

Rebecca tried to get up, to run away, but the pain in her shoulder stopped her.

Blood dripped down her arm, streaming away to join the rivers from the dead girl and her momma, forming a moat around her and Daddy. She tried to push against the car she was leaning on, to stand up, but her blood-slicked hand slipped, and she fell, splashing into the gore.

The tide came in like a tsunami, knocking her sideways. Her shoulder burned, and she tried to scream, but she couldn't tell which

way was up. Trying to use her arm was futile. It wouldn't move.
She was drowning and couldn't find her way out.

"Saltwater is the key. And God gave us plenty of that."

A young woman screamed...

Rebecca's throat ached from screaming as she tried to raise her arms to save herself, but they were numb, heavy. Her heart hammered in her chest. Louder, harder.

Finally, she was able to open her eyes.

She was sitting in the middle of her bed, blankets flung halfway to the floor.

Gasping with relief, she started to lie back down, but a throbbing in her shoulder distracted her, and she turned her head to stare at it, confused by the pain. Her right arm was wrapped in the blanket and pinned behind her body. Lifting her hips, she pulled the blanket out and untangled herself.

Her arm was still asleep, pins and needles dancing through it as blood started flowing again. Moving to the side of the bed, she leaned forward, hanging her lifeless arm down, and shook it. Mobilizing the joint, her physical therapist had called it. She continued to shake her dead arm while reaching for her phone with the one that worked.

Thumbing the lock button, she saw the time.

Quarter 'til four.

If I go back to sleep now, I can get almost four more hours of sleep before work.

She did the math out of habit. But thanks to the experiences that had taught her that habit, she also knew there was no way sleep would come. With a long-suffering sigh, she stood and made her way into the kitchen, rubbing at her shoulder and feeling the knotted scar of her gunshot wound.

In the kitchen, she filled the kettle with water, then set it on the stove top. It took her a few tries, but she finally found the cabinet where the mugs were and pulled one down. Tea was the only way she'd be able to get any more sleep tonight.

She pulled the hair tie from her wrist and looped her shoulder-length hair into a messy bun.

"Saltwater is the key. And God gave us plenty of that."

Rebecca froze. She'd heard that line before. Not in the innumerable nightmares she'd had since finding her parents gunned down in their home. She was sure of that. But someplace.

"Saltwater is the key...to what?"

She shuffled over to where she'd left her laptop on the kitchen table. That phrase seemed significant enough that she opened her browser and searched. The number of results was staggering.

Saltwater was suitable for all kinds of things, according to the internet.

"Healthy living, relaxing the mind, healing wounds...oh, taffy." A video popped up, and in spite of herself, she was mesmerized as the saltwater candy was pulled.

She shook herself free of the sugary rabbit hole she was about to get lost down in her sleep-addled state. "What the hell am I doing?"

The sooner she got this case settled, the better. Once it was done... "Solving Mom and Dad's murder didn't fix anything. Why would solving this case be any different?"

Rebecca didn't want to feel hopeless, like everything she'd accomplished in her entire career as a law enforcement officer meant nothing. But really, what good was she doing, catching criminals after they'd already destroyed lives?

She paced around the kitchen. The water should have been boiling by now. But staring at the spout as she got closer, she didn't see any steam coming out. Lifting the lid showed no bubbles either. Rebecca groaned and slammed the lid back down, glaring at the burner knob still set to off.

"Water boils faster if you turn the stove on." She grumbled, then smiled. That was something her father would have said.

Suddenly, she missed her father more than anything— even more than sleep.

A glance at the coffeepot showed that it was still half full. "This is gonna be gross, but I have to have something." Picking up her mug, Rebecca filled it with the day-old coffee and popped it in the microwave. She clung to the handle as if it were a lifeline, watching the beverage spin. As soon as it beeped, she burned the tips of her fingers grabbing the rim of the mug. "If anything's going to make this coffee palatable, it'll be seawater." Carefully holding the handle instead, she retrieved her laptop and headed for the back door.

The door stuck as she tried to open it, so she yanked harder, annoyed at everything so early in the morning. It creaked but refused to budge. "Why are you being an asshole?" Yelling at the door didn't seem to work.

After unlocking it, she tried again. It opened with a groan. Frowning, she took her coffee and laptop onto the back patio.

More than anything, she was glad her deputies couldn't see her now.

Sitting in one of the comfortable cushioned chairs, she took a few minutes to breathe and enjoy the peace. The night was dark, with the moon mostly hidden in the sky. The ocean stretched out, dark and majestic, nearly invisible in the night. Just a giant presence whispering to the island. The coffee was bitter and thick, but the salty night air soothed the unpleasant tang on her tongue.

For that brief moment, Rebecca forgot about the nightmare and everything in her life that had been rolled into it. Then, more relaxed, she settled into the plush cushion. Unfortunately, the throbbing in her shoulder flared.

Slightly more awake, Rebecca flipped open her laptop.

Signing into the department's website, she ran through the case files again to see if anything else had been added. Bailey had loaded the picture of the note found in Bryson's pants, and Rebecca scrolled to make it larger.

The writing looked masculine to her, but then, she'd only ever taken the basic intro to handwriting analysis, so it was, at best, a guess. One that could be influenced by her lack of sleep. She'd need to think about sending it to an expert if nothing else came up.

The only new evidence was a forensic report on the glass pieces she'd found. The glass contained trace amounts of alcohol and was identified as a popular brand of beer. The minute traces of blood that were on it matched Bryson's type. That didn't mean much. Bryson was O-positive, like one-third of the world population.

Having exhausted her research on the victim, Rebecca began to dig into Albert Gilroy's life. The first page of search results contained links to his social media and business websites. Of course, she'd already looked up his social media information. They were all the basic PR posts you got when you paid an expert to maintain everything. Just fluff pieces and glowing reviews of a lobbyist who could afford to have someone else polish his image.

Moving on to the second page of results, she skimmed over them. Those were mostly stories about a wealthy man making even more money by working with the rich. Forming connections, making deals, and influencing powerful people.

As a lobbyist, the man could practically do as he pleased without the general public knowing who he controlled or what legislation he influenced. Plenty of innocents had likely been hurt by the backdoor deals he'd brokered. Albert Gilroy was ruthless and didn't hesitate to step on people to get what he wanted. Collectively, the stories indicated a large pool of suspects with motives.

A few political blog posts suggested shady dealings regarding a big-ticket appropriations bill. It stopped just short of calling them bribes, but Rebecca had spent enough time on The Hill to understand what wasn't said in the articles. Still, there was no reason for anyone to go after his son instead of attacking him directly.

One article included a picture of a triumphant Albert Gilroy shaking hands with one of the senators whose bill he'd helped to push through. Senator William Morley.

A chill ran through Rebecca as she checked the article's date and reread it. It was written one full month before her final run-in with the crooked senator. At the same time, she'd been working on finding the person behind her parents' murders.

It was the case that had ended her career with the FBI and brought her to Shadow Island. And because life hadn't thrown her enough curveballs, she was now trying to get justice for the man who was cozy with the senator.

Bitterly, Rebecca wondered what dark secrets the two men shared. How intertwined were their lives? Did Gilroy donate to Morley's reelection campaign? Hand him a check? Pay for a vacation to an exotic resort? Or did he take him out on superyachts to have his choice of young women or men to keep him company for a night?

Had he been sitting back and drinking with the Gilroys on their yacht before he'd showed up in that parking garage the night she was nearly killed?

Rebecca shivered at the thought, then realized it was more than just that. A cool breeze was blowing in off the ocean. Lifting her head, she saw there were no ominous clouds, but it sure felt like a storm was building.

"But is the storm coming for me? Or am I the storm?"

13

Hoyt had just finished making his first cup of coffee at the station when a commotion broke out at the reception desk. It had become a fairly standard occurrence for people to wander in and view their late sheriff's memorial, or even stop for a quick chat. When he'd first heard the chatter, he'd thought it was just another one of those. But the voice sounded surly, if not angry. He needed to check it out.

Viviane's back was ramrod straight. Still, she wasn't using her overly professional tone...yet.

Sipping from his steaming cup, Hoyt's stroll was casual and slow while his expression remained peaceful and blank.

"But I thought she was the new sheriff. If she's the sheriff, then why isn't she here?" Nathan Warner's double chin jiggled as he complained.

Nathan ran the Sunrise Cove Motel down by the beach. He came in here often enough, asking for help to get rid of a problem guest or to file claims for a trashed room.

On hearing his light shuffle, Viviane glanced back at Hoyt and rolled her eyes. "See, Nathan, Deputy Frost can help you.

Now if you'll excuse me, I need a cup of coffee too. Mind the dispatch, Hoyt?"

He nodded, flopping down in her seat as she made her way to the back, heels slamming on carpet in what, he supposed, was an effort to let the world know of her displeasure.

"What's the problem, Nathan? Did someone leave their car parked in your lot overnight again? I can call Henry up if you need a tow."

Nathan shook his head and took a deep breath. He removed his ball cap, pushing his thinning gray hair back, and then readjusted the cap to keep the hairs in place.

Hoyt braced himself for another wild story that could only happen with tourists who thought reality didn't matter when they were on vacation.

"I wish that were the problem. But no. I've just had my third cancellation of the season." His bushy eyebrows shot up to where his hairline should be.

"Okay…" Hoyt waited for Nathan to continue but only got a bug-eyed stare in response. "That's not really a police matter, Nathan. Certainly not something the sheriff needs to look into personally."

Nathan slapped an age-spotted hand down on the counter. "But it's because of the sheriff that all my customers are canceling!"

Hoyt took another sip of coffee and stood. "How would our sheriff get your customers to cancel their reservations?" If this was the story Nathan had been pouring out to Viviane, he understood why she'd gotten so mad.

"It's because of those kidnapped girls!" Nathan threw his hands up in the air as if it should be the most logical thing.

Hoyt chewed that over. "I can see how some parents might be scared off, hearing about kidnappings happening at the beach."

"And now, because of her, I'm losing business!" Nathan jerked his head in a nod.

"You're going to have to explain how this is Sheriff West's fault."

"She's the sheriff, isn't she? She should've stopped this."

"She did. The first kidnapping wasn't even in our jurisdiction. It happened in Lynnhaven. If you wanna blame someone, go yell at Lynnhaven PD for letting it reach us." Hoyt was getting tired of the man's antics.

"Lynnhaven PD didn't make front-page news."

Hoyt stared Nathan right in the eyes, hoping the man would see the error in his line of thinking, but the older man was too worked up. "Nathan." He dropped his head and took a deep breath, telling himself he would not yell. "The story made the news because our new sheriff saved those girls. From human traffickers. From a life of sexual slavery."

"Well, I—"

"Are you standing here complaining that she saved those three little girls from that, Nathan? Is that what your complaint is? 'Cause if it is, I'll be happy to pull out a complaint form right now and write it all down, with your name attached to it so that it can be read at the next town hall meeting."

Nathan looked like he'd swallowed a beetle. His lips flapped as fast as his second chin as he shook his head. "I'm not saying that, dang it. I'm just saying it's bad for business, is all."

"And having a missing child in the two tourist towns north of us isn't? Hell, man, that's just as likely to stop people from coming as anything else. At least we found our missing girl and the others and sent them home safe. The papers all called West a hero." Hoyt was leaning across the counter and had to remind himself to not appear threatening. He stepped back.

Nathan put his fists on his hips and raised his chins. "Then where is she?"

"West? She's not in yet."

"It's already past eight. Why isn't she here? Is she already returning to her vacation? I know she rented that Sand Dollar house because she came here for vacation. Not to take a job. And now she's the sheriff, but she isn't in the office? How are we supposed to trust someone like that?"

Hoyt rubbed the bridge of his nose. "West's shift doesn't start 'til nine. If you want to see her, try calling back then."

"Nine?" Nathan went back to shaking his hands in the air. "What if something happens before then? How is she supposed to protect our town if she comes in so late every day?"

That was enough. Hoyt knew when someone was bitching just to bitch. He leaned forward again.

"First of all, I feel like you're personally attacking my deputies and me. Are you saying we aren't competent? Because we are."

Nathan shifted his feet. "No, I—"

"Way back in eighteen hundred and fuck-if-I-know, there was this man named Alexander Graham Bell. He did the craziest thing and went off and invented something called a telephone. Now there's one in just about every pocket."

Hoyt drawled out the words real slow so Nathan would know just how stupid his complaint was.

"Now we use this newfangled gadget, the tell-ee-phone, to call up the boss whenever we need her." He set his cup down and mimed spinning an old rotary dial while holding the other hand up to his ear. "When we call her, she can get into her automobile, another brilliant invention you might have heard of, and drive out to wherever we need her. It's a small island. You might have noticed that too. Doesn't take very long to get from one side to the other."

Nathan stuck his lip out, and it was not a good look on a man of his age and standing. "I don't appreciate being made fun of, Deputy Frost."

"And I don't appreciate you insulting me, my fellow deputies, and my sheriff, or wasting my time with something that should be obvious to anyone with a brain. Why aren't you at the hotel? Don't you have any guests?"

Nathan's pride kicked in just a step faster than his brain did. "Of course I still have guests. It's the start of the high season. I'm almost at capacity for the whole summer."

"You mean to tell me your business is still running even if the boss isn't on the premises? You're a twenty-four-seven operation where anything could go wrong at any time. Yet, somehow, you expect me to believe that all your guests are safe and happy without you being there?"

"Of course my guests are fine. And if anything happens, the front desk phone is routed to my…"

It was a beautiful thing to witness realization kick in.

Still, Nathan was determined to complain about something. "But Wallace was always the first one in the door every morning. You could set your watch by him. He was reliable and dependable and, most importantly, we voted for him." Nathan gave a sharp nod, as if that settled matters.

Hoyt groaned. "Nathan, Sheriff Wallace didn't work twenty-four-seven. None of us did. And for your information, I asked our new sheriff to swap shifts with me so I could spend the evenings with my wife. Now I open the office, and she comes in when things are picking up and stays late into the evening. You can set your watch by me, I guess. Don't try to do that with her. She's worked overtime every day since she started here."

"I still don't like it."

Hoyt picked up his coffee and took another sip, pissed that it was cooling down. "If you want to complain about this when special elections are held, take it up with the mayor. Sheriff West's got no say in the matter. Goes against county bylaws."

Nathan flapped his lips a bit more but seemed to be running out of steam.

"Look, Nathan, I get that you're worried. New face, new problems, you don't know how good of a job she's going to do. But I can tell you one thing, after working with her for the last couple of weeks, when the election does happen, she's got my vote."

"You can't be serious. Surely you're going to run for it. You're sure to win."

Hoyt chuckled. "West's got the brains, the training, the experience, the drive, and the balls to do the job. I've got the balls, but they're basically just for decoration nowadays. And more to the point, I don't want it. Being sheriff is a hard job. Hell, you could rescue three children, stop an international smuggling cartel, and save a puppy all in one day and people still find reasons to complain about you. Does that sound like a job you'd want?" He smiled. "And don't call me Shirley."

Nathan, either not appreciating or understanding the Leslie Nielsen quote, turned on his heel. "I'm leaving."

"Yeah, didn't think so."

Pushing away from the desk, Hoyt was about to track down Viviane when the phone rang. Instead, he snatched up the receiver. "Shadow Island Sheriff's Department, how can I help you?"

"May I speak with Deputy Frost?"

"Speaking."

"Deputy, this is Arthur Carson, manager of Sandpiper Bank. Our lawyers have informed me that you filed a warrant for the security footage on our ATM."

Hoyt clenched his jaw. "Well, Mr. Carson, you did tell me

in no uncertain terms that that was the only way to get that from you. So of course, I did."

"I'm calling to let you know that the warrant has been issued. We did not dispute it."

Hoyt frowned at the phone. He'd been prepared to fight to get that footage. "Well, good."

"I always intended to cooperate with the police. I simply needed that warrant to protect my business. In fact, the footage has already been compiled, if you'd like to come get it. Or I can drop it off later in the day."

Hoyt relaxed and even started to smile a little. This was a pleasant change of pace. "I can come over right now."

"That would be perfect. We're not open for business yet, so just knock on the door once you get here, and I'll let you in."

"I'll see you in ten minutes."

❄

HOPING his doctor didn't see him driving, Hoyt pulled into the bank parking lot and headed to the front door. A woman was waiting just inside, so he didn't need to knock. Instead, she opened the door as he approached, then closed and relocked it as soon as he was inside.

"Gotta keep it locked. Otherwise, people will just wander in. Mr. Carson is waiting for you in his office. Second door on the right."

Nodding his thanks, Hoyt walked toward the office as the woman headed for her workstation. The first office door stood open but the second was closed. Arthur Carson was printed on a black nameplate on the door. Hoyt knocked.

"Come in."

A middle-aged man sat behind a large cherrywood desk, shuffling papers around. "Right on time. Have a seat. Could you close the door behind you? I need to protect our customers' privacy."

"There are no customers."

"Oh, right. Habit." Mr. Carson set the paperwork aside and typed on his keyboard. "Again, I apologize for the delay, but red tape can get so tricky. Still, I know time is of the essence."

Hoyt sat in the plush leather chair across from the manager. He didn't know the man well. Working for the sheriff's department allowed him to use the state employees' credit union. Still, he'd always heard good things about Arthur Carson.

He was considered a real pillar of the community and a levelheaded man. After being denied access to the cameras, Hoyt had started to doubt that, but his actions now were more than making up for it.

Mr. Carson handed over a thumb drive and a sheet of paper. It was a copy of the signed warrant. Hoyt hadn't even managed to get that yet.

"This contains all the footage shot from midnight on the twenty-second until nine a.m. of the same day, as requested. Our cameras didn't run the entire time. In fact, they don't record videos at all. They take pictures once someone approaches the machine and then every two seconds while the machine is being operated."

He spun his monitor around so that Hoyt could see the screen.

"I know you were primarily focused on the footage around five-thirty, and I've wasted enough of your time, so I have that ready for you now. The angle is meant to focus on the customer's face, so we can verify it's them using their cards in case anything happens."

Hoyt scooted to the edge of his seat. "Is that gravel in the background?"

"It sure is. It's not much of a view of the parking lot, but as soon as I saw this transaction, I thought this was what you probably needed to see. It happened at five forty-three."

He hit play, and the video started. It was like a stop-motion film, with a woman walking up to the camera, using the screen. She reached for her cash and completed her transaction.

"After this, there's nothing else recorded because her transaction was complete." Arthur Carson closed the file on the computer and opened another one.

"I'd like to get a look at that parking lot again. There was a car parked there. Maybe I can pull a partial plate."

The bank manager nodded. "If you look here," he pointed toward a dark shape in the gravel parking lot. "That's not her vehicle. It's still there in the next group of photos that start at five fifty-seven."

He played the next group. This time an older woman walked up, made her transaction, and left. The car was still there but not in focus, and Hoyt couldn't even make a guess at its make and model. It was so blurry he wasn't even sure if it was a sedan or a coupe. All he knew was that it was a car.

"You always have this many customers so early?"

"Shift change at Shadow Island Community Health Center is six o'clock. So yes, we tend to have a small group now and then, which came in real handy here. At six eleven, the car is gone." He waved his hand at the screen, which showed a person walking up, using the ATM, and leaving without incident, with only an empty parking lot behind them.

"So not much help. I'm sorry." He shrugged, turning his monitor back to face him.

"It's more than we had before. We at least have an idea of when the car left the lot. Thank you for this. I'm sorry it was such a runaround to get it."

The bank manager waved Hoyt off and reached out to shake his hand, standing up as Hoyt did. "I'm the one who's sorry. If there had been any way for me to speed things up even more, I would have. Like I said, I know time is of the essence in any criminal case, which was why I went ahead and assembled that slide show presentation while I was waiting to hear back from our lawyers."

He pointed at the thumb drive in Hoyt's hand. "Those are the full-resolution files. Hopefully, your people can do something with it. And good luck with your case."

"Thank you." Hoyt headed out of the office, Arthur Carson following behind him.

"My pleasure, Deputy."

As Hoyt stepped into the doorway, he noticed that the bank was now open for business. And right there, at the front of the line, was Nathan Warner handing something to the teller. Coming up on the teller window from an angle, Hoyt watched as the woman counted a stack of crisp hundred-dollar bills. Nathan licked his lips and smiled, clearly quite pleased.

Hoyt stayed in the doorway while the owner of the Sunrise Cove Motel completed his transaction.

"Is something wrong, Deputy?" Mr. Carson asked from behind.

Nathan turned away from the window and froze when he saw Hoyt. His face went white as a ghost, and he stuffed the deposit slip into his back pocket before scurrying from the building.

"Nathan's motel is a cashless business, isn't it?"

Mr. Carson shrugged, looking out the door where the man in question had just disappeared. "I'm not sure. And I'm sorry, but if you need that information, I'll need another warrant."

Hoyt turned everything he'd just witnessed over in his head. "What other services does your bank offer?"

Catching on that something was amiss, the bank manager stepped around Hoyt and gave him a meaningful look. "Well, we offer international wire transfers and other ways to move large sums of money around. And we're more than happy to help the department any time they can get the proper warrants."

"Thank you, Mr. Carson." Hoyt nodded and headed for the door.

"Oh, and Deputy Frost."

Hoyt turned back to Arthur Carson, who was smiling. "Please tell Sheriff West I'll be voting for her in the special election. I have high hopes for what she can do for our little town."

14

Rebecca pulled into the parking lot of the Seaview Marina. She'd hesitated to drive the cruiser, so her well-loved truck stuck out like a sore thumb parked between a Benz and Rolls-Royce.

Let people wonder who it belongs to.

They might not have known there was a new sheriff in town, but they would soon.

Walking into the marina was like entering one of the many upscale luxury clubs in D.C. Leather club chairs and couches, a full-service bar, an espresso bar, and white granite counters sprawling from end to end greeted her.

She wondered what type of business was conducted at each of the three separate countertops. Maybe counter one was for the members who preferred brunettes, while counters two and three were for redheads and blonds?

Or were they divided by girls' ages?

The thought made Rebecca's stomach roil and fueled her anger. She tamped the growing rage down. She'd never get the answers she sought with her fist down someone's throat.

You'll catch more flies with honey than vinegar.

As a child, Rebecca never understood why her mother told her that so often. Why would she want to catch flies in the first place? It didn't make sense when she was little.

It made sense now.

"Welcome to my parlor," said the spider to the fly.

Ah, look. There's one now.

As expected of such a high-class establishment, she was greeted almost instantly. The man striding her way appeared to be in his late twenties or early thirties. Despite being dressed in designer clothes tailored to his body, there was something slovenly about him. His suit hung properly, but he hadn't bothered to straighten his shirt or adjust his tie. A tie that didn't even match.

Despite his unkempt appearance, he carried himself with an air of arrogance and surety that he belonged. He almost reminded her of the schoolyard bully, all grown up.

A man-child.

Yes. The description rang true.

"Ma'am, this is a members-only establishment. If you're not a member, I'm afraid I'll have to ask you to leave immediately. And take that hideous *truck* with you." He said the word "truck" like Hoyt said "fuck" when he was really pissed off. "And if you've scratched the paint on any of the cars, we'll hand over video footage to the owners so they can sue you."

And just like that, Rebecca's mood lifted, despite the nightmares that had plagued her sleep. Without needing to search for carefully concealed cameras, he'd just told her there was video surveillance if she ever needed it.

She smiled sweetly and debated batting her lashes but decided to save that tactic for later. She pulled her badge instead. "Well, if you'd like, I can come back in my other vehicle. It has all the latest bling. Flashing red and blue lights. A shiny cage for the back seat. I can even run the siren. It's really loud and will grab everyone's attention."

The man-child's badly bloodshot eyes blinked in double-time as his mouth snapped shut like a fish.

Rebecca sensed his arrogance fade away faster than her last day off. "So should I?" She lifted a brow to emphasize the question.

He blinked again, running a hand through his wavy brown hair. Rebecca took note of the gaudy ring on his middle finger. "Should you what?"

"Get my other car. The one with the lights and sirens?"

"No! No, ma'am." He held up his hands, and she counted a total of three large rings decorating his fingers. "That won't be necessary."

Oh, yeah, this dude is going to squeal.

"It's sheriff, actually. Sheriff Rebecca West."

He took a step back. "Let me get Mr. Longmire. He's the owner. I'm sure he'd be happy to talk to you."

Before he could flee, she sought to engage him. "What's your name?"

He licked his lips. "Um, Jake Underwood."

"Nice to meet you, Jake." She pulled out her notepad and jotted it down. "How long have you worked here?"

"Um, ten or eleven years now." He sniffed hard and ran a hand under his nose.

Cold or coke? It could be either or both.

"Eleven, I think. Yeah."

"Is Mr. Longmire a good employer?"

He frowned, clearly thrown by the random question. "What?"

"Mr. Longmire, the owner. Is he a good employer?" Rebecca repeated with the patience and cadence of a kinder-garten teacher.

"Yeah, I guess so. Why?"

Rebecca waved his question aside. "Do you have an

employee parking lot? Or do all employees park out front with the members?"

"There's just the one lot, but the employees have to park in the farthest corner, so the members don't have to walk as far."

"I see. And do you ever valet a car for a member? Or drive them home if they're intoxicated?"

Her random questions were throwing him off, just like she'd hoped.

"We don't have a valet service. Not really. If they're too drunk to drive, they usually get picked up by a friend. I guess." Jake's eyes grew wide. "I've never run into that issue."

Rebecca nodded sagely and started a list of things that needed fixing around her rental home. Let him wonder and worry about what she was writing down. "So what happens to the vehicles of your members who are too drunk to drive and catch a ride with someone else?"

"They...sit in our parking lot?" It seemed more like a guess than an answer consistent with an employee who'd worked here for over a decade.

"Is that a question or a statement?"

"A statement." He fiddled with the badly tied knot at his throat. "We don't mess with the members' vehicles, no matter how long they've been parked here."

"And do you know who owns the vehicles in your lot?"

"What?"

"Say 'what' again! I dare ya! I double dare you, motherfucker!" The iconic line from *Pulp Fiction* played in Rebecca's head, but she managed not to say it. Instead, she smirked.

This seemed to confuse Jake Underwood even more.

"Do you know which car in your parking lot belongs to which member of your little boat club?" Rebecca watched him nearly swallow his tongue when she said the last two words.

Such a stupid name. It could be worked into any conversation.

He recovered and lifted his chin. "We're not affiliated with any clubs."

"Then what would you call it, if not a club? A boat society? Boat ring?" She tapped her chin with her pen. "Or maybe yacht is a better word? I can never remember which one it is. Boat, yacht, ship, they're all pretty much the same to me." She shrugged as if it didn't matter.

"Seaview Marina can accommodate one hundred and twenty *yachts* up to three hundred feet long. In addition to the slips, members enjoy a host of services."

I bet they do.

She batted her lashes. "I didn't see the list of services on your website. Do you have a brochure, perhaps?"

He swiped at his runny nose again. "Membership is invitation-only, so we have no need for marketing material."

She changed direction. "How do you know if the vehicles left in your parking lot are taken by their rightful owners if they're allowed to park here for an indeterminate amount of time without issue?"

"Well, we know our members, and we're familiar with their cars. But we've never had any issue with theft or—"

"And what about the boats? Sorry, the *yachts*." She added a snooty twang to the word. "I assume you know who owns each vessel."

"Of course."

"What about Bryson Gilroy?"

"Who?"

Rebecca couldn't stop the amused grin from lifting the corners of her mouth. Though Jake was at least ten years Bryson's senior, she had little doubt the pair knew each other. Fortunately, Jake was a terrible actor whose nonstop micro expressions gave away most of his feelings.

"Bryson Gilroy," she repeated slowly. "You said you know all your members and their boats. Sorry...*yachts*. Surely you know Bryson Gilroy. He and his father, Albert Gilroy, are both members of your boat club, which isn't a club. Surely you recognize their names."

His face turned an interesting shade of pink. "Oh, yes, of course. The Gilroys."

"I'm just asking about Bryson. Do you know Bryson Gilroy? Twenty years old, short brown hair, green eyes, drives a silver Jeep."

"Of course I know Bryson Gilroy." The response held an edge of snotty elitism.

"Then you know which yacht is his?" Rebecca turned to the window and examined the obscene display of wealth lined up in neat little rows at three individual docks.

"Uh, yeah. Well, it belongs to his dad. The *Mermaid's Clam*, dock two, slip seven."

Rebecca grimaced at the awful name but flipped her notepad to a fresh sheet and wrote the information down. "Thank you. I'll have someone come by later to tow it away."

"Tow it?" Jake looked close to passing out. "What? You can't take Bryson's dad's yacht!"

Rebecca raised her eyebrows on purpose but also smiled out of reflex. Jake didn't just know Bryson. He was a friend and was trying to protect his dead friend's stuff.

"I'm not *taking* his boat. It needs to be properly searched for evidence." She forced her expression into a mask of sympathy. "Oh, dear, did you not hear? Bryson was murdered on Tuesday."

Jake's nose began to run in earnest, and he strode to a counter and grabbed some tissue. He blew his nose. Rebecca noticed spots of blood when he pulled it away.

Coke for sure.

After tossing the tissue, Jake faced her again. "Yeah, I

heard all about it. But what does that have to do with the yacht?"

"Well, poor Bryson was found in a park, but that's just where his body was dumped."

As a law enforcement officer, she was allowed to lie in order to get at the information she wanted. By acting more confident than she felt about the details leading up to Bryson's murder, she could gauge how much or little Jake Underwood might know, or had heard, about the crime.

Jake reached for another tissue. "That's terrible, but I still don't see how that—"

"At this point, we're looking into every possible theory. That the yacht was used in either the murder or the transport of his body. Or that the murderer used Bryson's Jeep in a similar way." She paused, waiting until Jake met her eye. "We're going to search under every rock and look into every corner on this island until we find the person who did this."

Jake backed up a step, his hand back at his tie. He was alarmed, but why? Rebecca didn't think he was a killer, but she did think he'd go to lengths to ensure his precious members' safety. Again...why? Because he was afraid, or because he enjoyed the fruits of the club's debauchery? It was another place for her to start digging.

Jake cleared his throat. "The *Mermaid's Clam* didn't leave the marina the day Bryson died. And he didn't drive here that day either. He caught a ride here with Luka the day before though, and they boarded Sam's new superyacht."

"So they got on this superyacht Monday evening? What time?"

He lifted a shoulder. "Monday, yeah. Around seven I guess."

"And they went out on the superyacht to party?" It was a guess.

He rolled his eyes. "Why else?"

"But you weren't invited."

He threw up his hands, clearly offended. "Of course I was invited. But I had to work in the morning, and they planned to be out until sunrise, so I couldn't go." His chin went up again. "They were all bummed I couldn't make it. Luka said he'd toss back a few shots for me."

Rebecca smiled. "What a nice friend. Any idea how many shots he tossed back in your name?"

Jake lifted a shoulder. "No idea. Probably not enough, because he said things got rowdy, and they ran out of supplies early. Had to call it a night just after five."

Rebecca wrote it all down. "Luka who?"

"Huh?"

Damn.

Jake was back to feigning ignorance.

"Luka, your friend who tossed back the shots in your honor. What's his last name?"

"He's not my friend."

Interesting.

"So he tosses back shots for strangers?"

The knot in the tie was down a couple inches now, and Jake scratched at the scruff on his neck. "Why not?" His laugh was forced. "Any excuse, right?"

"What's Luka's last name?"

"I don't know. I just heard Bryson call him Luka."

"What was Bryson wearing before he and Luka got on Sam's superyacht?"

Alarm widened his eyes. "I don't know."

"Luka would know, though, right?"

Red welts started to sprout on Jake's throat. "I guess."

"Luka would also know where he last saw Bryson, too, right?"

"Maybe."

"What about Sam and his superyacht?"

Jake gulped so hard she heard the click in his throat. "Who?"

Rebecca lowered her notepad and gave Jake her most sincere fake smile. "Do you want to find out what happened to Bryson?"

"Of course."

"And you said the boats outside all have their owners listed in your registration. Since you want me to find out what happened to Bryson, I need both Luka and Sam's contact information. I can wait right here while you get it."

Jake's eyes darted around the room. He might be willing to defend a dead friend who was a member, but not if it meant throwing other members to the wolves. Maybe *especially* if they'd been involved in murdering one of their own.

Loyalty was such a strange and fickle thing.

"Jake, who are you talking to?"

A man appeared in the doorway behind one of the white counters. His shirt was perfectly pressed, and the collar was flat and sharp, precisely where it should be. His jacket was done up neatly with his buttons in a perfectly straight line. This was a man who took care of himself and had the confidence to back it up.

Understated, elegant, polished…and displeased. He wasn't quite frowning at Rebecca, not yet. She figured it was because he wasn't certain if she was the guest of a member.

Jake jerked as if he'd just been caught with his hand in the cookie jar, spinning around to face this man. Clearly his boss.

"Mr. Longmire. Um, this is, uh, West. She wanted to look at Bryson Gilroy's yacht, but I told her she couldn't do that. I was just telling her she needed to leave." He stumbled on nearly every word.

Rebecca stepped forward, her hand out. "Mr. Longmire, so nice to meet you."

He gave her a single shake. "Who are you?"

She pulled out her badge. "Rebecca West. Sheriff with the Shadow Island Sheriff's Department."

Two deep lines appeared between his eyebrows. "Why are you interested in a member's yacht, and why are you interrogating one of my employees? What business do you have here?"

Rebecca tucked her notepad away. With this man, it was better to look as nonthreatening as possible. "I came to talk to you, but I was just chatting with Jake first. Your employee is excellent, very helpful, and knowledgeable."

The frown lines grew deeper as Longmire's gaze slid from her face to Jake's.

Jake was trying to smile, but his misery snaked out instead.

Longmire's attention came back to Rebecca. "Well, if you came here to speak to me, let's take this to my office, where we can have some privacy."

Rebecca nodded graciously and followed him down a narrow hallway. Longmire's office, like the man, reflected a refined and understated classic luxury.

No gaudy knickknacks or gold-trimmed anything. Just fine wood furniture and top-of-the-line electronics. The office was set up so the guest in the leather visitor's chair either felt like they were the most important person in the room or that they were out of their league and didn't belong. The occupant made all the difference.

Sitting, Rebecca made a show of adjusting her holster before crossing her legs and leaning back against the buttery-soft leather.

Lewis Longmire knew precisely what she was doing, she could tell. He didn't even bat an eye at the flash of her gun. Most likely because he was so used to seeing them.

"What is this about?" He sat primly behind his desk, his manicured hands folded in front of him.

"Murder," Rebecca enunciated slowly.

Surprise and something else flashed on Longmire's face so quickly that she couldn't say with any certainty what the second emotion was. Dismay? Disgust?

He ran a finger down his tie. "Yes, a tragic thing. Bryson Gilroy was taken much too young. He was a good boy from a loving family. He will be missed."

"Honestly, Mr. Longmire, you're the first person to say that." She leaned forward, projecting a sorrowful expression. "His own father didn't even say that. Nor did his stepmother. Neither of them shed a tear after learning their son was dead."

"Well, people all deal with grief differently."

Rebecca gave a slow shake of her head. "I've been telling myself the same thing for the last two days, trying to make some sense of his father's behavior." Rebecca wanted a reaction from this man. "I even checked to see if Bryson was adopted, which might have explained why his father was so detached. But nope, Bryson was Albert's biological son. He was even there when he was born. I saw a picture of it. It looked like it was the best day of his life. Now?" She shrugged, interlacing her fingers across her waist.

"Ms. West, I—"

"On Monday, Albert Gilroy's son was alive and heading to a party. Today, his son is dead, splayed open in the morgue while we determine who put him there. And all Mr. Gilroy seems to care about are threats and his own privacy. What happens to a man that turns him from a loving father into such an emotionless robot?"

Rebecca suspected the line about watching his son born would get to Longmire. She'd already combed through his online presence. He, unlike Albert Gilroy, seemed to be a doting father who shared pictures of his sons and daughter. On their birthdays, he posted photos of himself holding them as newborns in the hospital, and he'd looked like he'd just been handed the most coveted prize in the world.

She was right. Longmire was visibly disturbed.

"I'm not sure. You would know about that better than me. Since you're law enforcement."

"Me? No." She shook her head in easy denial. "I deal with the sickos and the drunks, the down on their luck, and the psychopaths, but I only do that for a few minutes at a time. And I never cater to them."

Curiosity lifted his eyebrows. "What do you mean?"

"I don't ask them if they would like something to drink before they sail off to commit heinous crimes. I don't offer to mop their floors when they return from purchasing a human or raping someone who was too drugged out of their mind to know what was happening." She sharpened her gaze. "And I've never turned a blind eye and a deaf ear to a sobbing victim and wished their abuser a safe trip before going home to kiss my kids goodnight. No, Mr. Longmire, you would know about such men far better than I ever could."

Longmire swallowed hard, his Adam's apple pushing against the tight collar of his pristine white shirt. "I don't know what you're talking about, Sheriff West. I've never been around such men. I run a reputable and exclusive marina with carefully selected clientele. All of whom must have at least two references from current members to be considered for entrance."

Rebecca nodded along as if she already knew this song and dance. "That's what the Crips say too."

He jerked his chin back, pulling himself up high in his chair. "We are not a gang, Ms. West. I—"

"Are you aware that what you just outlined as your membership policy is also a general requirement to join any gang? Whether it's the mafia, a street gang, a biker gang, or the Yacht Club. They all have the same requirements. And the funny thing is, they all say the same thing too." She raised her hands to air quote the next words. "'We're a legitimate but exclusive group of like-minded individuals who just like to get together and party sometimes.'"

Okay. So maybe it wasn't a direct quote, but still...

"And when one of their own dies, they all band together. They shut out the cops so no one can see what they're doing behind closed doors."

The marina owner had gone from offended to disgusted back to offended and was now stuck on resigned with his hands tightly clasped on his desk. "You didn't let me finish. I'm more than happy to help in any way I can to find out who murdered one of our members, but—"

"But you can't invade any of the other members' privacy by divulging any information that might paint them in a bad light?" Rebecca supplied, lifting one eyebrow.

Longmire showed her his teeth. "Similar to attorney-client privilege, if you will."

"Except you're not an attorney or a doctor, are you, Mr. Longmire?"

His gaze darted around the room. "No."

Uncrossing her legs, Rebecca leaned forward, resting her elbows on her knees. "That's the same line a gang leader of MS-13 fed me when I investigated the murder of one of his dismembered members. Of course, he didn't call himself a gang leader either. He was the 'chapter head' of a 'legitimate and exclusive group.'" Rebecca made a point of looking around his office. "His office was similar to yours too."

"I assure you." Longmire's chuckle was full of mockery. "I am not the head of any organized crime syndicate."

Rebecca *tsked* and sat back in her chair again. "That's too bad for you. If you're not a part of the gang, then you're not protected by them either. And if they find out you helped protect someone who killed one of their own, they'll get their revenge."

His mouth popped open, but no sound escaped.

She spread her hands. "It's just good business. Someone takes from you, and you take back twice as much. What do you have that Albert Gilroy will see as compensation for his son's life, Mr. Longmire?"

Rebecca had to hand it to him. Lewis Longmire lasted a full minute before his shoulders fell. "What do you want?"

"Answers. The truth."

He scoffed. "As you can imagine, I am not in a position to do that."

"We can protect you."

It was a promise she didn't know she could keep, but he didn't need to know that. She held little sympathy for anyone who covered the monstrosities she suspected the Yacht Club committed daily. But she needed to get him talking and would have offered him the world at that point.

His nostrils flared. "I highly doubt that. Tell me what you want to know, and I'll decide how open I can be."

"Was Bryson Gilroy here Monday evening?"

Longmire closed his eyes, unconsciously blocking himself from the question. "Yes."

"Did he arrive with a man named Luka?"

"Yes."

"Did he and Luka board the superyacht of a man named Sam?" She badly wanted to ask for both Sam and Luka's last names but was afraid the question would shut the flow of information off. She'd try a bit later.

"Yes."

"Did he come back, dead or alive, on any of the vessels moored in your marina?"

Longmire opened his eyes, and a twitch made the left one

jump. "He did not return on any vessel, in any condition, Monday night or Tuesday morning, which is when the superyacht he left on returned to its slip."

"What was the name of the superyacht he left on?"

Longmire was so tense that his neck muscles clenched as he answered. "The *Tide Bagger*."

Rebecca winced at the name. *These guys should be brought up on charges for bad boat names alone.* But with that knowledge, she could track down ownership if Longmire refused to share.

She forced a grin. "I can see why you don't make it known which yachts dock at your marina."

Longmire had the good grace to look embarrassed. "People can be overly creative when choosing names."

That's one way to look at it.

"If Bryson Gilroy didn't return on the *Tide Bagger*, can you tell me how he might have gotten off the superyacht and back onto the island?"

One side of Longmire's mouth tipped up. "Swim."

She wasn't amused. "How else?"

"A few homes have private docks."

"Do the Gilroys possess such a dock?"

Longmire picked up a paperclip, turning it between his fingers. "I don't think so, no."

"Do you happen to know which private dock Bryson might have used?"

"I'm sorry, no."

Rebecca scanned her brain for more questions. "Other than the private dock option, how else might Bryson have made it to shore?"

He unfolded the paperclip. "An individual can be dropped off at 'most any point on the island. They can either sleep it off on the beach or walk home if they're able. We charge extra for cleaning up vomit, and we won't clean any vessel until they're one hundred percent vacant."

Was he trying to sidetrack her?

"How do the yachts get in close enough to drop the passengers off? Doesn't that damage the hull or engine?"

His twitching eye narrowed. "It would, yes. That's why they typically use jet skis or a small raft."

"Gas engines?"

Longmire inclined his head and used one edge of the paperclip to scrape under a fingernail. "Yes."

"May I see the receipts for the fuel bill for the *Tide Bagger*?" When he hesitated, she smiled. "I can get a warrant."

He sighed. "There's no need. On Tuesday morning, one of the *Tide Bagger's* jet skis needed its fuel topped off, and it had marks that needed to be buffed out, indicating it had been driven up onto a beach. Based on fuel use, it was an extremely short trip. A mile, tops."

Strange.

"Do you always top off tanks like that?"

"Yes. It's part of the service we provide. Full tank after each excursion. I wouldn't have paid attention to how much gas was added but had to sign off on the maintenance service to fix the body damage."

"Would a mile be just far enough to drive Bryson to shore, then make it back to the superyacht?"

"Yes."

"Was there any blood or damage to the jet ski other than the scraped bottom?"

"No, nothing."

He unfolded the paperclip until it was a straight line. Was he planning to stab her?

"Any blood or signs of violence on the *Tide Bagger* when you cleaned it up that morning?"

"No, of course not."

Rebecca nodded, knowing she could have forensics luminol the entire ship...*if* she could get a warrant.

"Do you have any members who are judges?"

Longmire lifted his chin. "I can't say."

That would be a yes.

"What are Luka's and Sam's last names? And when did the *Tide Bagger* leave and return to the marina?"

His lips thinned. "You'll need to present a warrant for any additional information." He crossed his arms over his chest. "I've already said too much."

Deciding not to press him any further, Rebecca stood and held out her hand. "Thank you, Mr. Longmire, for your cooperation. That's all I need for now."

Longmire tossed the paperclip into the trash before standing and taking her hand. "Like I said, we're a legitimate company. We're more than happy to fulfill our civic duties so long as it does not interfere with our clients' need for privacy."

Rebecca snorted inelegantly and handed him a card she'd written her cell phone number on. "Did you just hear yourself?"

He leaned forward, planting his knuckles on the desk. "This club has been around for a lot longer than you or I have, Sheriff West, and they will be here long after we're dead and our grandchildren have moved away."

"Oh, that I believe." Rebecca ran a lingering gaze around the expensive office. "Slave trade and smuggling go back to the Vikings. And no matter how many laws we pass in an attempt to halt it, there will always be people who value money over humanity." She turned on her heel and headed toward the door.

Longmire gave an exasperated sigh and hurried around the desk to follow. "I'm not involved in any form of criminal activity. I am simply the owner of a marina where people happen to park their yachts. Think of it as a glorified parking lot for overpriced boats. I have nothing to do with anything that happens once they leave the marina."

Rebecca faced him. "That's what everyone says during their RICO trial."

Lewis blinked at her rapidly, and she thought she saw him start to sweat.

"A what?"

"RICO. It's short for Racketeer Influenced and Corrupt Organizations Act. You can look it up. A smart guy like you, I'm sure you know all about those kinds of things."

"I'm unfamiliar."

Rebecca wasn't buying the innocent act. He'd only shared what he had so far to make her go away. In the end, he'd told her nothing that would sully his or the marina's name.

"RICO can not only lead to criminal charges against everyone involved, but also lead to the seizure of personal possessions when you're found guilty. Things like your cars, house, boat, pension funds, college funds, trust funds, all that fun stuff. Of course, since it's federally prosecuted, they'll go after any holdings, even if they're not in the United States, and lock those up tight too. Then the IRS gets involved, and things really get messy."

Watching Longmire's eyes quiver, Rebecca thought she had finally gotten through to him.

"You wouldn't."

She took a step closer to him. "I assure you, Mr. Longmire, if I find out the Yacht Club had anything to do with Bryson Gilroy's murder or any illegal activities were committed that led to his death, I will come after the club and take down anyone who gets in my way."

She turned and headed out. Reaching for the doorknob, she stopped when Longmire grabbed her arm. "But the Gilroys are members of the Yacht Club as well as Luka and

Sam. Why would someone in the Yacht Club kill one of their own?"

Rebecca stared at his hand until he dropped it away. It gave her a few precious seconds to ponder his question.

In all honesty, she didn't have an answer. At this time, there didn't seem to be any motive for Bryson's death. And if it'd been a Yacht Club member, why stage him at the park instead of dropping him into the water for the sharks or other marine life to consume?

Dismissing her own questions, she met Longmire's gaze, prepared to fake her way through it. "I already said I don't understand men like these or why they do the horrible things they do. But ask yourself this, why wouldn't they kill Bryson Gilroy? How many of them have changed their habits since he died?"

He paled. Just from his expression, she knew the answer. No one in the Yacht Club had missed a single party or trip since one of their own was murdered.

"I don't know."

She turned the knob. "Me either, but I intend to find out."

Before she could pull the door open, he lifted a hand, not touching her this time. "Sheriff?"

She raised an eyebrow. "Yes?"

"Another thing to keep in mind." He lifted his gaze to hers. "When kings and queens fight, their servants die first."

15

Now that the adrenaline rush of breaching the lion's den had faded, Rebecca was not only tired but in a foul mood. Pushing open the door to the sheriff's department, she expected to receive a hint of joy seeing Viviane's smiling face, but there was none to be had.

For the first time since she'd started working here, the receptionist desk was unoccupied.

Rebecca's frown deepened into a scowl. She didn't want any nasty surprises today. She unlocked the half door and went into the bullpen.

Empty.

She dragged herself over to the coffee station and flipped over a paper cup. Picking up the pot, she groaned as she realized it was too light. Empty. Not even a sip.

"Sheriff West, that you?" Hoyt called from the locker room.

"It's me. And I would like to report a crime." She slid the pot back onto the burner. "Someone drank the last cup of coffee and didn't make more. And it's not even ten yet."

Hoyt's laugh preceded him up the hallway, and Rebecca debated if this would qualify as a justified homicide.

She leaned on the little table that made up most of their kitchenette and dropped her head. Sleep had been impossible after she'd woken up before the crack of dawn, and she still had another eight hours on the clock, at least. There was no way she would get through this day without an excess of caffeine.

"Don't worry, Boss. I got your back."

Hoyt, an angel in his navy-blue shirt and uniform pants, held out an extra-large cup with one of those little thermal sleeves. She snatched the coffee and took a greedy sip. Finding it the perfect temperature, she drank down a few swallows. "Aah! That's just what I needed. What's up with the coffeepot, and where's Viviane?"

"She got a little upset this morning, so she started cleaning to calm down. There's vinegar in the reservoir." He jutted his chin toward the nonworking coffee maker.

"Where is she now?"

He took the last cup from the carrier. "Not sure. She ran out to get these before you got here and came back madder than ever. She handed them to me, then stormed out again. Said it was 'official business,' so I'm not gonna question it." Hoyt took a sip of his coffee. "I'm not the boss, after all."

Touched by the thought that Viviane had made sure she had coffee, Rebecca ignored the "boss" part. She would call her friend in a minute.

"Are you covering the phones? And did we get that warrant yet?"

"Phones have been quiet, thank goodness, and you're not going to believe this. The bank manager, who'd insisted on the warrant, called *me* to say he'd received it and had everything ready for me before they even opened. Was happy to do it, just didn't want to get in any trouble."

"What did we get?"

Hoyt sat down on the corner of Locke's desk. "A tiny view of the park's parking lot over the shoulder of a person using the ATM. It's black and white and out of focus, but I could see part of a front quarter panel on a car. Maybe."

Disappointment slammed into her. "That's not much."

He shrugged. "I got the pictures, if you wanna see 'em." He checked his notes. "I ran the video back and, best I could tell, the vehicle arrived at the park at midnight and left at three minutes 'til six. Odd hours to visit a park, wouldn't you say?"

She nodded. "Very. Any sign of the driver?"

"You guessed it. I hoped to have something to show you when you finally decided to roll out of bed and make it into work." He pointedly looked at the clock while hiding a smile behind his coffee cup.

She pointed to the dark circles beneath her eyes. "Does this look like a person who's had much sleep?"

He chuckled, but his expression was concerned. "You work late again?"

"Yes…and also started work early. Went through more of the files."

"Find anything useful?"

"You could say that. I followed some leads and went to the Seaview Marina this morning as soon as they opened."

Hoyt nearly spit out his coffee. "You went there without backup?"

Rebecca snorted. "The only danger I was in was of Jake Underwood pissing his pants and splashing my shoes. Were you going to take that bullet for me?"

Hoyt grimaced and shook his head.

Rebecca laughed. "Yeah, I didn't think so. Some battles you have to face on your own. Thankfully, he didn't spill his bladder, but he did spill some of his guts. And so did Lewis Longmire."

When Hoyt nearly choked on his coffee again, he set the cup on the desk. "Instead of going around obstacles, you smash into them like a battering ram."

"Around, through, over." She shrugged as she flipped through her notes. "I'm flexible. But I did discover some of Bryson's movements on Monday."

Hoyt clapped his hands together. "That's a good start."

"It helps, but it opens up even more questions. Here's what we know so far." Rebecca went over to the whiteboard to write as she spoke. "Bryson left the Gilroy home at an undetermined time on Monday, driving his Jeep. Bryson met his friend, Luka No-last-name, at an unknown location. Luka drove Bryson to the marina, and they both got on the *Tide Bagger*."

"What the hell is a *Tide Bagger*?"

"Sam No-last-name's superyacht."

"Super small dick compensator maybe." Hoyt shook his head. "Never mind. Keep going."

Rebecca bit back a smile. "The *Tide Bagger* left the marina at an unknown time with Bryson aboard and returned to the marina sometime after five a.m. without him. Longmire said a jet ski was missing enough fuel to cover about a mile, so a theory is that the jet ski grabbed Bryson from the big boat and dropped him off at an unknown location that we can only assume was the beach near the park."

Hoyt grimaced. "That's a lot of unknowns."

She nodded and drew a crude map of the beach, the park, and the Gilroy home on the board. "The assumption is that Bryson cut through the park on his way home." She placed a red X in the middle of the park.

"What do we know about this Luka and Sam?"

"Practically nothing. And right now, we don't have enough for a warrant to seize any information from the marina." She didn't mention that she suspected a judge was a member. That was something to worry about another day.

Hoyt waved a hand, and she realized she'd been staring out into space. "Sorry, what?"

"I was just telling you not to get down. You might not have enough for a warrant yet, but you will."

His faith in her lifted Rebecca's spirits. "You know, these are adult men, but the more I learn about them, the more immature they sound. The Gilroys named their yacht the *Mermaid's Clam*, and I can only hope that Bryson was the one doing the naming. I thought they were called boys because they were the younger generation of Yacht Club members. Now I think it's because they're man-children."

"Alleged members of the Yacht Club."

She waved that off. "No, that was another thing I learned today. Longmire was adamant that this club has been around for generations. And he's scared. He also believes no one in his lifetime has ever tried to stop them, which is why the club is getting more brazen."

Hoyt shifted uneasily. She wondered if he was thinking of Wallace.

Her phone beeped, and she held up a finger while she opened the email. "Forensics tested the pieces of glass and the hair entwined in the bark I found. Both the blood and hair belong to Bryson. I think we can safely identify that location as the starting point of the attack since that bark fits the missing section from that tree."

Hoyt moved over to the whiteboard and added the information. "Another puzzle piece is in place, but it doesn't help home in on the killer."

She groaned. "I know. Cyber is still working to unlock his phone and computer. Though we had access to Bryson's living space earlier, I'd feel better having an official warrant.

His Jeep is still missing too. We, quite honestly, don't have much to go on."

Her deputy reached down to pick up his cup. He fumbled, and coffee spilled onto the mouse of his fellow officer's desk. "Shit."

Locke's screensaver disengaged, and Rebecca did a double take when she glanced at the screen. "You've got to be kidding me." Not only had Locke not password-protected his computer, he was still logged into his account. The Gilroy case file was open for anyone to see.

Hoyt came back with a handful of napkins. "What?" Following her line of sight, he cursed. "He knows better than to do that shit."

Leaning over the desk, Rebecca logged Locke out of the server, then started the shutdown routine. Twice now, Gilroy had been a step ahead of them, possessing information he shouldn't. With lax security like this, she wasn't surprised.

"I'll have a talk with him later." Hoyt's voice echoed with defeat. It was clear from his tone that he'd had that talk before.

Rebecca shook her head. If she stuck around, she might have to look into Locke's personnel file to see what kind of training he'd had or still needed. But not now.

Since she and Hoyt were the only two people in the office, she wasn't going to waste precious conversation time on someone like Trent Locke.

"I'll have a word with him, but let's go back to the case. Lewis Longmire should have been anxious and worried when I showed up at the marina today. Instead, he seemed confused and surprised. Is it because no cops ever bothered to show up there, even though they knew that was where the Yacht Club gathered? Did no one ever think it would be a good idea to pop in while on patrol, just to let them know law enforcement was aware and watching?"

"No."

"Why not?"

Hoyt scrubbed his face with his hand. "Wallace told us to leave them alone. Said he'd handle it all. He was getting a lot of pressure about not letting anything impact tourism. And…" He clamped his mouth closed.

Rebecca wasn't going to let him off that easy. "And?"

"We were getting anonymous death threats. Bad reviews. People were complaining."

She scoffed. "You ignored wrongdoings because of a few complaints?"

Looking miserable, Hoyt shook his head. "One time, Wallace took a weeklong vacation and, while he was gone, there was a drunk boating accident. Destruction of private property, serious injuries. We were doing our jobs, taking witness statements, the usual stuff. Well, people got riled up, and lawyers showed up. Wallace came back to work three days before he was supposed to and took everything over. After that, things settled down."

Rebecca was speechless for a second before sputtering, "That's part of the job."

"What is?"

"Death threats. Screaming lawyers. Complaints." She started to pace. "Darian pulled over a drunk driver last week. He spewed threats the whole trip back to the station. And you know what happened? Darian added those to the list of charges against the guy. Because *that's our job.*" She threw up her hands. "Kowtowing to the rich bastards won't stop us from getting death threats. Just not from them anymore because you all stopped doing your jobs when it came to them."

Hoyt stared at her, slack-jawed, his cup dangling from his fingertips. He looked like he'd just had the world's most significant epiphany.

"Hoyt, firemen get burned. Doctors get sued. Hell, cashiers get death threats all the time. Why do you think our job should be any less dangerous than everyone else's? We knew that was a possibility when we signed up. That there was a chance we would be killed on the job. They give us guns for a reason."

She took a deep breath, trying not to sound as judgmental as she felt.

"But now you've got an entire generation of kids who are threatened by this Yacht Club and what these men might do to *them*. You've got teen girls being harassed, assaulted, and hauled off in the dark of the night."

Unable to look at him any longer, Rebecca picked up her cup and headed toward her office. Halfway there, she turned back. She wasn't quite finished yet.

"Hoyt?"

He didn't even lift his head. "Yeah?"

"Do you feel better putting your uniform on every morning knowing kids like Cassie Leigh and Dillon Miller are being threatened, hurt, and harassed instead of you?"

His head dipped lower. "No."

"Good. Then let's do something about it."

16

For the next four hours, Rebecca stayed in her office. She heard Viviane come back in and have a conversation with Hoyt. But it was barely discernable through her closed door. Every time she thought of her senior deputy and his excuses, she got angry again. Working behind a closed door, she felt alone and isolated. That hurt more than she'd expected. A lot more.

You were starting to feel at home here. That was a stupid move. You're just the interim sheriff, after all. Stop trying to fit in here when you didn't even fit in at the FBI.

Rebecca berated herself. Benji had more authority, better resources, less to lose, and had known and worked with her for years. If he hadn't been willing to go up against corrupt politicians, why did she think a career deputy on this small island would be?

Still, it hurt.

Some ever-hopeful part of herself—the part that tried to see the good in people and believed in the oaths she'd sworn to uphold the law—was hurt. Again.

You gotta get over it. When you leave, they'll forget about you as quickly as they forget about any other tourist.

She hated the cold, calculating part of herself that had only gotten stronger over the last few years. But, just like now, it was so often right. It had been right the whole time she'd investigated her parents' deaths, about who was behind them.

Well then. If I'm just temporary...

She looked around the mostly empty office. Sure, there was furniture, but there were no touches of personality in the room. There wasn't even a nameplate on the door.

If she was temporary, it wouldn't matter if she stepped on a few toes. Even if she ended up leaving, she could still make them wish to God they'd never met her in the first place.

Feeling better, Rebecca logged off and left the office. Spite was as good a motivator as anything else she'd ever found. Second only to love, which was running on empty in her life.

She waved to Viviane as she walked out the door. "I'm heading out. Call if you need me."

"Be safe."

Just those two little words coming from the lips of someone who gave a damn eased a little weight off Rebecca's heart. Hopping into the cruiser, she punched in the address she'd looked up that morning.

Cottage Sports was an old family-run sporting goods store specializing primarily in fishing, scuba, and other beach-related gear. But they were also the only store on the island that sold ammo and a selection of guns for hunting or personal defense.

A little bell on the door rang as she walked in.

A man at the counter looked up from some type of ledger. One eye squinted, his mustache twitched back and forth as he examined her from head to toe. Finally, his gaze dropped to her waist, and he gave a slight nod. "Afternoon, Sheriff. What can I do for ya today?"

She stuck out a hand. "I'm hoping you can provide me a bit of information. Are you Ralph Montgomery?"

His shake was firm. "I sure am, and I'll do my best."

"Are you aware of the recent murder of Bryson Gilroy?"

Mr. Montgomery's smile faded. He took his glasses off and tucked them in his breast pocket. "'Course I am. Everyone's talking about it. Wondering what it means. Got a lot of people worried."

Rebecca knew what that meant. Worried people tended to take steps to protect themselves. Unfortunately, he'd probably seen a lot of customers in the last couple of days, and not for the snorkel sets currently on sale.

"I'm interested in learning who might have purchased .22s recently."

He closed his ledger and slid it behind the counter. Rebecca very politely didn't look down at it, keeping her gaze on his pale blue eyes.

"Why? That's their business. Why do you think it's yours?"

"Bryson Gilroy was shot with a .22."

He shrugged, clearly not worried. "It's popular."

"You're right. I'm hoping you'll give me a list of people who purchased that caliber. If you do, I might be able to track down his killer a little faster."

"And harass a lot of innocent people while you're at it." Mr. Montgomery bristled, his mustache twitching over the scowl. "I can't go sharing people's details and trampling on their rights...'specially not for the likes of one of *them*. That would put me out of business. And, more importantly, it goes against my morals."

That was interesting.

"Them who?"

He waved a hand in the direction of the ocean. "Those rich bastards who think they own this place."

"Mr. Montgomery, I'm not interested in trampling anyone's rights or damaging your reputation. I just want to do my job and catch a killer." She shot him her most earnest smile.

"Then you'll need a warrant first." He seemed a bit mollified.

"I like you, Mr. Montgomery. You're my kind of people."

Mr. Montgomery seemed like he wanted to say something but pressed his lips closed.

"I heard you're a good businessman who wouldn't sell guns under the table."

He squared his shoulders. "That's right. All my guns are sold properly, with proper permits and paperwork, each and every time. I do all the paperwork myself."

"I'm glad. That's why I was hoping you could help with my investigation into the ammo. I felt sure you'd keep good records on that type of thing."

"Well, like I said, you'll need a warrant first."

Rebecca nodded, though she knew she had little chance of getting one. "I'll look into that, because it's not up to me to decide who gets justice and who doesn't. Far as I'm concerned, we're all equal under the law, and the laws should be applied equally as well. Coming from money shouldn't change that, whether you're the victim or the perpetrator."

Mr. Montgomery chewed his bottom lip for a full thirty seconds. "That's how it should always be. I agree. But you understand, I can't help you with that."

Rebecca grinned and tapped the glass countertop with her nails. "You still can. I need some .45 hollow points. I used up some of mine last weekend and need to replenish. Maybe you heard about that too? Sheriff's office doesn't stock mine, so I thought it would be easier and involve less paperwork to get my own."

Mr. Montgomery nodded, his eyes gleaming with just a hint of respect. "Heard about that, yeah." He pulled out the box of ammo, and she walked with him to the register to ring it up.

As she took her bag, he cleared his throat. "I file all my revolver sales through the ATF. They keep records that you can search through, as you probably know. Also, when it comes time, you've got my vote, Sheriff West." He gave her one last nod and turned to go back to his bookkeeping.

He'd seemed to stress the word "revolver." Was that a hint?

Even though she already knew she could search those records and planned to contact ATF, Rebecca also knew it was a paper chase that could take days. But she appreciated the show of solidarity. Both to justice and to the laws that protected people's rights. He hadn't needed to mention that or the revolver sale.

Did Mr. Montgomery have his own suspicions about the Yacht Club? His wave toward the ocean led her to believe he might. She couldn't help but think he wasn't happy about the club or how it'd been handled in the past.

Walking out of the store, ammo in hand and feeling a little less alone, Rebecca took a deep breath of the clear ocean breeze. There was just a hint of something, an aroma in the air. Her stomach growled in response. Then, realizing that she hadn't eaten since breakfast, she followed her nose to see where the delicious scent was coming from. A small café seemed to be the culprit and was within easy walking distance.

As she got closer, Rebecca realized the place was familiar. It wasn't until she got inside that she remembered coming here with Wallace a couple of weeks ago. She took in the long bar with the metal edging, and another memory surfaced.

She'd sat there as a child…

She and Mommy had been out playing at the beach. They were sitting at the counter, all smiley and sun-kissed, waiting on Daddy to join them. She was finishing a strawberry milkshake, her first of many. He came in and kissed the top of her head. The waitress helped her get down off the tall swivel stool and showed them to a booth.

It had been the first time she'd had a double-decker sandwich too. Funny, that memory hadn't surfaced back with Wallace. So consumed by the case, Rebecca hadn't bothered to take in the space to stir her recollection. Of course, they'd dined on the patio that day.

"Ma'am? Can I help you?" The hostess looked concerned. Appearing to be in her early sixties, she had fine lines feathering away from her light blue eyes. Her bright pink lips were a sharp contrast to pale skin and the silver top knot pinned securely at the crown of her head.

Feeling her cheeks heat up a bit, Rebecca laughed. "Sorry, I was caught up in memories. I came here as a child with my parents. This place has changed a bit since then."

The woman straightened, glancing around the restaurant with a proud smile. "Oh, a fresh coat of paint, some new booths, new owner," she pointed to herself, "but still the same delicious food and family friendly service."

Rebecca walked up to the hostess stand, finally leaving the entryway where she'd been reminiscing. "Family friendly is right. I remember there was this waitress. She was so sweet to me. She gave me the whole metal cup with my milkshake because there was extra in it. Even helped me carry it to the booth and—"

"You couldn't finish your meal because you kept drinking

that milkshake. Had pink ice cream from your eyeballs to your kneecaps." She laughed.

Rebecca peered deeper into the older woman's face. "Betty?"

"You remember my name?" Stepping forward, Betty wrapped her in a hug. "I haven't seen you in years, Katey Cat. I heard about your folks. I'm so sorry."

Rebecca held onto her smile despite the spear of grief that sliced deep. Her dad had given her that nickname. And it had stuck 'til college. Somehow, though, standing here with sweet Betty made the pain more bittersweet than brutal.

"What are you doing back here, sweetheart? Come to visit again? Maybe bring your own family? Restart the tradition?"

Laughing, Rebecca tapped the badge on her belt. "Actually, I'm the interim sheriff."

"Rebecca West! Sheriff West! Of course. The one who found that kidnapped little girl." The woman clapped her hands over her mouth and hugged her again. "I heard what you did, putting up that memorial in the sheriff's department. That was real decent of you. But look at me, blathering on when you're probably starving. Let me get you a menu."

"Thank you. I'm looking forward to a good meal."

Betty picked up a giant laminated card. "Did you want to sit at Wallace's table?"

Rebecca frowned and glanced around. "Um, is it available?"

"It's right outside on the edge of the patio. He used to love chatting with people who walked by. Wallace used to come in here every Thursday for lunch. Became a thing. People knew he would be here, so they'd come over and have a chat about whatever was bothering them."

"Wallace was a kind man." A twinge of guilt hit Rebecca as she said the words. She'd started to say "good man," but changed it at the last second. She couldn't forget everything he'd overlooked while wearing the badge.

Betty rubbed Rebecca's arm in a motherly way that she missed. "It'll be good for people, seeing you sitting in his place. It'll put down all that talk Nathan is doing too. Don't worry. No one is listening to him anyway."

Rebecca didn't know who Nathan was or what he was saying but sitting outside on her lunch break sounded like bliss. The breeze and the sunshine would revive her waning energy.

Not that she needed to agree, as Betty was already leading the way to a side door. It was a good table, if chatting with people was something you wanted to do on your lunch break. The patio came right up to the sidewalk, separated by a decorative post and chain rope. It gave a clear view of the majority of downtown.

Rebecca sat on the wrought iron chair, setting her package in her lap because it didn't seem right to put ammo on a diner table.

"What can I get you now, dear?"

Rebecca didn't even have to look at the menu. "Club sandwich and a strawberry milkshake."

Betty laughed, putting her hand on Rebecca's shoulder in a motherly way again. "One double-decker sandwich with crispy bacon and an extra-large strawberry milkshake."

A surprised laugh burst out of Rebecca. "How can you remember that?"

Betty winked. "It's a gift and a curse, believe me." She gave Rebecca's shoulder another squeeze before walking away.

Alone and relaxed, Rebecca closed her eyes and enjoyed the sun on her skin. Even if she did end up not being sheriff after this was all over, she still loved this town. The people here were just so open and caring. They deserved so much better than what they'd been getting.

A shadow fell over her face, and Rebecca looked up.

Steven Campbell stood on the sidewalk, blocking the sun. Albert Gilroy was next to him, his face screwed up in a disapproving scowl.

Shit.

17

"Afternoon, gentlemen. Lovely weather we're having today, isn't it?"

"I'm finding it rather gloomy." Gilroy scowled up at the sky. "Don't you have something better to do than sitting around enjoying a meal while there's a killer on the loose?"

"Well, I worked through my lunch, and we're still waiting on some reports to come in. It seemed the best use of my time to eat now since I'm sure I'll be working late into the night again. Rest assured, my deputies are working on Bryson's case as we speak."

"Well, I—"

"I'm sure you understand how important proper delegation of the workload is." Rebecca waved at the empty seat across from her. "Would you care to join me? You must be exhausted. You haven't even had time to be with your wife."

That last one was a guess, but she saw it hit as his eyes widened slightly.

Whether he thought it was unseemly to continue to criticize her while standing so far away or really was tired, she wasn't sure. Still, Gilroy gestured at Campbell, who unhooked the chain so he could join her.

Rebecca sat up straighter, years of manners taking over. Slouching at the table when alone was one thing, but not with company.

Gilroy walked in like he was thinking of bulldozing the place. As he lowered himself into the chair opposite her, he continued to give everything a baleful, contemptuous glance. Campbell was left to fetch a chair for himself from another table.

"I hope you've set aside the foolish idea that my client's son had anything to do with that criminal you were investigating yesterday," Campbell started off, setting his seat down next to Gilroy. "We expect more focused work from law enforcement around here. There's not a lot of crime on Shadow Island. I don't understand why you can't stick to what's important."

That's the subject on the forefront of his mind?

"Mr. Campbell, as a lawyer, I'm sure you would agree that every crime is important, and since it seemed you were concerned about that case file, I looked into it deeper. And you were right. Mr. Gilroy's son didn't seem to be associated with that dealer at all."

Campbell smirked. "It would have saved you time if you'd listened to me."

"But that drug dealer *was* bailed out by one of Bryson's friends, who was later charged with a hit-and-run. I know they were friends because Bryson was the one who gave him the alibi, so those charges were dropped."

Gilroy leaned forward, eyes blazing. "Are you claiming this is some kind of conspiracy? That my boy was wrapped up in some kind of criminal enterprise?"

Campbell pointed a finger. "That sounds like slander to me."

Rebecca smiled sweetly. "Not at all. In fact, I've said from the beginning, and several times since, that the two cases don't appear to be connected. You two," she waved a finger back and forth between them, "are the ones who keep bringing it up. The only connection I could find was the most tangential one, an acquaintance of a friend from years ago."

"And that friend was the reason you went down to the Seaview Marina to speak with Mr. Longmire?" Gilroy leaned his arm on the table, causing it to tip slightly. "Because you *don't* believe those bullshit rumors about some club? It's because of those damn rumors that I'm forced to take my lawyer everywhere I go."

Interesting.

Rebecca forced her eyes wide open. "Is someone harassing you, Mr. Gilroy? If so, you can come down and file a report. No one should have to walk around with legal representation at all times for fear of harassment. If you could tell me who's done this, I'll investigate it immediately."

"You!" he bellowed, throwing his hands out. "My son was murdered, and you're investigating my marina. For what? Some ridiculous rumors?"

Rebecca jumped on his slipup. "*Your* marina? I was under the impression you merely rented a slip there." Rebecca adjusted a pile of napkins and tried to relax her shoulders.

"I do have a slip there," he blustered, his cheeks reddening.

"I was at the marina because I'm being thorough. Since your son's Jeep wasn't at the park where his body was found and since his friends seemed hesitant to have a conversation with me, I had to check into the possibility that he had been on a yacht when he was killed."

"He wasn't shot dead at that picnic table?" Gilroy seemed shocked and genuinely disturbed by the news.

Interesting.

Gilroy and his associate seemed to know too much about this case but didn't know this important detail?

So maybe her deputies weren't the ones feeding Gilroy information?

That epiphany made Rebecca realize just how much trust she'd lost in them, and maybe it wasn't deserved. Worse than that, she was profoundly disturbed to realize this information hadn't been conveyed to the deceased's next of kin.

She leaned forward, dropping her voice, setting aside her ire. "Mr. Gilroy, this should have all been explained to you by the medical examiner's office. I know they've reached out to you repeatedly. Have you not contacted them?"

Gilroy glared at his lawyer. Campbell shook his head slightly. He didn't know either.

"Mr. Gilroy, check your phone. Or call your maid."

"Well, you're here now, so you can tell me."

Rebecca shot a glance at Campbell. "Are you sure you want to talk about this in front of your staff? It's personal. And a bit distressing."

Gilroy waved a hand. "He's fine. Just tell me."

Regardless of his assurances, Rebecca kept her voice low. "Mr. Gilroy, the evidence we've uncovered points to your son being attacked while walking home through the park sometime between five and six Tuesday morning. An unsuccessful attempt was made to suffocate him with a plastic bag before he was strangled to death." She refrained from telling him it was a suicide bag, because she didn't want that detail getting out. "After that, he was moved to the picnic table. The killer then put a round through his forehead even though he was already dead."

All color had drained from Albert Gilroy's face as she'd explained the circumstances of his son's death.

For a moment, Rebecca debated telling him about the

note that had been found but decided against it. With how upset he already appeared to be, she wouldn't be able to tell his genuine reaction to hearing the killer had connected Bryson to the Yacht Club.

If that was what the note meant, she reminded herself.

"You understand now why I don't think this was a simple murder. This type of murder is personal. And despite being stonewalled everywhere I've looked, I have found that your son had no real enemies, very few people who even had a real dislike for him. Yet this person knew where his friends dropped him off and that he would be alone, an easy target. We need to consider the fact that this may not have been one of his enemies, but one of yours."

Gilroy shook his head, the glare returning in his eyes. "I don't have those kinds of enemies, Rebecca." He spat her name out.

Her cheek twitched as he used her first name as if she were some kind of child he was berating. "You don't think you've made any enemies with your dealings in Washington?"

Campbell cut in, leaning forward. "Those transactions are private and not in the public record."

Rebecca didn't turn away from Gilroy. "Nothing is ever truly private, though, is it?"

"I pay a premium to protect my privacy." Gilroy was back to his usual pompous, unsympathetic self. "Sure, there have been threats from environmentalist groups and those who ended up on the wrong side of bills I helped get signed into law. Nothing real ever comes from it."

"Until the day it does. You may think you have no enemies who would do this. You may think your son had no enemies either. Yet it takes a strong personal vendetta to watch someone struggle and die the way your son did. Who would want to do something like that?"

"That's your job to find out," Gilroy growled, standing up and leaning over the table. "At least it is until the board meets on Monday, and you're removed from your post. I've already found a candidate to take your place. One who knows how to do this job and get results."

Rebecca wasn't surprised that a man with his power would try to plant one of his stooges in the role, but she was caught off guard that a date had been set for the meeting.

She worked to keep her tone neutral. "Is that so?"

"Then you won't have that badge to hide behind."

His blatant threat was a bit shocking.

She smiled, showing all her teeth. "I've never relied on a piece of tin for protection. I prefer lead." The .45 rounds landed with a heavy thud as she dropped the bag of ammo on the table. "And I will make sure to prosecute the killer to the fullest extent of the law, as well as anyone who hired or conspired with them."

Betty appeared, carrying a tray. She cleared her throat. "Gentlemen, if you'd like to eat, you can have your own table. There's no need to harass my other customers."

Gilroy sneered at the kind woman. "I wouldn't eat here—"

"Then you can leave. The patio is for paying customers only." Betty set Rebecca's order down. "And you." She flicked her chin at Campbell, who was staring back and forth between Betty and his boss. "Put that chair back where you got it before you go."

Gilroy stomped off, having to unhook the chain himself as Campbell returned the chair before following his master.

"Good riddance to bad rubbish," Betty muttered, straightening the chair as Rebecca got up and set the chain back in place so no one walking on the sidewalk would trip on it.

"Sorry about that."

Betty smiled and patted her shoulder. "Lunch is on the

house, dear. Anyone who pisses that old dickhead off deserves a free meal."

Rebecca choked on a laugh. "I imagine you'll eventually go bankrupt if you make that a hard rule." She hadn't pegged Betty for a curser. Gilroy really knew how to push people's buttons.

Clearly, the Yacht Club was not welcome around here. Surprisingly, she was. That warmed Rebecca's heart as she took a big slurp of her shake.

It was just as delicious as she remembered.

18

As I watched the new sheriff sit down in the café, I had trouble understanding how her presence made me feel. It was weird seeing her where Alden had sat so many times.

Before the world changed.

Rebecca West was just another sign that everything was now different. That nothing was how it used to be. And never would be again.

I thought about crossing the street for a chat. See how she was doing. It had to be rough for her. Rumor had it, she'd lost her parents a few years ago under tragic circumstances. It might be nice to talk to someone who understood the pain.

Ready to take a step in her direction, I stopped when Albert Gilroy showed up. His lackey opened the gate like a servant to a king, and my teeth ground together as the pair sat with the sheriff like they were old friends.

Rage flooded me, turning everything red. It was hard to see through that haze. I stepped back into the alley. No one could see me like this.

They would know. And they couldn't know. Not yet.

Maybe Gilroy would see it one day. Yes. That seemed fitting. Later, though. First, I had to check a few more people off my current list. Gilroy was old. His time had come and gone. Now he was just a name. A shadow of who he once was, anyway. Because whether he showed it, he was suffering now too.

That made me smile.

On second thought, I figured he should pay for the things he'd done, but my list of those who had to die and in what order had to come first.

Once the actives were dealt with, I'd add new names to the list. The old guard would be next, the one who'd taught these boys how to not be men. How to be a disease that ate the heart out of everything good. How to corrupt and destroy innocence.

My plan was already in place. There was no turning back now.

The haze grew redder and hotter as Rebecca and Gilroy leaned toward each other as if they were sharing secrets. They almost looked chummy. Maybe the new sheriff wasn't that different from the old. I'd heard she'd worked in D.C. before moving here. Was that where she'd met Gilroy? Would I have to add her name to the list?

No!

The rich bastard jumped up, looming over her. I almost crossed the street again. I wasn't armed, but I couldn't just stand by and watch another young woman be bullied by the Gilroys, even if I was unsure about her.

Rebecca slammed a bag on the table.

Cottage Sports was the logo, and the shape made the contents clear. I clapped my hand over my mouth to hold back my laughter as the bastard scum turned white.

She wasn't going to be bullied. That's what that ammo told me. Instead, Rebecca was going to fight Albert Gilroy.

Betty came out and chased them off. Betty was good people. She'd always made sure the sweet potato fries were fresh when I'd come here with...

I closed my eyes against the memories.

I couldn't think of her right now. I had a list to attend to.

Everyone in town hated the Gilroys and all the others. We all wanted them gone. The club no one dared to talk about.

Yet I was the only one willing to do anything about them.

Rebecca looked like she was willing to do something too. Maybe she'd even be on my side if I told her everything I knew.

Bryson Gilroy's bulging eyes flashed in my mind. The way they'd turned red as he'd fought to breathe. The terror as he'd realized his angel of death stared him in the face. The rush of vengeance as his lips had puckered and flapped like a fish. The way his eyes had pleaded for his life.

No. I couldn't give that up. It was the only thing I had to look forward to in this life anymore.

Rebecca wouldn't be interested in vengeance. She wanted justice. I respected that, but I wanted more. I needed more.

Pulling the phone from my pocket, my thumb moved across her face as I keyed in my code. I relaxed before I even heard her voice.

"Today is the day we start our new lives..."

The haze cleared, and peace descended. For a minute.

It wouldn't last long.

19

H appily humming to herself, Rebecca walked back into the sheriff's department, sipping on her to-go cup.

"Rebecca Rose West! You went to Seabreeze and didn't bring me a milkshake?" Viviane grumped, glaring at her with ire. Whether it was real or fake, Rebecca couldn't tell.

Rebecca's mouth popped open. "Did you just middle-name me?"

"You're dang right I did. And you deserve it for this heinous crime."

In truth, Rebecca did feel bad for not thinking about bringing a milkshake to her new friend. But that was the thing…she still wasn't quite used to having a friend.

When tears pricked at her eyes, she made a show of sucking greedily at the straw to cover up the sudden surge of emotion. "This isn't just a shake. My childhood memories are in this cup, Viviane Adorabele Darby."

Viviane dropped her face into her hands. "Oh goodness, she knows my middle name."

Rebecca laughed. "Of course I do. Learned how to track that stuff down on day one of FBI training. It's *adorable*."

Viviane groaned. "I'm gonna have to quit my job now, aren't I?"

"Nope, 'cause if you do, I'm telling the world. Your secret's only safe with me if you promise to never quit."

Dark eyes appeared between Viviane's fuchsia-tipped fingers. "Am I being blackmailed?"

"Yep."

Viviane sighed dramatically as Rebecca let herself through the half door. "And to think I've been going around saying so many good things about you too. Then you go and pull this. I see how you are, not sharing and pulling skeletons from closets."

Rebecca laughed. "You've been saying good things about me? What kind of good things? To who?"

Dark eyes twinkling with mischief, Viviane tapped her chin with one of the fuchsia nails. "I was telling people that you were a good friend who would always share her milkshake with someone who's been slaving away at her desk all day and only had crackers for lunch."

Feeling genuinely bad now, Rebecca extended the cup, not expecting Viviane to actually reach for it. She did, snatching it from her hands before she had time to blink.

An instant later, Viviane popped the top and drank from the cup.

"Ahh, I needed that." Viviane licked her lips. "Talking is such thirsty work."

"Must be."

Viviane's giggles were so filled with joy that Rebecca's heart squeezed. "Sorry. I have a slight addiction when it comes to Betty's milkshakes."

After another sip, Viviane extended the cup back, but Rebecca waved her off. "Keep it."

"You sure? I don't have cooties."

Rebecca laughed. "You look like you needed that as much

as I needed my first one. Betty made me that one for the road."

"Oh, well, I don't feel in the least bit bad then." Viviane opened a drawer and pulled out a straw.

"So...about those good things you were saying about me?" Rebecca batted her eyelashes.

"Oh, right. Nathan over at the Sunrise Cove Motel was going around talking nonsense, so I set him straight." Viviane returned to the drink, batting her eyelashes innocently in return.

"That's it? That's not worth almost an entire milkshake."

Viviane opened her mouth, but Hoyt popped his head around the corner. "There you are. I was just about to call you. I followed up on that footage." He waved some papers in his hand.

Mourning the loss of her milkshake, Rebecca headed to her office and stowed the bag of ammo in the desk drawer. "Please tell me it's good news."

Hoyt plopped into a chair, wincing a little as he did.

She frowned. "When are you supposed to get those stitches out? It's been two weeks now, right?"

He scratched his nose. "Well, since I've not exactly been following doctor's orders, Doc said they needed to stay in until Monday or so."

Guilt reared its ugly head. "I'm sorry. I really am."

Hoyt waved a hand. "Catching killers and saving little girls was worth it." He turned his attention to the papers in his hands, clearly done with the subject. "Despite the clearer resolution of the footage on the thumb drive, Cyber wasn't able to even identify the make or model of the car seen in the ATM footage. Hate to say it, but it's a big dead end."

He slid a picture across her desk so she could see for herself. It was pixelated as hell.

"Well, I appreciate you following up. Every lead has to be

followed." Rebecca opened the case file on her computer and saw that the final autopsy report still hadn't been added. There must have been some holdup at the M.E.'s office.

She quickly ran through the rest of the file, a terrible idea forming in her mind. Everything Albert Gilroy had known about his son's death was in the file. The one thing he didn't appear to know about—the note—wasn't listed.

Rebecca checked who'd last accessed the file and when. So far, it had only been Hoyt, Darian, Locke, and one tech. She'd already crossed Hoyt off her list of possible leaks. Darian and Locke had checked the file as soon as the report was created on Tuesday and, as they should have, had checked it every day since. As would be expected from an office with so few officers. Everyone worked on every case.

Had the leak come from a person or the server itself? Or an unsecured workstation?

Rebecca wrote a quick note to check into the cybersecurity of the station. "Well, I had an interesting lunch. Albert Gilroy and his lawyer stooge paid me a visit."

"Wow, he really goes everywhere with that guy, doesn't he?"

"He says it's because he gets harassed. I think it's to cover his ass. He also threatened me."

Hoyt's shoulders went tight. "What happened?"

"Said my badge wouldn't protect me for long. I think he's grossly overestimating the size of my badge. Which is either an insult or a compliment. Hard to tell coming from such an asshole."

"He threatened you?"

Rebecca lifted a shoulder. "It was a pretty weak one, all things considered. More of an 'I'll have your job' kind of thing." Rolling the stress from her shoulders, she contemplated whether to share the next bit but went ahead. "Said the board was meeting on Monday about replacing me."

"The bastard."

She couldn't disagree. "Oh, and he didn't know how his son was killed. Even after the scene he made at the park, he never bothered to go down to the morgue or answer Bailey's calls."

Hoyt shook his head. "That shows how much he cares about his son as a person. This is just business for him."

"Yeah. He's protecting his ass and his assets. Doesn't want to look weak. Looked real shook when I hinted that this could be because of his involvement in the Yacht Club, though."

Hoyt groaned. "Is that when he threatened you?"

"Yup." Rebecca turned back to her computer, looking up how to requisition body cameras for her deputies so they could be protected.

"Boss."

Rebecca gaped at the cost. "Yeah?"

"Rebecca!"

She jumped. "What?"

"This is serious." Hoyt ran his palms over his cheeks, making a rasping sound. "Albert Gilroy threatened your job. And don't give me that line about how a drunk driver could do it too. These people have serious money. They can hire people to take you out."

"Yeah. I know," she mumbled, turning back to her screen. "That's why I bought more bullets, and why I'm going to requisition body cams. I can't believe you guys don't have them already. You only need four."

"Wallace talked about getting them. And well, we just never had a need."

Rebecca pressed her lips together to stop herself from saying something she shouldn't about the real level of crime on this small island.

"Until we get the cameras, use your phone to record all

your interactions with Gilroy and the rest of the Yacht Club doofuses. And their lawyers. Those organized crime guys do love their lawyers. So cover your ass."

Hoyt's entire body went still. "You know who the members of the Yacht Club are?"

Rebecca shrugged and went back to filling out the order. She needed to get this done and approved before Monday. That way, at least the deputies would be covered if something happened, no matter who took over as sheriff.

"Not yet, but it shouldn't be too hard to put it together. I just need to go down to the marina again and look up who owns all the yachts docked there."

"They'll never let you back in that place."

"Maybe. If they don't," she waved her hand, "there's a whole ocean out there. I can sit out in a boat all day and work on my tan while waiting for them to sail past. Do yachts sail? If they don't, what do you call it when a sailless boat goes past you? Driving sounds weird."

"Er, with all due respect, ma'am, you're not taking this seriously enough."

Heat flashed through Rebecca, and she jumped to her feet so fast her chair crashed into the wall behind her. All the anger and pain she'd felt that morning came flooding back. And the sugar flowing through her system only fueled it further.

"No, Deputy Frost, you're the one not taking this seriously enough. You and this entire department have not taken this seriously enough for the last thirty years. At least. You've allowed criminals to invade your town. They're a threat to everyone on this island and the surrounding areas, while you've only cared about yourself and your coworkers. Wallace protected you guys, but who was protecting Cassie when she needed it? Or Serenity? And who knows how many others!"

She slammed her fist down on the desk, making the keyboard jump.

Hoyt held up a hand. "I didn't—"

"I will not back down and allow innocent citizens to be hurt. A crackhead can take me out tomorrow. An assassin could make a headshot from a passing boat while I'm sipping my coffee. McGuire's associates could come gunning for me tonight. Any one of the criminals I've already put in jail could come after me. Hell, I could drown, or choke on a doughnut."

Hoyt slowly pushed to his feet. "Listen to—"

"That never has and never will stop me from doing my job. Which is to uphold the law and investigate any and all criminal activity in my jurisdiction. So long as I have this badge, Shadow Island is under my protection."

As the words drilled from her mouth, Hoyt stood and took them.

When Rebecca was finished, a small part of her worried that she'd destroyed any possibility of friendship that might've been started. She regretted that, but not her words or her actions. She would never regret doing her job with an unbiased and fearless, but never reckless, heart. That was a promise she'd made to her father when she'd graduated from Quantico, and she'd be damned if she was going to break it now.

"Do you understand me, Deputy Frost?"

Hoyt stared at her, his body as stiff as a board and his face stony. She could see the wheels turning as he tried to process everything she'd said.

Finally, he reached over and closed the office door, then held out his hand. "I understand. Give me your keys."

Rebecca's eyebrows shot up. "Excuse me?"

"Your keys. I need them." He wiggled his fingers.

"For what?"

"Wallace was a lot of things, but corrupt wasn't one of

them. He kept his own files. Ones that were never digitized. He didn't trust computers for some reason. Maybe it was because he was old school, I don't know. But he kept everything he'd ever compiled against the Yacht Club in an old storage room off the locker room. He was the only one who had the keys to both the room and the filing cabinets in there."

Rebecca took the keys from her pocket and dropped them in Hoyt's hand. Opening the door, he closed it softly behind him as he left.

He had more files? Dammit, Wallace. If you'd let me know how dangerous the Yacht Club truly was, I never would have suggested confronting them that night with so little staff.

But Wallace had known. He'd known, and he'd gone ahead with it anyway.

Rebecca reached for her chair. As she did, it cracked. She'd broken the thing.

Dammit all.

Her phone rang. It was her direct office number, not the precinct's.

Sighing, she sat on the edge of her desk and answered it. "Sheriff West speaking."

"Sheriff, I'm calling to let you know we're still working on the Gilroy laptop. But we've managed to crack the password on the phone." There was a slight pause. "You're going to want to see this. We can mail it to you or—"

"No, I'll drive over and pick it up. I can be there in less than an hour." A peaceful drive with the windows down sounded like just the thing she needed right now.

"Yes, ma'am. See you then."

Pushing the broken chair out of her way, Rebecca left the office. She didn't see Hoyt anywhere. Instead, she walked up to Viviane, still sucking on the milkshake while engrossed in a Neal Stephenson novel.

Rebecca had never seen her reading on the job before and wondered if she was actually reading it or pretending to because she'd heard Rebecca yelling at Hoyt. She was embarrassed about that. She never should have done such a thing where other employees could overhear. Praise in public, rip them a new ass in private. That was her screwup, and now Viviane had to deal with that.

"Viviane?"

"Yeah, Boss?" Her eyes stayed glued to her book.

"I'm heading back to the locker room. Just wanted to let you know I wasn't sneaking out the back to go get another shake and not tell you about it."

Viviane smiled without looking up.

Feeling two inches tall, Rebecca walked back to the locker room and saw the open door. The storage room was brightly lit and crammed full of filing cabinets. Hoyt stood in front of one, pulling stacks of papers from it and putting them in a box.

"Frost, I've got to run out to forensics to pick up the phone. They were able to unlock it."

"Wait for me. I've got some reading for you to do. You need to know what you're up against."

Hoyt slammed another handful of files into the box, then slapped a lid on it. Rebecca stepped out of the room.

He secured the lock on the filing cabinet, grabbed the box, flipped off the light, and handed Rebecca the box so he could lock the storage room door.

The box was half full.

"That's a lot of reading for a short trip." She tried to make a joke, but it fell flat.

Hoyt looked miserable. "This is just some of the most recent stuff from the last couple years." He ran a hand down his face, then took the box back so she didn't have to carry it out. "And there's a lot more where this came from."

20

Rebecca drove while Hoyt organized the files into some semblance of order. Apparently, Wallace had started shoving files wherever they would fit before giving in and buying additional cabinets. What the deputy had pulled seemed to be all over the place.

He had only been sorting a few minutes, grumbling out random dates before he sighed. "You're right."

"About what?"

"I didn't take this seriously enough." He chewed on his lower lip, staring out the side window. "I need to confess something."

Rebecca braced herself. "I'm listening."

"Remember when I told you about getting those death threats?"

Her hands tightened on the wheel. "Yeah."

"Well, Angie and I...we were having some troubles. I won't make excuses. It was a stupid, unforgivable mistake, and I've tried to make amends every day since."

A chill lifted the hairs on Rebecca's arms. "Okay."

"Just looking at all these case files brings it all back. Seeing the sloppy job I did." He swallowed thickly.

Rebecca's nerves couldn't take it any longer. "You're stalling."

Hoyt chuckled, but it was dark, painful. "I am. I don't want to say it. This shouldn't even matter. But I want you to understand why." He sighed. "I'd been working a lot of overtime. Barely getting any sleep. The overtime was great for my family's finances, but I rarely saw them. One of the threatening letters was delivered to my house, so I sent Angie and the boys to stay with her mom on the mainland. I was lonely. And there was a woman. It was only a onetime thing."

Rebecca relaxed a little bit. "You had an affair."

"I had a one-night stand with a woman I met on the beach. She was pretty, and lonely too. Her boyfriend had dumped her while they were on vacation and just left. She needed a ride back to her room. It was the end of my shift, so when she asked me to join her for a drink, I thought, *why not?*"

He swallowed again, so hard she could hear it over the hum of the tires on the bridge. Rebecca gave him a minute as she noticed the slate gray clouds as they rolled in off the ocean. Sadly, there was not a lot of peace to be found there. The storm that had threatened yesterday was rolling in now.

"Somehow…"

When he paused, she looked over, seeing years of pain and guilt etched onto Hoyt's face, pulling his wrinkles tight.

"Angie came back a week later. Thank God she left the boys with her mom. Someone had dropped off pictures of me with that woman. Angie saw them. I thought it was going to tear us apart. Any other woman, it would have. But we worked through it. Took us a long while, but we managed."

Hoyt blew out a breath. Rebecca kept her eyes focused on

the road, so he wouldn't feel self-conscious about the tears in the corners of his eyes.

"They set you up with a honeypot. I'm sorry."

"A what?"

Rebecca shot him a quick glance. "A honeypot. An attractive woman who fauns all over you, plays to what will get you most interested. In your case, a damsel in distress. While her partner follows behind, snapping compromising pictures."

Hoyt ran a hand down his face. "No, she was just a young woman with a shitty boyfriend who needed a bit of help. Not some sweet-talking Jezebel."

"Yeah? Did you see the boyfriend? Any trace of anything of his in her room?" Rebecca couldn't believe she was going to have to explain this.

"Well, no, but he'd ditched her, so…" Hoyt's eyes filled with confusion, but he wasn't getting defensive, so that was good.

"So she decided to go drinking, with a cop, on her vacation, then sleep with him? While she's dealing with the heartache of being dumped just hours earlier. Did she cry prettily too?"

"She only cried a little. I thought that was odd at the time, but maybe they weren't too serious. What do you mean 'prettily'?"

"Did her face turn red, snot run out of her nose, makeup run? Ya know, the normal things that happen when a woman cries."

"Well, she was putting on a brave face."

Men could be so thick.

"Did the photos look up close and personal?"

"Yes."

"Were they in focus or did they look like they'd been swiped from a camera feed?"

His hands balled into fists. "They were in focus."

"And I'm betting there wasn't just a couple of photos but at least ten, if not twenty." When he said nothing, she went on. "Hoyt, think about it. If a friend told you the story of what happened that night, what would be the first thing you asked them?"

"I'd ask what...what she wanted from them."

He turned his face to the window, and Rebecca left him to his thoughts. There was no reason to rub salt in his reopened wound.

"Son of a bitch! Fuck." Hoyt slammed his fist on the dash. "I never thought about it like that. Thought the stress of things just led me into a bad situation I otherwise never would've glanced twice at." He turned in his seat to fix Rebecca with a solid stare. "I love my wife. I swear to you, that was the only time I ever did anything so stupid."

"I believe you. We all make mistakes. What matters is what we do after."

Hoyt sat in silence, alternating between chewing on his thumb and glaring out the window until they were nearly at their destination.

"What's in the box?"

"Boss?"

"What jarred this memory?"

With a long exhale, he opened the box and lifted a folder. "This date right here."

If Rebecca hadn't been driving, she would have snatched the folder from his hand. "Is that a file on the honeypot?"

Hoyt winced. "No, but the honeypot happened just a couple days after this." He tossed the file back into the box. "Two teen girls didn't come home one night, and their parents got worried and called it in. Wallace was working another case, so I went to the marina and questioned a couple bigwigs. Let's just say they didn't like it."

"What happened?"

"Couple of things. One, Wallace jumped my ass and told me I'd jumped the gun going there. And second..." He scoffed. "Just call me Winnie the Pooh, I guess."

Rebecca pressed her lips together to stop the smile. "What happened to the girls?"

"Well, they showed up at home saying they'd lied about the sleepover to spend the night in a tent in the woods with their boyfriends, but..."

When he didn't go on, Rebecca prompted, "But what?"

"They looked scared. Not the typical 'my parents are going to kill me' scared either. Couldn't keep their stories straight, shit like that. I think they'd been out on a boat and were told to keep silent."

Big city or small island town, it didn't seem to matter. Corruption and abuse knew no boundaries.

"Looks like the chickenshits in the Yacht Club didn't like getting their feathers ruffled."

Hoyt shook his head over and over until he slumped in his seat. "I'm going to nail those sonsabitches to the wall. That's what I'm going to do."

Rebecca nodded, glad to have him on board. But she couldn't help but wonder if the people who'd set Hoyt up had done something similar to Darian? To Locke? Maybe even to Greg?

Wallace had told her that he was just one man fighting against them. Perhaps he really had been. He might have gotten caught up in a web of his own.

She glanced over at the box of files in Hoyt's lap. Wallace may not have been able to prosecute anyone, but that hadn't stopped him from documenting everything. That was an ace up her sleeve, and the Yacht Club knew nothing about it.

The element of surprise was on her side now.

21

They'd arrived during shift change, and the three-tiered parking structure was busy with activity. Rebecca went up a level to avoid the commotion and parked. She hoped the cyber tech working on the case was waiting for them. It was always best to talk with the tech who'd discovered the evidence, instead of someone who just read the notes.

And it seemed the tech, Justin Drake, had a lot to tell them about Bryson Gilroy's phone.

As soon as she and Hoyt walked into his lab, he started talking, his green eyes wide behind his red-framed glasses.

"We had to brute force the password. That's why it took so long." Justin passed Rebecca a clone. The original would stay safely in an evidence box.

She tapped the screen. "What'd you find?"

"I gave it a quick once-over. Your victim was no Boy Scout. In fact, he was a dirtbag. If he'd survived, we'd likely be pressing charges against him. Careful looking at the pictures. I'm pretty sure most of those girls aren't legal."

Rebecca started flipping through the phone. "Not what I

wanted to spend my day looking through, but I have to admit, I'm not surprised. Can you go ahead and forward those to the FBI so—"

"Already reached out to ECAP and CPVA and let them know I had something for them."

The Endangered Child Alert Program worked with the FBI and the National Center for Missing and Exploited Children to find the identities of adults involved in suspected child pornography. In contrast, the Child Pornography Victim Assistance looked for the victims in order to help them.

Rebecca checked that off her mental list. "Brilliant. Thank you, Justin." If some of the Yacht Club crew got caught in this net and she didn't have to lift a finger, so much the better.

The tech perked up. "You remembered my name."

Rebecca frowned. "Of course I did. You've worked what, three of my crime scenes now?"

"Technically five. We count by the scene, not the case." Justin started ticking numbers off on his fingers. "The marshland body dump, the attempted homicide, kidnap staging area, but you'd already left from that one, the shooting, and this body dump."

"Yeah, that's right. And I think you were the one who verified the mud I found on the killer's boot was the same as what Cassie Leigh was submerged in."

Justin narrowed his eyes. "Oh, right. Cassie."

"What about her?"

He lifted a finger and tapped the screen. "You're going to want to look through his text messages in the month preceding her death."

"Okay."

With Hoyt watching over her shoulder, she started scrolling, then froze. Her eyes were wide as she looked up at Justin, who wore a grim smile.

"Thought that might be important. Good luck piecing all this together. You've got a hell of a tangled web to unwind."

Rebecca smiled her thanks and kept scrolling as she walked out of the office and toward the parking structure.

Behind her, she heard Hoyt thanking Justin properly. But by the time she hit the parking garage, he was by her side. "Tell me about this tangled web."

"You sure?" She glanced up from the screen. "You'll have to walk into my parlor first."

❄

"Did anyone tell you that you can be pretty scary?"

Rebecca chuckled. "Oh yeah."

You have no idea.

"Okay, I'm in the parlor, Madam Spider, so please tell this lowly fly what you know."

"Our victim wasn't just a dirtbag. He was a pimp. Not only did we just get his client list, we got the contacts for the girls he 'partied' with. And, like a good dealer, the first parties for the girls were free. After that, they had to exchange services to get invited back. The girls didn't even know they were being prostituted."

Hoyt pressed a hand to his stomach. "How the hell does that work?"

"From what I've read in Bryson's messages so far, it looks like he and some other people were targeting teenage girls. That makes sense, because that age group is typically unsure and insecure, and they want to prove how grown-up they are. My guess is that the members would tell Bryson what they were looking for, or a name if they had a favorite girl, and he would get them on the boat any way he could. Bribes, drugs, blackmail, and manipulation appear to have been his common tactics."

"Sons of bitches."

That was an understatement.

"Common grooming tactic. Make the girls feel good about getting invited, then tell them they aren't good enough. Not wild enough. Not open enough to new experiences. Or a combination. And I quote," she glanced back down at the screen, "*'Is the reason you told him no because your tits are too small? It's okay, babe. Older men like small titties.'*" She turned up the second parking ramp and then looked back at Hoyt. "He got a thousand dollars for that girl."

"Older men paying a young man to manipulate even younger girls into sleeping with them? That's disgusting."

Rebecca was clenching a fist and had to shake it loose. "Agreed. But effective. And now we've got some evidence."

"Enough?"

She shook her head. It wasn't enough, not even close to bringing charges against anyone. But it was a thread she could start pulling.

"Not yet. We have some first names, but mostly only phone numbers. I'd bet my truck those belong to burner phones. He used apps that hide identities too. They were pretty careful. Look here."

Hoyt leaned over her shoulder. "Cassie. Cassie Leigh?"

Rebecca nodded grimly. "I'm pretty sure that's her phone number. We'll need to double-check, but I'd bet my truck on that too."

Hoyt pinched the screen to expand the message. "There's four people in that group message. Does that mean three men ganged up on Cassie and verbally manipulated her into being part of their sicko club?"

"Yeah. That's exactly what this looks like. I wonder if they always ganged up on girls like that or if she'd been more challenging?"

She scrolled quickly, trying to answer her own question.

She stopped when she spotted a familiar name—*Dillon*. "Whoa, look at this."

Hoyt expanded the screen again. "Is that Dillon Miller? Cassie's boyfriend?"

"That's my guess." She glanced up at Hoyt. "It looks like Bryson Gilroy was the person texting Dillon. Bryson's the one who set up the meeting on the beach."

Rebecca didn't need to remind Hoyt which meeting that had been. Or how it had turned out. She'd never forget the day Sheriff Wallace had died, and neither would his deputy.

"Fucking hell," Hoyt bit out.

Rebecca continued walking, absent-mindedly looking for their cruiser. A vehicle approached them, entering the ramp from below, so she moved to the left side of the aisle.

"It gets worse. The text messages harassing Cassie continued after she was killed because no one in the Yacht Club knew she'd died. And Bryson's phone indicates those messages were read by everyone in the group."

Hoyt stopped a few feet away from her and stared. "Who has Cassie's phone now?"

Rebecca felt sick. "Her parents."

The vehicle coming up the ramp sounded closer, so Rebecca checked to make sure they wouldn't be in the way when it reached their level. She started toward their cruiser but stopped when a black SUV backed out of a spot in front of her.

Instinct pulsed from Rebecca's gut and through her veins before her brain could register the problem.

The car wasn't turning. Instead, it had backed straight out of the spot, blocking them off.

Behind her, an engine roared.

22

R ebecca didn't think. There was no time.

Grabbing Hoyt, she was forced to reach across her body with her left hand to pull her weapon.

The front sight snagged on her holster as she tugged it out, as that was not how it was designed to be unholstered. But, after her last ambush in a parking garage, Rebecca had started practicing different maneuvers to protect herself. That included not only shooting with her nondominant hand but drawing the weapon too.

It wasn't easy, but she managed to push her deputy between the two parked cars.

Hoyt bounced off one of the car doors. "The hell?"

Ignoring his outburst, she darted for shelter beside him.

On seeing her gun, he cursed and dropped into a crouch, following her lead.

She prayed to anyone listening that he was pulling his gun too. There wasn't time to look. She had to keep an eye out for what she knew was about to happen.

Over the sound of squealing tires, Rebecca peeked over the hood of the cover car. The second SUV, a dark gray

Tahoe, slid up at an angle, blocking off the ramp from below like the first car, a black Suburban, had blocked the upper ramp.

"Ambush. Stay down."

Rebecca pulled the cloned phone from her pocket and slid it next to the tire she was crouched beside. She removed her own phone, began recording, and placed it back in her breast pocket.

Bryson's phone was the only reason she could think that someone would be stupid enough to try and ambush two officers right next to a police building.

"What the hell is going on?"

"Call for backup."

Rebecca's heart pounded way too fast. And hard. Too hard.

Blood on the counter.

Her arm hanging useless at her side as the SUV raced toward her, headlights bobbing.

Rebecca scraped her thumb over the diamond design of the wood grip on her 1911 to orient herself to the here and now as Hoyt made the call.

"Dammit. No signal."

Dammit indeed. She'd had a signal in the garage earlier. Were the men carrying a blocker?

She pushed back as two men got out of the Suburban. "Two above." She rattled off the make and models of both vehicles, then the descriptions of four men as two more exited the Tahoe. All of this was done while she thought through their options.

Which weren't many.

The back door on the passenger side of the Tahoe opened, and a man dressed in a long, black trench coat strode toward them. The other four waited, looking entirely too at ease.

They should have been looking over their shoulders. Worried about other—

Dammit! It's after the shift change! Everyone is either long gone or working inside. They timed this perfectly. But how did they know we would be here?

Making the decision, Rebecca lifted her gun and sighted in on Trench Coat, using the car as a shooting stand.

"Sheriff's department. Stop where you are and raise your hands."

"You were warned to stop sticking your nose into business that does not concern you, Sheriff West." Trench Coat stopped and raised his hands to shoulder level. He did it all with a sardonic smile. None of the others even moved, staying tucked next to their vehicles.

Why is he so comfortable coming out in the open like this? No mask. No care about cameras.

It was a question she'd have to think about later.

"Are you telling me that the murder of a Yacht Club member isn't my business? That's funny. I thought Albert Gilroy wanted his son's killer found."

Rebecca felt warmth on her back and realized that Hoyt had slid up behind her, covering the other side. He literally had her back.

"You've been asking around, digging into people's business. People who had nothin' to do with Bryson Gilroy's death."

"How do you know that? I'm not sure where you're getting your information, but everything I've done so far is to track down Bryson Gilroy's movements in an attempt to find his killer."

"Is that so?"

"Yup, that's so. Maybe if you tell me what I saw that I wasn't supposed to see, I can stop looking there." Rebecca kept her barrel pointed at his chest but kept her peripheral vision homed in on his goons. They were all standing still, feet spread, hands clasped over wrists, Mafia-style.

The man in the coat took a deep breath and chuckled. "Things around here work a bit differently, Ms. West. We're used to being treated with a certain amount of…respect."

"In that case, respectfully go fuck yourself." Rebecca shifted. Staying crouched for so long was playing havoc on the balls of her feet and knees. "Now, how about you respectfully lace your fingers behind your head and get down on your knees?"

Trench Coat laced his fingers behind his head but didn't otherwise move. "Like this? Why must you be so coarse when we're having such a friendly chat?"

"Got movement." Hoyt was so quiet, his warning barely reached her ears. "Someone's in the back seat of the Suburban. Can't make them out."

Shit. Shit. Shit.

"Do they have an angle on us?" The cruiser was on the other side of the makeshift barricade these men had formed.

"Oh, yeah." Hoyt chuckled. "Just about every angle you can think of."

Ah, that was the kind of humor she liked. The one shared in the face of danger.

She refocused on Trench Coat. "Let's make this chat real friendly then, and everyone gets out of the cars and down on the ground in perfect harmony. We can even sing a little 'Imagine' while we get better acquainted, if you like. This can be done peacefully."

It was getting hard for Rebecca to stay focused on this "friendly chat." She was also trying to judge shooting angles, priority of kill, and whether the concrete corner behind her was likely to shatter bullets or ricochet them into her back once the shooting started. She wished she'd stayed to chat with Justin just a little longer.

Trench Coat laughed, and it nearly made her jump. Her finger twitched on the trigger. If this all went to hell, she didn't want it to be because she got jumpy. But if it did go to hell...she hoped she went down so she wouldn't have to face Angie Frost. And she'd take as many of them with her as possible.

"My employers would not like that. And I do not like to disappoint my employers. And they are very disappointed at the moment."

The men behind Trench Coat, back at the Tahoe, leaned in to talk to each other.

"Then have them come down to the station and tell me what's wrong."

"When they need a message sent, they send me. There's no reason for such men to do such a tiny task like convincing you to do what's reasonable. They have more important things to do."

"Well, you're not very good at it. See, when men like you show up like this, we cops tend to get trigger-happy. Are they too busy being important to come down to the morgue to identify your body?"

The man on the passenger side of the Tahoe reached for his pocket.

"And if your man doesn't keep his hands where I can see them, you're all going to need another party to identify your bodies."

Trench Coat turned and must have mouthed something because the man stopped moving and even held his hands out to his sides.

"We didn't come here to start a gunfight, Ms. West. Just to deliver a message. Mr. Gilroy is distraught. Nobody can blame him for that. Your investigation is upsetting. He wants the name of the man who killed his son, not for you to harass your betters."

Betters? Fuck that.

"I'm sorry about that. I've done my best to be compassionate and sympathetic with Mr. Gilroy in his time of grief. I was so sympathetic I didn't even tell him that his son had been castrated." The lie slid easily from her tongue, and she enjoyed the way the men all winced. "If you'd like to file a report with my superiors, I'm sure they'd be happy to force me to go to victim sensitivity training. Why don't you come down to the station, and we can—"

"Do not play games!" Trench Coat shouted.

The idiot was going to end up getting shot if he kept startling her. Rebecca debated taking the shot anyway. If the second car hadn't had higher ground, she might have.

"You good, Frost?" Rebecca kept her voice low, and her eyes locked on her three targets below. Frost had the guys above.

"As can be. Mine have stopped moving."

"I'm not playing games." Her command voice was back. "You're the one out here slowing me down, interrupting my work. If you want answers, then tell me what I need to know, and don't get in my way again."

"Ask your questions elsewhere. You will not find Bryson's killer in our ranks. Goodbye, Ms. West." Trench Coat lowered his hands and spun on his heel.

As soon as he was in the Tahoe, the other two men piled back in, as did the two guys by the Suburban, and both vehicles turned to exit the structure.

Rebecca didn't try to stop them, just focused on their plates, saying the numbers out loud, hoping her phone recorded them clearly or she remembered them until she could write them down. Not that it would matter. She doubted they were authentic plates.

"Clear," Hoyt called out.

She didn't move. Just kept her gun tracking the vehicle

with Trench Coat inside until it was out of sight.

When the sounds of their engines disappeared, Hoyt pressed a hand to his heart. "What the hell was that?"

Rebecca lifted a finger as she jotted the plate numbers down in her notepad. When that was done, she moved to the back of the cover car, rested her arm on the cement wall of the ramp, and threw up. Once she'd finished, she strode back, hoping her lifted chin would cover her embarrassment.

"You okay?"

"Smell of oil, engines, tires. Gets to me every time." Rebecca blew her breath out. Her club sandwich had tasted better the first time through. She closed her eyes, taking a slow, deep breath. "I hate parking garages."

"Yeah, me too." Hoyt's smile was filled with so much sympathy that she was forced to turn away.

She reached under the car and scooped up Bryson's phone before stopping the recording on her own. She had a signal now. They'd definitely been carrying a blocker. Bastards. "They never even asked about his phone. That seem odd to you?"

"Everything about that seemed odd to me. Why are they coming after us? We don't even know who was involved with Bryson's murder." He pulled a piece of gum out of his pocket and handed it to her.

Smiling gratefully, she unwrapped it with fingers that shook more than she liked and popped it into her mouth.

"They're not. You didn't see his face, but he looked shocked and disgusted when I said Bryson was castrated."

"Hell, any man would react like that. If I hadn't been so busy shitting myself, I probably would've cringed too."

"Hmm, hadn't considered that. Guess I should come up with a better lie next time."

"Wait." Hoyt's eyebrows jerked together. "Wait. He wasn't...you know?"

"Castrated?" She said the word just to watch Hoyt squirm. It helped her mood a little. "No, you would've known about it. But Trench Coat doesn't know that. I'm still guessing the Gilroys are pretty high in the food chain, if one of the head muscles was sent as a warning."

"You made all that up on the spot, in the middle of an ambush?"

Rebecca shrugged and headed toward their cruiser. "Lying under pressure became second nature when I worked as a Pentagon intern during college."

Hoyt chuckled. "I didn't know you interned at the Pentagon."

"I didn't. I'm just really good at lying." She grinned back at him. "And now, we wait to see who hears about my latest lie and how long it takes. That's when we'll know who Trench Coat reports to."

❄

AFTER FILING the report and answering all the questions Coastal Ridge PD had for them, Rebecca and Hoyt finally made it back to their little island.

Shoving the Explorer into park, Rebecca kept a careful eye on her surroundings as she climbed out of the cruiser. Behind her, Hoyt grunted as he climbed out too.

"Your shift's over, Hoyt. Head home. I'll take this in." A thought occurred to her. "Need a ride, or is Angie coming for you?"

"I'll call her, but are you sure?"

"Yep."

Hoyt went for the box of files.

"Hold up there. I shoved you pretty good back there. Let me get that." She pulled out the keys of her Tacoma and pressed the unlock button.

"Will do." He gave her a little salute. "Angie'll be glad for us to have supper before midnight."

Rebecca grabbed the box out of the SUV and locked it up.

As Hoyt walked away, a little bounce in his step, her smile faded. What was it like to have someone waiting at home? The only thing waiting on her was her beloved air fryer. Different town, same issues. *At least my "fella's" hot,* she thought, grateful for retaining her sense of humor after that stressful encounter.

Setting the box inside and locking her truck again, Rebecca headed to the station entrance just as a shadow slid around the corner.

Adrenaline spiking, Rebecca dropped her keys and reached for her holster. As a tall figure emerged from around the building, her thumb hit the snap on her holster, and her fingers curled around the grip.

"Stop!" Her command voice was a bit shakier than she would have liked.

The figure jerked to a halt, arms shooting for the sky. "Rebecca, it's me. Ryker."

Rebecca blew out a shaky breath, snapping her holster as she faced Ryker Sawyer. She felt more than a little silly reacting like that. But then again, those instincts were also proving to come in handy lately.

"Shit, Ryker."

"Sorry. Did I startle you?"

"A little, yeah. It's been a rough day." Bending over, she picked up her keys. "What are you doing here? Wait. Is something wrong?"

Ryker laughed, exposing the dimples that sat high on his tanned cheeks. "Nothing's wrong. Just wanted to check in. See how you're doing. I haven't seen you since Wallace's funeral."

Rebecca massaged her temple, where a headache was

starting to form. She hoped to drop like a rock into her bed later. Lack of sleep and back-to-back adrenaline rushes were leaving her exhausted.

"Yeah. I've been busy."

"Work's that bad?"

"It's a killer." She snickered, then realized she was talking to a civie who probably wouldn't appreciate her dark humor. "Sorry, cops tend to have a twisted sense of humor."

Ryker shoved a hand through his sandy-blond hair. "No worries. Construction workers also have a terrible sense of humor."

"Is that what you do? Construction?"

It was strange. She'd seen him a couple of times since coming back to the island but hadn't learned what he did for a living.

He scratched the stubble at his neck. "Used to. Now I'm the local handyman. I specialized in large construction but started getting more and more calls for smaller jobs. I was trained in all of it, so I decided to quit my day job and just stay on the island. Larry, a guy I work with, is close to retirement and can't handle it all, not anymore."

"Larry, right. He comes into the station to help out. Handyman is a good trade."

Ryker chuckled. "It's not anything as spectacular as an FBI agent, but it's a good living, and I enjoy the work."

"That's *special* agent, thank you very much," Rebecca replied haughtily, making him laugh. Ryker had one of those laughs that was contagious. One that made her want to hear it more often. "Being a former special agent was not all it was cracked up to be."

They were already at the door to the sheriff's department, and Rebecca's brain fizzled out. She enjoyed talking to him, but she needed to get back to work, hopefully without looking like she was trying to ditch him.

"It's got to be the end of your shift, right? Do you want to grab some dinner?" He gestured over his shoulder, but she didn't know what he could be pointing at.

Butterflies stirred in Rebecca's stomach, which made her realize her breath probably still smelled like vomit and mint gum, hopefully more of the latter. "I'm sorry. I've got work to finish up."

He lifted his hands, palms out. "That's cool. I can wait. Maybe later this evening?"

That sounded like a much better plan...for a moment. Then she realized just how tired and gross she felt. As great as it would be to spend more time with Ryker, she knew she'd be bad company if she didn't get a chance to calm down and relax first. And take a shower and brush her teeth.

"It's going to take a while. A couple hours. It would be way too late to have dinner then."

Ryker stuffed his hands in his pockets. "Hey, no worries. Just thought I'd ask. Have a good night."

"Rain check?" she nearly shouted in panic.

He looked over his shoulder with a smile. "Rain check."

Rebecca watched him walk away. As much as she hated seeing him go, she enjoyed the view. Yeah, he definitely had the body of a man who did physically demanding labor all day. Sighing, Rebecca turned and pulled the door open.

Darian, Melody, and Viviane all stood there grinning. Clearly, they'd just seen her acting like a schoolgirl and ogling Ryker's butt.

Rebecca threw up her hands, going on the offensive. "What?"

"Quick, somebody go get the sheriff another milkshake." Viviane's dark eyes were teasing. "I think she needs something to cool herself down."

Shit.

23

Tonight, I timed it perfectly. It was moments like this when I knew my plans to eliminate the scum of the earth were approved by the gods.

The streets were quiet as the asshole's Porsche Cayman pulled into his drive. It wasn't as dark as I would have liked, but that was okay.

The bastard had the gall to whistle as he got out of his car. Not a problem in the world, the whistle seemed to say.

It was wrong.

Stepping back into the darkest corner, I waited for him to stroll to his front door. This area wasn't like the Gilroys', but it was still obscene. No getting to know your neighbors in this area, not like where I lived.

The neighbors couldn't have known the beast who lived among them. They couldn't know the rotten heart that beat inside his chest.

Would they even miss him? Or would they simply be afraid for themselves and purchase another security camera or lock? My money was on the latter.

As he drew closer, I thought I recognized the tune. I did.

I'd heard it often enough at its height of popularity. "I'm Too Sexy."

I almost laughed, but rage tamped down any humor.

Go ahead and sing, you bastard. Go ahead and enjoy your life for the short time you have left.

I'm too angry for my shirt.

Too angry for my shirt.

So angry it hurts.

As my own lyrics played out to his whistle, I crept closer to the door as he turned his back on me. Keys jingled, mixing with the melody of his surprisingly on-pitch tune.

The door opened. Light spilled out.

My pulse had become an ocean in my ears, *swoosh-swoosh-swooshing* like the crash of waves on rocks. A dark abyss inside me, pounding to get out.

Just as he set one foot inside his home, I sprang.

He whirled back around, and I smashed my gun into his teeth before he could speak. He stumbled back, shock and blood covering his face.

Slamming the butt down harder this time, I stepped into his house as he fell, bringing my weapon down on his face again and again, tearing it up.

Just like that, his world turned upside down. I grinned at him as understanding filled his one good eye. His whistles were replaced by groans, and I enjoyed their symphony.

I'm too vengeful for my car.

Too vengeful for my car.

Too vengeful by far.

I pulled the bag from my pocket.

Fear clouded his features. The stench of piss reached my nose.

I stepped around, avoiding the growing puddle, and dropped to the floor. Pulling the bag over his fat head, my only regret was that the blood from his injuries coated the inside, hiding his face from me.

"How does it feel?" I hissed, leaning over him, pressing down. "How does it feel to not be able to breathe? How do you like it when it's done to *you*? You never thought about it before, did you? Did you?"

Like a beating heart, the bag pumped in and out.

The bag fluttered.

Stuttered.

It slowed. Weaker now.

Stopped.

Waiting, I hoped the plastic would move again. It was over too soon.

You're too dead for your party.

Too dead for your party.

No way you're disco dancing.

Breathing hard, I picked up my gun and pushed to my feet.

I pulled the hammer back, pressed it against his forehead.

I'm too—

The boom silenced the song running through my head.

24

R ebecca stared at the cold air fryer, then at the knob. It was definitely turned on and definitely plugged in. *Dammit.*

She'd planned on tossing a chicken breast into the basket for an easy meal, but now? She didn't trust her knowledge of the electric stove to avoid overbaked meat or food poisoning.

"RIP, my friend."

Tossing the fryer in the trash, Rebecca dug around in the cupboards until she found a suitable pot. She dumped a jar of tomato sauce into the bottom, added some extra garlic and Italian spice before setting it on the stove, then double-checked to make sure the knob was set to low. Her mother had always lectured her to let the sauce simmer for at least half an hour. Once the sauce was hot, she would throw in one of the packets of precooked ravioli from her fridge. Setting the oven to 400, she prepped a tray for some garlic bread.

With that set up, she decided to take a quick shower while she waited. After the day she'd had, combined with the tiny amount of sleep she'd gotten the night before, there was no way she'd have the energy to get cleaned up after her belly was full.

Grabbing a coffee stout from the fridge, she headed to the bathroom. Drinking the cold beer while standing in the hot shower, she finally relaxed. The residue of the day washed down the drain, leaving her muscles so loose she felt weak. Scents of coconut and lemongrass filled the steamy air, making her almost feel like she was on vacation.

Well, the vacation she was supposed to have had.

After brushing her teeth to rid her mouth of the vomit aftertaste, Rebecca sprayed leave-in conditioner into her blond mane and combed it through, deciding to let it air-dry. After that, it took all her energy to pull on clean shorts and a tee.

Walking out of the bathroom, she looked longingly at her bed. She could turn off the stove and put the bread in the freezer. Put everything away and simply go to sleep right now. The evening sun hadn't yet met the horizon, but she didn't care. She was tired. Stretching out on the soft, smooth linen would feel so good.

But...after throwing up earlier, if she went to bed without eating, she would sleep poorly and maybe even wake with a hangover, even though the amount of alcohol she'd consumed thus far was minuscule.

Back in the kitchen, Rebecca dumped the ravioli into the sauce before she could change her mind. *A quick meal, then bed.*

A meal with lots of cheese sounded even better.

Rebecca pulled the bag of shredded mozzarella from the fridge as well and placed the bread in the oven to toast.

She just had to stay awake until the pasta cooked. Ten minutes, tops. That was doable, with a little bit of help from Mother Nature. Picking up her beer, she walked to the back door and watched the clouds blow toward the north.

She'd eat on the deck, she decided. Listening to the waves washing up on land would soothe her nerves.

Taking hold of the door handle, Rebecca tugged. It didn't move. She double-checked that it was unlocked. It was. She pulled again. Then yanked. With a loud squeal, the sliding door jerked open and leaned at a crazy angle.

Of course.

Examining the top track, she saw that one roller was twisted, and only a single screwhead showed. Pushing against the door itself, she tried to smash it back into place and folded the roller plate more, making a bad situation even worse.

Shit.

There was no way she could sleep with the door like this. It wasn't safe. And she didn't want to think about the number of bugs that would fly in overnight.

Back in the kitchen, Rebecca went through all the drawers, searching for a hammer or a screwdriver. Anything that might help with the situation. Nothing.

Slamming a drawer closed, she jammed her fists on her hips. "Screw this."

And just like that, Ryker Sawyer's handsome face flashed through Rebecca's mind.

Face heating, she plopped down on the chair. Maybe a good screwing was exactly what she needed. But with a childhood friend?

"Why am I thinking about sex?"

Dropping her head on the table, she gave her forehead a few good raps, hoping to knock some sense into herself. All it did was give her a headache.

With a growl, Rebecca grabbed her phone and did a search until his name popped up. Sawyer Handyman Service. Was it a business phone or his personal cell?

Tapping the number, she chewed her fingernail while it rang. And rang.

Just when she thought a voicemail would pick up, the call was answered with a breathless, "Sawyer Handyman Service. How can I help?"

Had he been running or doing something else?

Her mind immediately went back to the gutter. She forced it out.

"Hi, Ryker. It's Rebecca. Um, about that rain check…"

✳

WHEN THE DOORBELL RANG, Rebecca had been kicked back with a second beer on the patio, listening to some Black Flag on her phone. Her hair was still damp, so the best she'd been able to do was pull it up into a loose ponytail.

Instead of walking all the way to the front, she stood at the broken door and shouted, "Come in!"

The front door opened, and Ryker appeared. A tool belt was slung over one shoulder, a cordless drill dangled from one hand. Spotting her, he lifted the power tool. "No reason to panic, ma'am."

She wrinkled her forehead, confused. He sounded like an old public service announcement from the radio. "Huh?"

"This is just a drill. If this had been an actual emergency—"

Rebecca burst out laughing. "That's bad."

"Oh, come on. That's my favorite joke." Grinning broadly, the smile fell away as Ryker examined her door. After a quick inspection and a slight shake that made the door tip, he shook his head. "Yup. You really beat the shit out of it." He sounded impressed with her ability to destroy large, stationary objects.

Rebecca shoved her hand in a pocket. "What can I say? It pissed me off."

Ryker made a show of checking out her biceps. "Remind me never to piss you off."

"Always a good plan." She had a sudden thought. "Do you have kids?"

"No." He narrowed his eyes at her. "Are you asking because I made a dad joke?"

She nodded, hiding her grin behind her beer. "If you're not a dad, does that make that joke a faux *pa*?"

Ryker groaned. "You can never, ever call my jokes bad again." He nodded to the can she held. "Is that...coffee-flavored beer?"

"It's a coffee stout, and it's delicious. Want one?"

He looked dubious. "I think I'll keep my coffee and my beer separate, thanks." He checked the bit in the drill, then got to work removing the screws from the mangled roller plate.

Rebecca shrugged and took another sip. "Your loss. I like mixing my uppers and downers. It's more efficient."

Ryker chuckled and pulled out the screws. "Is that Henry Rollins on your phone?"

It was still outside, but she couldn't hear it now that he was taking up most of the doorway. "Probably. There's a big chunk of eighties Black Flag on that playlist."

"I didn't figure you for a punk rock kinda girl." He set down the drill and pulled a screwdriver from his pocket and worked on prying the bent roller off.

"What kind of girl did you figure me for?" Rebecca raised one eyebrow, her finger tapping the side of her can.

"I've suddenly remembered that you're the kind of girl who carries a loaded weapon." Ryker turned back to the project at hand. "Oh, look, a broken door that needs to be fixed."

She hadn't laughed this much in a while.

"Have you eaten yet? I have a pot of ravioli and garlic bread in the oven."

His tawny eyes twinkled. "Are you sure you didn't break this door on purpose because you regretted turning me down earlier?"

Rebecca shrugged, ignoring the butterflies in her stomach that were chasing away her exhaustion. "Happy coincidence."

"Then I'll be more than happy to take you up on dinner." He turned back to the door, replacing the twisted roller with one he pulled from his kit. "As it turned out, I got a call after leaving the station, so I haven't eaten yet either."

Rebecca headed to the kitchen. This was nice. Having company. Someone she could laugh and joke with. She glanced back.

He held the door in place with one hand while the other worked the drill. His muscles were toned from constant use, and his skin possessed a golden glow from all the time he spent in the sun.

She licked her lips. "Dinner with a view."

"What's that?" He laughed, and she realized she'd said the words out loud.

Mixing lack of sleep with a long workday and a couple of beers, she'd have to be careful. "I said dinner with a view. We can eat on the back porch."

Ryker's eyes trailed over her, and it made her insides sizzle. "Dinner with a view. I like that."

Oh yeah, sleep was the last thing on her mind now.

❄

"Wow, you work fast."

Ryker slid the door back and forth a few times, ensuring it latched, locked adequately, and opened again. The corner of his lips twitched as he looked at her. "When the job requires it, sure."

Rebecca picked up the plates she'd assembled and walked toward him, unsure if there was innuendo in that statement. Not that she was trying to get closer to him. It was just because he was between her and the table on the back porch. And if she told herself that enough times, she might even believe it.

"Otherwise, I prefer taking my time."

Oh yeah, definitely innuendo there.

"Well then, would you like something hot and steamy?" She lifted the plates. "And cheesy."

He grinned. "I like cheesy."

From the way his eyes were sparkling, she felt damn sure he did.

Ryker moved aside, barely enough for her to squeeze past him and onto the back deck. The night was cool but not chilly—a perfect setting for a romantic dinner. Rebecca set the plates down, stepping around his tool bag as she did so. When she looked back, he walked out with her beer in his hand.

"Oh, I forgot to get you a drink."

He stooped over and pulled a bottle from his bag. "That's okay. I brought my own."

"I like a man who's always prepared." She gestured to the chair closest to the door and sat in the one she was starting to consider her own.

"That's me." He sat down and passed over her drink. "I never go anywhere without protection."

Rebecca nearly dropped her fork.

Ryker set the container on the table and gave her a stern look. "Sunscreen is essential out here. Don't forget it."

Oh yeah, this man was pressing all her buttons. He was funny, good with his hands, had a flexible schedule, was witty and amusingly provocative. A man who could keep her on her toes with his verbal jousting.

She fanned herself with her left hand while stabbing a ravioli with her fork. "Is it getting hot out here?"

"Must be the company." His voice was all innocence.

Rebecca popped the ravioli in her mouth and swallowed it as she thought about jumping his bones.

From the way he looked at her, he knew exactly what she was doing. Or more to the point, what he was doing to her. There was nothing more appealing to Rebecca than a man who could make her laugh, even after a super crappy day.

Sitting here, bantering with Ryker, she felt better than she had all day. Better than she had all week. Maybe it had been a blessing in disguise that her air fryer had died.

"To get the question everyone is talking about out of the way, are you planning on sticking around?" Ryker kept his eyes on his plate, so she couldn't tell how he felt about that. It was also the first time he'd not looked at her since he'd arrived.

Rebecca took a swig of her beer. "Everyone's wondering?"

"You're kind of the talk of the town right now. A big-city federal agent shows up and starts setting things right. There's been a couple of people grumping about how this will make us look bad as a tourist attraction, but there's always people complaining about that."

Rebecca felt some of that heat that had been building between them start to disperse. Had he been buttering her up all night to get information from her?

"Oh, so you're wondering if I'll keep the job?"

"Well, yeah. But also, no. It's not the job I care about." He looked up from his plate and met her gaze. "I'd like to know if you're planning on being here for a while. Or if you see this as just some kind of summer fling."

The sincerity in his eyes brought the heat rushing back way south of Rebecca's cheeks. "Um..."

Ryker held up a hand. "With the job market, prospects can be fickle around here. If you're looking to settle down, though, this is a good place to do it."

"I hadn't planned on it." Her heart squeezed when his smile faded a bit. "Originally, I just came here for some downtime. A place to rest and recover. But the longer I'm here, the more reasons I'm finding to stay."

Ryker's smile returned, and he reached out to touch her hand. "I'd like that."

Rebecca's phone rang, cutting off her music. "Excuse me." Fumbling with her chair, she reached across the table. Darian Hudson's name was on the caller ID.

"Darian, please tell me this is a social call."

"Bad timing?" The question came with an undercurrent of amusement.

She slid a look at the man across from her. "Oh yeah."

"So now's not a good time to tell you that we have another dead body?"

Ryker licked some sauce from his thumb, glancing at her with a dimpled half smile.

She closed her eyes.

Son of a bitch.

25

"And this is what I get for thinking I might have an evening off," Rebecca groused the second she spotted Deputy Hudson.

There were no markers on the porch or steps leading up to where Darian stood in the tiled foyer. It was a lovely house, not entirely on par with the Gilroys' but more than she would ever be able to afford or need.

White walls and floors seemed to be a theme in these luxury houses. Something she did not understand at all. The layout and décor screamed rich-boy bachelor pad, complete with a giant home theater system and speakers she could see from where she stood. Minus the blood and brains leaking into the entryway of this one, of course.

"Sorry. I knew you'd never forgive me if I didn't call."

Rebecca sighed. "You'd be right. Gimme the camera and fill me in on what you know."

"I believe the victim is Jake Underwood. This is his home, and he's the correct height and build. M.E. is on her way."

Rebecca understood at a glance why Darian was iffy on the identification.

The victim had taken a beating and was unrecognizable with the swelling and the blood she could see through the bag. But Rebecca recognized the attire the second she set foot in the house.

She sighed. "I talked to Jake this morning, and those are the same clothes he was wearing then." A glance at his hands provided more confirmation. "I also recognize the rings."

Rebecca went through the pictures Darian had already taken and continued documenting the scene from where he'd left off.

"His neighbors, the Brookers, are just beyond the trees. Mr. Brooker reported hearing a single gunshot shortly after eight thirty. I came out to investigate and saw the door wide open and the interior lights on. I called you as soon as I verified he was dead."

Rebecca appreciated that. Even though there was a bag over the man's face, which was coated in blood, Darian had followed protocol and checked for a pulse. Touching a body like that wasn't for the faint of heart.

"You cleared the house?" She thought it best to ask, just in case. It would suck to get shot in the back of the head while taking pictures.

Darian stopped reading his notes and gave her a flat look. "I know my job. I'm not Locke." He mumbled that last bit. It was starting to appear that Locke hadn't been well-liked before her arrival.

Rebecca stayed quiet on the subject and continued to take photos from every angle. She lowered the camera. "What's that?"

Darian squatted low and followed the direction of where Rebecca's finger pointed. It could have been the tag of Jake's shirt sticking out, but she didn't think so.

Grabbing an evidence bag and a pair of tweezers, Darian pulled a piece of paper tucked inside the victim's collar.

Not so exclusive after all.

The same note as was found on Bryson. *Not so exclusive after all.*

Rebecca ran a forearm over her brow. "Well, the good news is that these deaths are related, so more than likely just the one killer. The bad news is that these deaths are related, so we have to contend with that. We need to check for signs that our unsub was waiting here for Jake."

Darian dropped to his haunches and examined the floor. "I'll check for footprints."

She noticed the keys on the floor beside the vic. Then, turning around, she inspected the frame of the door and doorknob as well. While there was a dead bolt, it looked pristine. "No sign of forced entry. Looks like he'd just let himself in when he was attacked. He lives alone?"

"Far as I can tell. I haven't found anyone else listed at this address, but I also haven't checked other than to make sure no one was currently inside. No cameras at first glance, but like I said, I've not done a proper search."

Debating how much to share, Rebecca decided to trust this deputy with what she knew. "He's connected to the Yacht Club. He'd previously partied with Bryson, was even invited to the party that ended up being Bryson's last. He didn't go since he had to work. And now, two men associated with the Yacht Club are dead."

Darian looked as disturbed by the realization as she felt. He pushed to his feet. "There's your link."

She hoped so. "Let's check to see if they had anything else in common. Their membership may not have been what got them killed."

❄

WITH BAILEY'S HELP, they confirmed that it was, in fact, Jake Underwood killed in his own home. His approximate time of death lined up with the report for the gunshot.

When Trent Locke arrived, Rebecca put him to work, roping off the crime scene and managing the murder logbook outside. She and Darian searched the home, inside and out, more thoroughly. The attack appeared to have been quick and contained near the entrance.

Nothing inside the home seemed to be out of place. Rebecca stood in Jake's office. They'd already taken his computers, but she was going through the paperwork on his desk, tagging anything that looked important. Considering who she was dealing with and the people he worked for, she expected lawyers to show up any minute now. Or, more likely, his father to show up with lawyers.

In all his glorious incompetence, Jake Underwood had a nicely labeled pad in a desk drawer that listed his usernames and passwords for various accounts and social media. That was going to make Justin Drake happy, at least.

She glanced down the list as she dropped the pad into an evidence bag and noticed that there were two passcodes for a phone.

Does that mean he's got a burner around here somewhere?

"Hey, Darian!"

"Yessir?"

Rebecca smiled. "Keep an eye out for a second phone."

"Roger that."

The filing cabinet wasn't locked, so she went through it next. Taxes, payroll stubs, and insurance all went into the boxes to be taken as evidence. They needed to find what linked Jake and Bryson since the Yacht Club wasn't an official organization.

A legally valid argument. At least until someone was willing to state on the record that the Yacht Club existed.

There wasn't time to read every paper, but she got enough glances to learn something else. As she'd expected, Jake didn't own this house. His father did. Jake rented it from his father for a dollar a month.

His father appeared to live on the island, too, at an address where Jake sent his "rent." Nothing unexpected or case-breaking there. She grabbed files and dropped them into the boxes to be hauled back to the station.

And then she hit the mother lode.

Rebecca very nearly missed the false door under Jake's desk. If she hadn't dropped a folder and run her hand along the underside of the desk to brace herself when she'd bent down to retrieve it, she wouldn't have felt a device taped there.

Heart hammering, she got on her hands and knees to peer up at the putty knife-looking tool taped under the desk. She peeled it from the wood. Then she picked up the file folder to reveal a cutout in the hardwood floor beneath it. The putty knife fit perfectly in the crevice.

Prying the floorboards up revealed a metal box about the size of a shoebox. Jake might be careless with his passwords, but he'd taken care to secure whatever was in this box.

It was locked, of course.

After searching for the key, Rebecca headed back to where Jake's body lay.

Dr. Bailey Flynn glanced up and smiled. "We've really got to stop running into each other like this."

Rebecca chuckled at the medical examiner's sweet sense of humor and knelt by the keys dangling from the Porsche key fob on the floor. The ring contained three other keys, but none were as small as the one she'd need to open the box.

"Can you check his pockets? I'm searching for a small key."

Bailey did as asked, turning the pockets out as she went. "Nothing."

Rebecca was about to turn back to do another search of the office when the biggest ring on Jake's hand caught her attention. It was a monstrosity. She peered closer. *Is that a hinge?*

"Bailey, can you check that ring for me? See if it opens."

The medical examiner directed the crime scene tech to video her actions. When he nodded that he was ready, Bailey pulled the ring from Jake's left middle finger.

"Hm…I think you're right." Taking a device that looked like a thin ice pick from her bag, she poked around the metal. The face of the ring popped up.

Heart increasing in speed, Rebecca smiled at the contents. A small metal key.

Waiting while the key was photographed and dusted for prints felt like an eternity. But soon enough, it was in her possession.

Back in Jake's office, she fitted the key in the box's lock and turned it. The lock opened.

Reams of paper were inside. Scanning quickly, Rebecca had to bite her lip to keep from *whooping*. She settled for silently pumping a fist. These were photocopies of names, dates, and contracts. There were ledger entries from the marina. It contained details about how much the slips cost, and who rented each one, with a diagram of which space belonged to who.

The annual rent of each slip was astronomical. Those numbers were more than enough to buy silence from the staff. All this was exciting information to have but didn't help much with the investigation into Jake Underwood's death. Or Bryson Gilroy's.

Unless someone from the Yacht Club had killed them. Had someone learned that he'd been making these copies?

Was he killed to keep his mouth shut? Was Bryson somehow wrapped up in this too?

Rebecca took pictures of every piece of paper from this file, just in case it went missing later. She was no longer willing to blindly trust anyone or any "secure" space moving forward.

Once that was all photographed, Rebecca pulled out another stack of folders.

"Hey, Darian!"

"Yessir?" His voice was muffled, so she spoke even louder to make sure he could hear.

"I need more boxes. And the tape."

"I'll see if the techs have some spares in the van. I'm filling up the ones I've got out here too."

Rebecca paused to think about that. Last she'd seen, he was digging his way through the entertainment center. "Do I want to know what you found out there?"

"Uh…" There was a long stretch of silence.

She knew from that silence it was going to be something terrible. While she waited for Darian to form an answer, she went back to reading the files in front of her.

The one on top was marked *Clients*. Flipping it open, she found a spreadsheet of men's names. Some she recognized from the slip rental paperwork, others she didn't. To the right of the names were columns with coded headers she couldn't understand—intentionally cryptic. In-line with each name, some were filled in with a number, and some were left blank in each of the columns' cells.

It reminded Rebecca of the menu cards she used to fill out at her sub shop in D.C. A set of columns for meats, then another for the cheeses, then the toppings…

Darian finally answered. "Home movies, I'm guessing."

Considering what she was currently looking at, Rebecca didn't want to know more. Not tonight.

"He had them out in the open?"

"Nope. I found a false bottom in the entertainment center."

She wasn't surprised.

"I'll probably have to buy the techs some booze to make up for having to watch all of those." A dark chuckle made its way down the hall. "Maybe some bleach too. For their eyes."

Rebecca's stomach lurched as she turned the next page and found a spreadsheet marked with the same codes. But before each column was a list of feminine names. First names only. In a hot second, Rebecca put it together. It was a menu. The men's cells were marked with a number corresponding to a girl or girls on this page, those who matched their desires, or so it seemed.

"Are those DVDs marked with first names only?"

"Yeah. How'd you know?"

"I think I have a similar list of names here. Make sure you make a list so I can compare them later."

Darian grumbled, but she ignored it, sure he would do his job, no matter how distasteful. This was the link. Bryson and Jake were working together in the prostitution ring. And now she had a list of some of the victims' first names. Or pseudonyms. It was a place to start.

Rebecca opened the next folder. With mounting horror, she flipped through the stack of names. This folder was marked *A–F* at the top. There were dozens of names. *Alexandra, Amanda, Anna...*

Rebecca kept turning pages.

They were filed under their first names with contact numbers, social media handles, and pickup locations. There was also a short list of which drugs or drinks they preferred. What was required to get the girls to join the parties when their services were requested.

Halfway through the folder, Rebecca stopped. Cassie was

on that list, with a description that matched Cassie Leigh to a T. And, ominously, her name was crossed out with a black marker.

Hearing the voices of the techs getting closer, Rebecca realized she didn't have time to waste reading each file as she sat there. She started taking pictures instead, so she could sort through them later.

When she was finished, she crawled under the desk to search the space beneath the floor more fully. Though she didn't really want to, she stuck her hand into the hole and felt around.

Her fingers brushed against something plastic and solid. Even before pulling it out, she knew what it was.

A burner phone.

26

"You trying to show me up, coming in this early? 'Cause if so, you might want to brush your hair first." Hoyt laughed as he leaned in the doorframe of the meeting room where he'd found his boss.

West groaned and rolled over. Her tousled hair had turned staticky from the pleather upholstery of the couch. She looked beyond ragged as she swung her legs down and tried to lever herself up. The coffee table in front of her was covered in paperwork.

He tried not to laugh at how bad she looked.

"The chair in my office is broken, so I worked here. Then it got late." Using both hands, West swept her hair back out of her face and lifted her red-rimmed eyes to his.

Hoyt grunted through lips pressed tight so he wouldn't smile and handed her a freshly poured cup of coffee. "Darian called this morning to say you'd gotten a new corpse last night and thought you'd end up working all night. I came prepared."

West took the cup, and Hoyt started poking through the

papers. They appeared to be printed pictures of paperwork. It must have taken her hours to print out so many on their slow-as-molasses printer. "How come you didn't just sort through the original paperwork? Or make copies?"

Looking up at him over the rim of her cup, West flicked her gaze to the open door.

As he pushed the door shut, the sound of a zipper being pulled made him panic.

Shit. Had she meant for him to leave so she could change?

Keeping his back to her, he cleared his throat. "Do you need some privacy or…?"

"No, why?"

He peeked over his shoulder to see her fiddling with the zipper of her bag.

Whew.

"Nothing." Dropping into a chair, Hoyt pulled out a notepad. "What's up?"

She pulled out a brush and raked it through her blond hair. It seemed oddly personal to watch her ready herself for the day, even though there was nothing sexual about it.

Okay, old man, you're not as woke as you thought. You'd have no problem sitting in a closed room with Wallace combing what was left of his hair. This is the same. She's your boss right now, not a woman.

After confessing to his downfall yesterday, Hoyt had been dealing with waves of guilt and shame all over again. The nightmares of his wife sobbing on the floor, taking their kids and running away, had plagued him all night, leaving him jumpy and unsure of himself.

"This is the paperwork we pulled from Jake Underwood's office. I took pics on my phone to review them right away." She shrugged, and he nodded in understanding. "There are so many names. I've been tracking them down. Matching names on his lists to the names on the slip rentals from the marina."

"The marina? How'd you get rental information from there?" Hoyt leaned over the table and started to read.

"That's the stack there." West pointed at the one tucked into the corner. "This is a start. It provides some first names that we can work off of. It gives us some threads to pull, at least."

Hoyt wondered if he looked as dumbstruck as he felt. They actually had evidence the Yacht Club existed? "You're kidding."

"Nope." West pulled her hair back into the low ponytail she seemed to favor. "It gets better. They're running a prostitution ring, among other things, and there's enough here to bust it wide open."

"It's too early in the morning to deal with all this." Hoyt groaned into a hand as he swept it over his face.

"Oh, that's just the tip of the iceberg."

There's more?

"I'm starting to connect some dots. None of them are pointing to our killer, though. Bryson Gilroy had his fingers in a lot of bad cookie jars, and so did Jake Underwood. Young girls, drugs—"

"Wait, where does Jake Underwood fit in with all that? He's rich but not the same level as the Gilroys. He worked at the marina, didn't own a superyacht." Hoyt flipped through the stacks of names, neatly organized into spreadsheets. Some weren't the names of people but rather businesses. An extra layer of protection for whoever was a member. They'd still have to dig to get all the names.

"West, we can't go to a judge with first names only." Still, he was impressed. And scared shitless. She hadn't just kicked one hornet's nest, she'd kicked hundreds of them.

After less than a month on the job, West had already gotten more information on the people running things behind the scenes than Hoyt had ever imagined existed.

"Bryson and Jake were thirteen years apart in age. So far, there's not much they had in common aside from their involvement in the Yacht Club."

She held up an evidence bag containing a phone.

"Is that…?"

West lifted an eyebrow. "A phone I found hidden underneath a floorboard in Jake Underwood's home office? Yes. Yes, it is."

Hoyt gaped at her. "What's on it? And shouldn't the techs have it?"

"They will very soon. I kept it because I thought I had the pin to open it, but once I got back here and turned it on, I saw it's protected by biometrics. Not facial recognition, but actual fingerprints." She wiggled her fingers.

He groaned. "Does that mean what I think it means?"

"What time does the M.E.'s office open?"

Hoyt checked his watch. "A bit over an hour."

West put her hands on her knees and pushed to her feet. "Just enough time for me to get cleaned up before we head over. We're going to get some real answers today. Hopefully, before we have another body on our hands."

❄

REBECCA HAD her laptop bag slung over her shoulder, the evidence bag with the phone secured inside. Before leaving, they locked everything securely away in a cabinet in her office, then locked the office for good measure.

She and Hoyt walked out the front door and turned for the parking lot. They'd not spoken much since she'd come back from washing her face and getting freshened up. He'd simply stood up and followed her out the door.

Her deputy seemed to be in a dark or introspective mood, responding to her mostly in grunts and head movements. She couldn't help but wonder if he'd recognized some of the names on those lists. Some of them had to be people he'd lived on the island with for years, both the villains and the victims. It had to be rough learning that about his neighbors, so she left him to it.

They'd just made the turn around the corner of the building when a car door slammed. Hoyt was as fast as she was this time as they reached for their sidearms.

Albert Gilroy came stomping toward them, his eyes lit up like a Christmas tree. Rebecca reached into her trouser pocket and hit the buttons she'd set to trigger the record function on her cell.

"You. This is all your fault!" Gilroy stormed up, trying to get in Rebecca's face, but she sidestepped him and kept moving. "Jake Underwood died because you couldn't get your job done."

Hoyt moved between her and the red-faced man.

"I can't talk about an ongoing case." She kept walking, which forced him to turn and tail her like a hungry pooch that smelled bacon in her pocket.

"I'll make sure the board of supervisors knows what a terrible job you're doing, and you'll be replaced first thing Monday morning. I'm calling for a special meeting to make sure it happens as quickly as possible."

"Until then, I still have a job to do. So if you'll excuse us." Rebecca hit the button to unlock the cruiser. Hoyt went around to the passenger side.

"Like hell you're doing your job. You never even told me about my son being chopped up! His corpse was desecrated, and you can't even find his killer."

So Trench Coat is Gilroy's bitch. That didn't take long at all.

She glanced over at Hoyt, who met her eyes and nodded.

"What do you mean desecrated? I told you he was shot in the head after he died."

"You didn't tell me this sick fuck cut my son's dick off."

Subtly sliding her phone from her pocket, Rebecca turned to face Gilroy.

"I didn't tell you that because it didn't happen. Where did you hear that?"

Gilroy jerked back as if he'd been slapped. "What?"

"Who told you that Bryson was castrated?"

"I...I heard a rumor," Gilroy floundered.

"You shouldn't listen to unfounded rumors, Mr. Gilroy. As I've repeatedly told you, if you'll simply contact the M.E.'s office, they can tell you everything you need to know about Bryson's death and how to claim the body. Have you still not done that? If it's too much for you, you can always send your lawyer to handle matters in your stead."

She made a show of glancing around, knowing she looked too pleased with herself. Gilroy had fallen into her little trap. "Speaking of, where is he? I believe this is the first time Steven Campbell hasn't been at your side. Why isn't he here with you now when you're talking to me?"

"He..." Gilroy stumbled over that as well. Obviously, the man wasn't used to being questioned or having his threats ignored. "He's taking care of personal matters."

"Well, you might want to contact him. If someone is spreading those terrible rumors about your son, you might want to have your lawyer look into it. I did try to warn you." Rebecca looked Gilroy dead in the eyes. "You seem to have more enemies than you thought."

His jaw snapped shut, and his glare turned deadly, but behind it, she saw what she'd been hoping for...a little worm of doubt. The Yacht Club would be much easier to take down if the members started to doubt each other and their henchmen.

"Think about it. Now, if you'll excuse me. I have a lot of work to get done this weekend…before I start my vacation on Monday and end up with all kinds of free time on my hands." Rebecca turned and slid into the driver's seat.

Hoyt folded himself inside too. It took some maneuvering to get out of the parking spot because Gilroy hadn't moved a muscle.

When he was clear in her rearview, Rebecca stopped the recording on her phone with the press of a button. But neither of them said a word until the station and the pissed-off millionaire were out of sight.

Hoyt finally broke the silence. "Do you really not care about keeping the job? Or are you just playing it cool with that asshole?"

She had to think about that. "I do care. I like this job. I like the people. I'd like to keep both of them in my life. But I don't want either of them enough to cave to a man like Albert Gilroy or his cronies." Not that she would stop digging into the Yacht Club even if she lost the job. "Men like that think they can bully me. I don't know if it's because they're rich and used to getting their way or because I'm a woman. Either way, they're wrong."

Hoyt burst out laughing and kept laughing. It bordered on hysterical.

Rebecca glanced over, wondering if he was okay.

"Bully you?" He wiped a tear from his eye. "After you used an armed ambush and turned it back on them to make Gilroy think his men are conspiring against him?"

He calmed down a bit, and she couldn't help smiling.

"You're handling them far better than Wallace or I ever did. And that lie, that was pure genius, Boss."

Using the lie she'd told Trench Coat to make Gilroy doubt his accomplices was one of her better moves.

Rebecca's cheeks heated, nonetheless. Taking compliments had never been her strong suit. Thankfully, he kept chuckling to himself, and she didn't need to respond.

"These guys don't know what they got themselves into, coming up against you. But they're going to find out."

27

Rebecca spotted Dr. Bailey Flynn as she was about to enter the hospital. She tapped Hoyt's arm to get his attention, and they waited at the door for the medical examiner.

Bailey didn't look up until she was nearly on top of them, her focus on a delicious-smelling breakfast burrito. She jumped when she spotted them. "Sorry, I about ran you both over."

Rebecca smiled. "I don't blame you. That burrito deserves your full attention."

Bailey pulled it close to her chest, mock horror on her face. "If that's a hint that you'd like a bite, forget it. Get your own."

Holding up both hands in surrender, Rebecca laughed. "I wouldn't dare."

The medical examiner shot her a wink and headed inside. "Smart woman. Now let me guess, you're here about our latest guest?"

"Nah, just here to make sure you didn't get lost or lose your nerve before tackling this one."

Bailey snorted. "Remind me to call you next time I get a shark attack victim."

Rebecca's eyes went wide. She had a strong stomach, but she wasn't sure how well she could handle something like that. "Do you get those often?"

Bailey shook her head. "Nope. People are friends, not food."

"Shark attacks are as rare as bear attacks," Hoyt added. "But you mainland folk seem to think they happen all the time."

Bailey waved her burrito. "Drowning victims are the worst. All bloated and leaky."

"You're saying I should send Hoyt down to handle the reports on those?" Rebecca teased.

Hoyt pressed his hand to his stomach. "Please, God, no."

Bailey's shoulders shook. "Not after last time."

"He dripped on my shoe." Hoyt pointed to the ground. "It got on my sock."

Rebecca shuddered at the idea of bodily fluids oozing between her toes.

"That's why you should never wear sandals to an autopsy!" Bailey scolded him as they walked into her office.

"I thought you said you were wearing socks." Rebecca stopped, whirling on the deputy. "Are you one of *those* guys? Socks with sandals?"

His mouth worked up and down for a few seconds before he managed, "You've clearly never gotten sand stuck between the leather and your feet. If you had, you'd wear socks too."

Oh, Rebecca was going to give him hell for that.

Later.

Now that they'd entered the autopsy suite, both she and Hoyt sobered.

Bailey found the only uncluttered spot on her desk and set her coffee mug down, throwing away her breakfast wrapper. With that done, the M.E. donned a professional persona. "Do you have questions about the preliminary report?"

Rebecca blinked. "You've done prelim already?"

Bailey lifted a shoulder. "Couldn't sleep. I got a few winks, no worries, but then got started last night. Should have the rest done by this afternoon."

Rebecca didn't know if she should be impressed by Bailey's work ethic or concerned. "We're actually not here about the results." She held up the phone. "We need a fingerprint."

Hoyt held up a hand. "We can, of course, get a warrant first."

Bailey waved him off. "The dead don't have rights to privacy, Deputy. There's no need." She tucked her bag in a drawer. "Unfortunately, he's already cold, so it may not work. We'll have to try and see."

"Was cause of death the same as the last one?"

Bailey frowned. "I don't think so. I have more tests to run, but I feel confident in sharing that your killer was patient enough to wait for the asphyxiation to work this time. No sign of strangulation. As we discussed at the scene, he was beaten pretty badly first." She waved for them to follow her. "Let me show you what I mean. Frost, you remember where the garbage cans are?"

Hoyt's neck turned pink. "Har de har, doc. I only threw up that one time."

Bailey grabbed a pair of gloves and pointed to the sink. "Can you get the hot water running?"

He blanched. "Are we going to boil his finger?"

Bailey rolled her eyes. "Yes, one by one."

Hoyt glanced at Rebecca, and she shook her head. "She's kidding."

The M.E. grinned. "Depending on the model of phone,

warming the flesh might help unlock it. I don't know what kind of scanner this phone has."

Hoyt headed to the sink. "That makes sense."

"Make sure it's hot but not scalding."

Unlike the morgues on TV, this one didn't have drawers to hold its bodies. Instead, sheet-covered stretchers were lined up in two neat rows in the spacious, refrigerated room. Bailey went to the closest one and checked the toe tag.

When Bailey pulled the sheet off Jake's face, Rebecca winced. It was hard to believe this was the same man she'd spoken to twenty-four hours earlier. "What's the damage?"

Bailey started pointing. "Blunt force trauma to the nose and mouth with multiple teeth broken or knocked out completely, and fractures to the zygomatic bone as well as the frontal bone. I've seen this before. He was pistol-whipped. You can tell by the shapes of the scrapes and bruises." She mimed holding a gun, then lashed out with it sideways at Rebecca's nose, then raised her hand and swung it down at her head.

Rebecca smiled at the theatrics. "You enjoy that way too much."

Bailey mimed holstering her gun. "Can anyone truly enjoy their job too much?"

"Yes!" Hoyt called from his place at the sink.

"Bah, spoilsport! I bet people say the same thing to you when you write them a speeding ticket."

Hoyt shook his head but ignored the jibe. "Water's ready. You want me to put this in something, or are you going to wheel him over?"

"Put on gloves and use the metal pan to your left." Bailey undraped Jake's arm.

Rebecca fetched a pair of gloves. Once they were on, she pulled the phone from the evidence bag.

Bailey splayed out the fingers of Jake's right hand first,

and Rebecca went ahead and tested it, pressing the scanner to his thumb. Nothing. Same for the other nine digits she attempted.

Hoyt arrived with the water, and they watched as Bailey dipped his right hand into the bowl. "This is giving me flashbacks of sleepover pranks from my childhood."

Rebecca had been thinking the same thing.

As they waited for the skin to warm, Rebecca prayed they'd get the phone open. Some devices required an electrical current from living flesh, though. She hoped this cheap model wasn't one of them.

Bailey pulled the hand from the water and dried it with a towel. "Here you go."

Holding her breath, Rebecca pressed the thumb to the scanner.

The screen came to life.

"Hell yeah," Frost murmured.

Rebecca went to the security settings and turned off the biometrics. Now that it was unlocked, she could take it to forensics to get them to make a clone while the original stayed safe in the evidence locker. But only after she downloaded some things for her own copy.

Relieved, Rebecca smiled at the medical examiner. "Thanks. Anything else we need to know?"

Bailey shook her head. "This one appears to be straightforward. Smash, smash, smash, smash, bag, dead, bullet." She went through the motions of each attack. "As soon as I get him open, I'll retrieve the bullet and get it to forensics. They'll be able to tell you if it's a match with the first .22. But based on the location, size, and angle of the entry wound, I'd guess yes."

After placing the phone back in the evidence bag, Rebecca stripped off her gloves and tossed them into the trash.

"Thanks, Bailey. Please let us know if you learn anything exciting."

"Will do."

Outside the hospital, the hairs on the back of Rebecca's neck stood up. They hadn't parked in the garage, but she still felt vulnerable as they made their way to the cruiser.

"Want me to drive?"

Rebecca did a double take. "You can't, doctor's orders."

Hoyt lifted a shoulder. "He's just being conservative. I'm feeling much better today."

She eyed him closely. As much as she'd love to let him take the wheel so she could dig right into Jake's phone, she couldn't risk it. "Just think of how much better you'll feel on Monday."

His face fell, but he didn't complain as he went to the passenger side.

Rebecca turned on the cruiser so they could have some air but didn't put the vehicle in drive. Jake's phone was calling to her.

"What are you doing?"

Cursing herself, she turned the phone over and over in her hand. Tapping the screen through the evidence bag, she was pleased when it responded. She hadn't necessarily screwed up the chain of evidence because it had never left her sight, but she'd likely screwed up a tech's ability to pull fingerprints.

In which case...would her taking a little more time with it really matter too much?

"Rebecca?"

"Ssshhh...I just want a peek."

Hoyt tapped his head a couple of times against the head-rest but didn't argue.

As she scrolled, a name caught her eye. Cassie. She

clicked. It appeared to be the same group message that had been on Bryson's phone.

"Look at this."

Hoyt leaned over the console to read the screen. He frowned. "That sounds familiar."

"That's because it's the exact same message we read on Bryson's phone yesterday. Jake was part of that group message."

He nodded. "So now we know that both Bryson and Jake took part in harassing Cassie Leigh into getting involved in the Yacht Club. But how does it help us solve their murders?"

It was a good question.

The phone buzzed, and Rebecca jerked. It buzzed again, but she didn't see any notifications. When it buzzed the third time, she realized it was coming from her pocket. Checking to see if Hoyt had noticed—which his wide grin confirmed—she pulled her phone out.

It was an email notification from her friend at the ATF. She tapped the screen and a list populated.

"What've we got?"

"A list of all gun sales at Cottage Sports for the last ten years."

Hoyt leaned his head close to hers, watching the names go by as she started to scroll. "Stop."

But Rebecca's thumb had already stilled. She'd seen it too.

Belinda Leigh, Cassie Leigh's mother, had purchased a .22 revolver four days ago.

28

"Dammit, dammit, dammit," Hoyt chanted under his breath as they drove to the Leighs.

Rebecca suspected he didn't like the idea that Cassie Leigh's traumatized mother could be their killer and was making no attempt to hide that. She didn't like it either.

But they had to follow every lead, no matter how unpleasant.

Plus, they wouldn't be throwing accusations around when they spoke to the woman. After all, they had no solid proof.

Not yet.

As they crossed the bridge back to the island, Rebecca was surprised to see how dark the sky had become. It was filled with thick, low clouds. And roiling gray-green waters peaked and crashed as directed by increasingly agitated winds.

"Looks like a storm's brewing."

Hoyt's head whipped in her direction. "You've not been keeping up with the reports?"

She was about to offer a smart-ass response about how

she'd been a little busy, but she bit her tongue. "Not this morning."

"Tropical storm brewing down south."

Rebecca's hands tightened on the steering wheel. "What? It's June, not September."

He held up his hands. "Don't shoot the messenger."

"Sorry. Is it supposed to hit us?"

Hoyt pulled out his phone and flipped through some screens. "Not too bad. It's set to hit the Carolinas first. It'll lose steam by the time it reaches us."

Rebecca couldn't wrap her head around it. "But it's *June.*"

"Official hurricane season here in the Atlantic runs from the beginning of June to the end of November."

Great.

She scanned the horizon. "When should it get here?"

He checked his phone again. "Not for a few more days. A lot can happen between now and then. This seems like your average storm."

Tearing her gaze away from the wall of clouds, she shook her head. "Well, let's keep our eyes open, but not worry about it until there's a reason to."

Hoyt snorted. "Yeah, like a serial killer running around on the island."

"That's not funny."

But she'd been thinking the same thing. Another killing, and she'd need to call in the FBI.

Hoyt slapped his hands on his knees. "Why are we heading to the Leighs' house again?"

She shot him a look. "Because Cassie was harassed by members of the Yacht Club, and her mom just purchased the same type of gun that killed Bryson Gilroy. If Cassie's parents found her phone and accessed those messages..." She blew out a long breath. "We need to make sure they aren't out for revenge." She reached over and patted his arm. "We're just asking questions, crossing off every possibility. That's all."

He was shaking his head. "It doesn't make sense. Why would Belinda...she taught Sunday school. Why would she start killing people? Why not just call us? Let us know what these men were doing?"

Rebecca knew the likely reason but struggled with how to put it in words.

Hoyt held up a hand. "You don't have to say it. Why would she or anyone trust us to do a damn thing when we spent years going out of our way to do nothing?"

"Or..." Rebecca drew out the word, "because she's mad with grief and wants vengeance, and calling the cops tends to hamper those kinds of plans."

Hoyt frowned. "I guess."

"Could be both. Maybe Mr. Leigh is the one going vigilante. Or we could be entirely off base. That's why we pull the threads, to see what, if anything, unravels."

A mile passed before Hoyt spoke again. "Maybe I should be the one who talks to her."

Rebecca pressed her lips together, thinking it through. "I was the one who interviewed Mrs. Leigh after Cassie's death. I'm also the one who caught her killer. Do you have a better rapport with her than that, but not so much it would hinder or bias you?"

Hoyt didn't say another word as they pulled into the Leighs' drive. They got out together, but he was slow to follow her to the front door.

Rebecca knocked three times, then waited. When no one answered, she knocked again.

"Maybe they're out." Hoyt pointed at the closed garage door. "Can't tell if their cars are here or not."

"Go look. I'll check the windows."

"Really?"

"Frost." Rebecca faced him. "When was the last time you saw either of them?"

Confused by the question, he had to take a moment before responding. "Not since Cassie's funeral."

"Three out of four people in that chat are dead. We don't know what happened to Cassie's phone after her murder. We know Belinda Leigh purchased a .22 a few days ago. We know .22 bullets were found in the brains of the two men in that chat and that their deaths were highly personal."

"Maybe someone registered the gun in Belinda's name in order to frame her."

Rebecca didn't want to argue, but he was being shortsighted. Still, it was a possibility.

"Could be. But we don't know who's innocent or guilty, and jumping to conclusions could get us killed. Stay cautious and call if you see anything."

Rebecca crept around the left side of the house while Hoyt went right. Remembering the house's layout from her first visit, she passed the kitchen where the window was too high to see through. Then, as she eased up on the tall windows of the den, she cupped her hands around her eyes and pressed them to the glass.

What appeared to be a person was curled up on the couch under a blanket. On their side, head tucked down, Rebecca couldn't tell if they were male or female. However, she could see they weren't moving. Something about the way they were lying there told her something was wrong.

Jumping onto the back deck, she ran for the sliding glass door and tried to pull it open. Locked. Making a tight fist, Rebecca pounded on the glass. The person didn't move. Not even a twitch. She pulled her radio from her belt and called Hoyt.

This time she used the radio to pound on the glass.

Still, the person did not move.

"Dammit! Leigh, open up! Sheriff's department!" She banged on the glass several more times and still got no reaction. Not even an involuntary twitch.

Hoyt jogged around the corner as she stepped back and kicked the glass.

"Hey! What are you doing?"

Rebecca kicked again, and the figure still didn't stir. "Exigent circumstances. I'm going in. Call a bus!"

"That's plexiglass," Hoyt warned as he pulled his radio out and called it in. "Hurricane-proof window."

"Shit!"

She ran to the back door and checked the knob. Also locked. Bringing her knee up, she smashed her foot down just below the handle. The door flexed but held. It took two more kicks before it finally gave. Hoyt was right behind her, calling out as he cleared each room while she ran for the couch.

Grabbing the shoulders, Rebecca was stunned by how frail and thin the person was. Flipping them over, Belinda Leigh's face rolled into view, her blond hair partially covered by a thick hoodie.

The woman was pale and cool to the touch despite the hoodie and heavy blanket. Her lips had a purplish tinge. Her breath reeked of alcohol, and she was breathing so slowly that Rebecca had to check her pulse to make sure she was alive. Ripping the blanket off, she checked for wounds and found nothing obvious and no traces of blood.

"Sleeping pills!" Hoyt skidded into the room, a prescription bottle in his hand. "It's empty, but the label says it was filled today."

An empty bottle of wine was beside the couch.

"Shit. Let the paramedics know and check the rest of the house. Toss me the bottle, I'll call poison control."

Hoyt chucked the bottle to her as she made the call. She

explained the situation and read off the details of the prescription.

Following the operator's instructions, Rebecca made sure Belinda's airway was clear and propped her up against the arm of the couch to help with her breathing.

"Belinda, can you hear me?" Rebecca slapped the woman's cheeks. "Mrs. Leigh, it's Sheriff West."

Belinda's eyelids fluttered.

"Come on, Mrs. Leigh. Talk to me. Where's your husband?" Rebecca struggled to keep her upright.

"Lemme...sleep." Belinda's arms twitched but didn't lift.

"Mrs. Leigh, you can't sleep now. You took too many pills."

Tears trickled from the woman's eyes. "Cassie...cries. In dreams."

Rebecca's heart shredded at the raw pain in those slurred words.

"Mrs. Leigh, where's your husband? Where's Robert?"

Hoyt called out from somewhere deeper in the house. "House is clear, and one car is missing from the garage."

Belinda shook her head and groaned. Her breath rattled in her chest. "Gone. Always gone."

"Okay. You're doing great. Keep talking to me. Talking will keep the dreams away." Rebecca shook Belinda again, forcing her to take a breath. That worked, at least a bit, and Belinda struggled to open her eyes again. "Talk to me, Mrs. Leigh. Do you have a gun? Did you recently purchase a gun?"

Belinda's face crumpled. "He took...he took..."

"He? Who took your gun?"

Belinda's breathing slowed down again, and Rebecca shook her again.

Hoyt came back into the room and knelt in front of them both. He took the woman's hand. "Belinda, it's Hoyt. Who took your gun? We need to report it. Can you tell me?"

"Bob. T'keep me…safe."

"Safe from herself?" Hoyt murmured. "Or safe from someone else?" He pushed to his feet and headed straight to an end table, pulling open a drawer.

"What are you looking for?"

He ran to the kitchen. "Her phone!"

Belinda mumbled something and tried to roll over on her back.

Rebecca stopped her, keeping her neck straight so she wouldn't choke as her breathing started to wheeze. "Hoyt, check her purse!"

"I can't find it, but I'm going to—"

His voice was interrupted by a loud knock.

"I got it," he yelled.

Rebecca heard voices and was pretty sure she recognized Greg Abner's.

"Sheriff, what can I do?"

She waved Greg over when he appeared in the den archway. "She needs to be held in place like this until the paramedics arrive. Rolled slightly forward, keep her neck straight."

"Keep her airway open and clear. Got it. What happened?"

"Looks like an overdose of sleeping pills and a bottle of wine. We need to make sure she doesn't choke and keep her warm. Keep her talking."

Greg knelt next to the couch with a few grunts. "Got 'er. You can step away."

Rebecca leaned down and put her lips next to the older man's ear. "Her husband has her gun. We've got to find him."

Frowning, Greg nodded. "You go. I'll take care of everything here."

"Got it!" Hoyt returned with a cell phone in hand. "She's got two phones synced to the find my phone thing. One is in the house, and I'm betting that's Cassie's. The other one has to be her husband's."

"Where is it?" Rebecca looked over his shoulder.

"Downtown." He zoomed in on a map. "Stationary, it appears."

Rebecca frowned at the map and the red dot. "I recognize the street names, but I don't know what's around there. Is that his job or…?"

"Shouldn't be. That's an office building."

Rebecca started typing the address into her phone. "What offices?"

"A CPA, a financial planner. Let's see, there's also a lawyer…" His eyes widened. "Shit."

Shit indeed.

She stared at the name on her phone. *Steven Campbell, Attorney at Law.*

Rebecca headed to the door. "Call Campbell to warn him. We need to get there now."

If they weren't already too late.

29

I covered my mouth with both hands to hold in the scream that had been building inside me for the past two weeks. If I started screaming now, I knew I'd never stop. And I needed to hold it in a little longer.

How had this all happened?

Why had my family been targeted?

And would it ever end?

They'd taken everything. Everything!

Nothing mattered.

I took a swig from the bottle on the passenger's seat to give my mouth something to do besides rant and cry. I hated wine, but it was the only alcohol in the house. Belinda loved her wine. Not in excess. She was a perfect wife and mother.

Oh, Belinda...I'm so sorry.

Cassie, baby.

I'd failed them both.

My fingers ran over the phone again. Even listening to my baby's voice no longer soothed me. I started the message I'd heard so many times since she'd died anyway.

"Today is the day we start our new lives. Leaving our childhood

houses behind, but never the ones that made it home. My mother and daddy..."

Cassie dissolved into giggles, and I smiled. Her laughter always had that effect on me.

"I can't call him Daddy in my speech. What's wrong with me? I'm going to be an adult. I can't call him Daddy anymore."

"You can always call me Daddy, baby." The first time I'd heard the recording she'd made to practice her valedictorian speech, I'd cried like a baby. Now, I couldn't stop smiling when I listened to it. For that moment, when she giggled and called me Daddy, my little girl was still alive with me.

My little girl. She was stripped from this world. Violently. Stupidly. All because she got involved with those damn bastards from the Yacht Club.

It wasn't enough that they'd been slowly taking over the island, buying up houses and building those awful McMansions. Or racing their boats around the island and making it so you couldn't even take your kids out to swim without worrying about getting run over by their stupid jet skis. They took everything and gave nothing back.

Except for pain.

Well, I'm returning the favor, assholes. How does it feel?

It's time to lose everything too.

It was getting stuffy in the car, and my hands hurt. They were white where I wrapped them around the steering wheel, clutching it so tightly. The rage was taking over. Killing Jake might have calmed the storm of my fury a little last night, but it was raging again this morning.

Raging out of control. I took another swig of wine to get a grip.

People were going about their business. No one noticed me. It was late morning, and nearly everyone had started their day already.

Except *him*. Him, I hadn't seen. Not yet. But I would wait

here until I did. I didn't know where he lived, but I knew where he kept an office, so all I had to do was wait.

A guy like him, pretending to be an upstanding, respectable member of the community, would show up to work sooner or later. It didn't matter that it was broad daylight. I had to do this now. Nothing else mattered.

Maybe I'd screwed up last night. I'd barely made it out of the house before hearing a dog bark. It was close. I should have at least shut the door before I killed Jake.

The cops had shown up not long after. I'd passed them on my way home, their lights and sirens flashing. I'd almost gotten caught because of my carelessness.

But that was then, and this is now.

Now I had to pay those pricks back for what they'd said to my baby girl in those messages. For taking her life. For taking mine. For Belinda.

Payback really is a bitch.

I wasn't so insane that I didn't understand that those three men weren't the ones who'd killed Cassie. Owen Miller had done that. And when Cassie's heart had stopped beating, my grandbaby's heart had too. Owen was in prison now, far beyond my reach. He'd spend the rest of his life in a cage. He'd probably die at the hands of a fellow inmate by year's end. That I could live with.

What I couldn't live with was knowing the three assholes who'd driven Cassie into Miller's arms were free, luring more innocent girls into their trap.

It was my job to stop them. *One to go.* Then I'd stop the men who'd spawned them. And so on and so on.

For my daughter. For my family that you destroyed!

I let go of the steering wheel and shook my hands, getting out all the pins and needles. I had to keep it together. I had a job to do.

Focus!

Oh, speak of the devil...

A car slowed, maneuvering into the reserved parking spot I'd been watching.

I fingered the revolver strapped to my leg. A chill ran up my spine. It was time.

Albert Gilroy climbed out of the passenger side.

"Your time is coming," I whispered.

I smiled as Steven Campbell stepped out of the driver's side. Campbell nodded as Gilroy yelled something I couldn't understand. His eyes darted around like he was looking for someone. Was he looking for me?

Had the sick bastard put it all together? Did he know he was next?

Gilroy shoved Campbell's arm, and the attorney nearly fell, which earned him another tongue lashing from his black-hearted boss.

Oh, this was too good. Too good by far. I could take out Campbell and Gilroy both at the same time. My only regret would be that their deaths would be quick, and I wouldn't get to watch them struggle for breath as they died.

Tucking my phone into the glove box, I pulled the .22 from its holster around my ankle, opened the door, and got out. I pressed the gun close to my body to conceal it.

Walk casually.

I didn't want to draw any attention as I crossed the street. Not yet.

30

R ebecca pulled onto Spring Street, gritting her teeth at the golf cart moving at a snail's pace in front of her.

"That's Robert Leigh!" Hoyt pointed at a man crossing the street.

It was the right build, but this man looked at least twenty years older than the forty-something-year-old who'd lost his daughter a couple weeks ago.

His attention was locked in on something. *Hoyt was right.* Rebecca followed his gaze and saw Steven Campbell and Albert Gilroy arguing in the parking lot of Campbell's office building.

Shit.

Fewer than twenty yards and a few cars and tourists separated the men from Robert Leigh.

Throwing on the sirens, Rebecca hit the gas and brakes, causing the engine to race and the tires to screech, making as much noise as possible. Heads turned to stare as she twisted the wheel and used the cruiser to block off the throughway, tires spinning and smoke pouring around the vehicle.

The loud spectacle worked as intended.

Campbell and Robert both turned. Red-faced, Gilroy threw his arms into the air, his mouth still firing on all cylinders.

Hoyt threw open his door as Rebecca slammed the cruiser in park.

Robert turned back to face his targets. That's when Rebecca saw it reflect the sunlight. His hand clutched a shiny, snub-nosed revolver. He aimed...

Shots echoed off the buildings as she and Hoyt drew their weapons.

Gilroy and Steven disappeared behind a row of parked cars. Glass exploded from a window in the building behind them.

Robert Leigh ran toward where the men had been standing.

Panicked screams rang out as people fled in different directions and chaos descended around them.

Robert managed to get behind one of the cars parallel parked on the road in front of the parking lot where Campbell and Gilroy were hiding. Using the line of cars as a barrier from the law, he was on his way to having clear shots of them both.

"Robert Leigh!" Rebecca couldn't even raise her weapon as people streaked past the front of the cruiser. "Get down! Get down!"

"Out of the way! Sheriff's department!" Hoyt bellowed, swinging one arm to wave an approaching woman to go around.

The tourist froze, staring at him before turning and running the other way.

Robert Leigh had ducked behind another car.

Another shot rang out, followed by a loud *tang* as metal hit metal.

Rebecca ran toward the gunfire, dodging fleeing pedestrians, her gun pointed at the ground. Hoyt kept pace beside her. There hadn't been any screams indicating physical pain, only screams of terror and confusion.

How many shots was that? Four? It's a revolver. Holds five or six. Eight, maybe. But how many shots? Does he have a reload? A speed loader?

"Don't come any closer!"

Rebecca recognized Robert's voice, though it sounded slurred from drinking. It came from farther down the sidewalk, past Campbell's car.

"Robert. It's Hoyt. Put the gun down and your hands up!"

Rebecca veered to the left, staying low and moving as smoothly as she could toward the front of Campbell's car, where she'd followed the trajectory of Robert Leigh's voice. Still, she was depending on Hoyt to talk him down.

"I can't. I have to end this! You didn't see what they said to my baby. What they made her do!"

Her senses on high alert, Rebecca estimated Robert was just in front of her, using Campbell's car as a barricade. She homed in on his voice and carefully lurched a little closer.

"I did see it, Robert. I saw it all." Hoyt's voice cracked. "We'll make sure they see justice."

"They have to pay. You caught Owen, and I appreciate that. But what about all the others? The other girls. The ones they'll lie to, like they did to my Cassie."

Another shot echoed, hitting stone or brick from the sound of it, and Rebecca dropped low, squatting mid-step. She'd made it up to the driver's door. Placing a hand on the pavement, she bent lower. Peering under the car, she saw the bottom of a shoe pointed at her. A man was laid out, his foot hanging over the curb, but she couldn't tell who it was. There was no sign of anyone else.

Was he hiding behind one of the tires? That would be the intelligent thing to do.

"We'll catch them, too, Robert. Give us whatever information you have. We'll track them down. And the girls." Hoyt kept talking, his deep voice echoing around the now-deserted area.

Rebecca moved around to the front of the car, her head on a swivel. The vehicle, a building, a broken window in a decorative brick window frame, a face in the next window.

She grimaced and waved at the person gawking at her, signaling them to get down.

The face disappeared.

Rebecca stepped left. There was another car closer to the building. Robert could be hiding there as well. Why hadn't he answered?

She backed up until she had the front bumper of the other car against her back. Stretching her neck and glancing around, she saw Hoyt looking at her. She waved two fingers, telling him to continue talking.

"Robert, don't let it go down like this. If you have information, give it to us so we can track down everyone involved."

A sob broke out behind her.

Rebecca slid to her right for added safety.

Dammit! She'd almost walked into it. Robert was hiding next to the car behind her, not Campbell's car.

"I don't have any more information." He started sobbing. "All I had were those three numbers. I found out who they were. That's enough for me. The rest is up to you. I just needed to finish this."

"Robert, we need to know what you know. This thing is bigger than three men, and you know it. Help us."

"I needed to finish this, Hoyt!"

Rebecca, still crouched, ran behind the second car she'd been pressed up against, using Hoyt's voice to cover the sound of her movement. She hoped it would distract Robert enough to get the drop on him. His choice of words scared her. His voice, his anguish. Not to mention alcohol was now involved. He was a man on a mission, and his mission was nearly over. What would he do once he realized that? And who was lying on the sidewalk next to the first car?

"What I know is they had to pay."

He'd moved again. He was now closer to the building. There were no other cars close enough for him to hide behind. That meant one thing to Rebecca. Nothing mattered to this man anymore.

Rebecca darted a quick look around the sedan. She didn't see him. Where was he hiding? After another glance, Rebecca spotted a row of decorative bricks that ran down the building wall, just like the ones around the windows.

It had to be an alcove for a doorway, just out of sight from here. She stretched to see it better through the car windows. She saw a foot low to the ground. She'd gone too far. Robert's voice had echoed, and she'd passed his new hiding spot by the door.

"It doesn't matter. I got the ones on my list. The rest is your problem. I'm done." Robert Leigh sat on the stoop of the doorway, shoved into the corner with the gun against his temple. Pain, grief, resignation, and despair were all etched deeply into his face. His hair had white streaks she didn't remember from their first meeting.

Rebecca, anticipating this, scrambled to the back of the car and peered around it.

"They *are* my problem, Robert."

He jerked. His eyes darted around, trying to find her, she assumed.

She moved out a little bit more so he could see her.

Robert's finger tightened on the trigger.

"But you, Robert, could be the solution," she said, stepping into clear view.

His finger eased as his eyebrows furrowed together. "What do you mean?"

Rebecca shifted slightly more to her right, exposing more of herself, but also freeing up her dominant arm, in case she needed to bring her gun into play.

"Tell us what you know, so we can stop them from taking any more girls from our island. You can be Shadow's deadline, our ticking clock to help us take this bastards down."

Robert paid no attention to her gun. But then again, why would he care? He was ready to blow his brains out.

"I can't." Tears poured down Robert's face. "It hurts too much. I've got nothing left. They took my daughter from me, and this morning..." His chest hitched as he took in desperate gulps of air. "They took my wife too. I have no family left. I got my payback. But that's all I had!"

She had to give him hope.

"Belinda isn't dead."

"Yes, she is! She killed herself this morning. I found her on the couch. I saw the empty bottle, and she was cold when I touched her."

"No, we found her. She's alive."

Robert was crying hysterically and shaking his head.

"I swear on my parents' graves, Robert. Belinda's alive."

His swollen eyes lifted. "Sh-she's not d-dead?" His entire demeanor shifted, relaxed.

"She's very much alive. Belinda was in a deep sleep from the meds. One of my men is with her now. That ambulance you hear in the distance is taking her to the hospital. She was cold because her heart had slowed, but it didn't stop."

A tiny gleam of hope sprang into Robert's eyes.

"She's not dead." His face crumpled again. "But I am. I killed three men. I'll spend the rest of my life in prison."

"You will be arrested, yes." She stepped around the car and moved toward him. Her gun was at her side, which she kept turned away from him. "I can't stop that from happening, but I can promise to help you get justice."

He blinked. "How?"

Rebecca lowered her voice. "I'll visit you often, and you can tell me everything you know about the Yacht Club. I won't stop until I take it down. I'll also make sure you're in witness protection, to keep you safe."

Robert lowered his gun until it rested near his neck. "I don't care if I'm safe or not."

"I do." Rebecca meant it. "You're one of the few people on this island who isn't scared of them." She kept her voice low.

Robert leaned forward. Finally, his gun hand came to rest on his knee and pointed off to the side. "What are you suggesting?"

Rebecca pressed her finger against her lips, giving him a sharp look. She leaned back, checking the area around them. She could not afford to be overheard. "Put the gun down so we can talk. I'm willing to work with you on this, but I'm not willing to get accidentally shot. Or have all evidence thrown out because I was caught conspiring with you."

Robert narrowed his eyes. "How can I trust you?"

"Me? You're the one who just killed a man." Rebecca blew out a harsh breath. "I know the rumor mill has been spinning about me since I got here. My past isn't exactly a secret, but I'm sure you know I went head-to-head with a senator. A senator. Because he was bought and paid for and complicit in illegal dealings."

A shiver ran up her spine as she realized how much she had in common with this murderer. He had been willing to destroy his entire life to take down the men he really blamed for the death of his daughter. The same way she had.

Reaching up with her left hand, Rebecca pulled her shirt down, exposing her shoulder and scar.

"I gave up everything, Robert. My career. My reputation.

My home. The love of my life. All to make sure the men who thought they were untouchable faced justice. I almost didn't survive. But I did."

"And then you ended up here, just to see the same shit happening again." A note of frenzy was evident in Robert's voice. "How are we supposed to stop these assholes and protect our kids?"

Again, Rebecca checked to make sure that no one had snuck up behind her. "If you repeat what I'm about to say, I'll deny it." She stared directly into his eyes. "Do you understand?"

Robert's gun came back up as his eyes narrowed. "How am I supposed to trust you? You could be corrupt the same way Wallace was."

"If I were corrupt, I would have shot you already. Or let you do it yourself."

"Unless you just want to take me in so you can figure out what I learned about the Yacht Club."

"I do want to take you in so I can learn what you know." Aggravation was taking over, and she knew that it wouldn't be much longer before she lost this opportunity. She spoke in a rush, trying to get it all out before she choked on it. "Robert, they killed my parents. Both of them. Shot dead in their home. That's the real reason I came back to Shadow Island, to the Sand Dollar Shores. To spend time in a place we were all happy together."

Blood on the cabinets.

Blood on the pillow.

Rebecca had to grind her arm into the bricks next to her. The memory was so strong she could almost smell the blood. Hear her own screams as she wailed for her dead parents.

Robert tracked her movements. "You're...touch-grounding. My therapist told me about that. To cope with...with the memories."

Rebecca took a deep breath, then blew it out, ignoring his comment. "Because of the evidence I've found during this investigation, I've found a possible link between Albert Gilroy and Senator William Morley."

Robert's jaw dropped open, and he stared at her in disbelief. "Really?"

She pointed to him, then herself. "You and me, Robert. We can do this. Together. We'll make every one of them pay. I have some evidence now, but I don't have what you know. How did you link these three men together? We couldn't do it, but you did. I need your help."

Robert Leigh nodded and seemed to be considering her words.

"Please put the gun down. Let me take you in. We don't want," Rebecca made a quote motion with her fingers, "'guards' to show up and stop you from helping me."

"First," Robert rubbed his face with his sleeve, "what's the evidence you found that makes you think I can be of use to you? To prove you're not working with the Yacht Club."

His finger twitched on the trigger, and Rebecca had a flash of fear that she hadn't talked Robert down. Instead, she'd made him more paranoid and redirected his fear and anger onto her.

She took a gamble and inched her way down the brick wall to a crouching position, which put her closer to eye level with Robert Leigh.

"You didn't go into Jake Underwood's home office, so you probably don't know. He and Bryson ran a prostitution ring, and he kept all that information where he lived. We've got his records, his clients, his victims. And the name of everyone who rents a slip at the marina. That's just what we've managed to read through so far. There's a list of girls, but their first names only. I'm not local. You can help figure out who they are." She spoke low and fast, saying whatever she thought might bring him to her side.

Rebecca dropped her voice even lower. "There are already three federal agencies working to link faces and names so the victims can get help and the men can be arrested. But with your assistance, it will go a lot faster. Once a crack is made in a case like that, it spreads fast. Don't you want to be around to see them all go down?"

"Yeah." Robert set the gun down and raised both his hands, surprising her with the suddenness of the movement. "I really want to see that. Even if it's from the inside of a prison."

Tension started leaking out of Rebecca's shoulders. "Great. I hate to do this, but I have to follow protocol." She reached for his gun, retrieved it in one smooth motion, and tucked it into her belt. "Okay, now let's stand up together, slowly."

He did as instructed.

"I need you to lace your fingers behind your head."

He turned around without prompting and followed her instructions.

Rebecca pulled handcuffs from her belt. He didn't flinch as she put the first one on and didn't fight as she pulled his arms down to cuff them behind his back.

Robert was smiling when she turned him back around. "These bastards are going to get everything they deserve."

Footsteps sounded behind Rebecca, and she knew she was nearly out of time.

She leaned as close to Robert as she dared, her voice a whisper. "Spoken like a man in the middle of a grief-based psychotic break. A man who knows nothing about a Yacht Club. A man who *only* went after three random men who bullied his daughter. Do you understand?"

He locked eyes with her, and she hoped that was a confirmation. Then he went limp, and Rebecca struggled to hold him up. Hoyt was at her side a second later and helped her lower Robert Leigh to the ground.

Robert swayed back and opened his eyes, blinking several times. "Hoyt...where am I?" He started jerking at his handcuffs. "What's happening?"

Rebecca mentally exhaled. The man caught on quick. He was intelligent and resourceful enough to have tracked down three men just from their burner phone numbers.

As the serial killer turned cohort began to sob, Rebecca did what had to be done.

"Robert Leigh, you're under arrest for the murders of Bryson Gilroy, Jake Underwood, and Steven Campbell. Anything you say..."

31

The state police came in to help with the cleanup. As Hoyt said, they were really good at directing traffic.

Rebecca had been buried in paperwork since Robert Leigh's arrest and had very little time to think through everything they'd said to each other. Neither of them had mentioned "Yacht Club" loud enough for anyone else to hear.

At least, she hoped so.

She wanted as many people as possible to believe that Robert was simply a man driven insane by the death of his daughter. A man who went after three people he'd learned had manipulated Cassie in her final days. Vengeance for his daughter, not a planned attack against an organization that would send lawyers to sway judges—or worse, assassins—to silence him in prison.

Rebecca had even managed to get Robert sent straight to Southwestern Virginia Mental Health Institute for evaluation and treatment and, eventually, competency testing. It was the safest place until she could get him into witness protection.

She had a lot to figure out before WITSEC could happen.

A knock sounded on Rebecca's door. Darian peeked in. She waved him inside.

He came bearing coffee and some good news. "Two pieces of good news. We found Bryson's Jeep on a lot near Beaman Beach."

Rebecca exhaled a long breath. "That is good news. We'll need forensics to process it, just in case any new evidence comes to light."

He beamed at her. "I've already called them."

Rebecca beamed right back. "Great. What's the second piece of good news?"

"Just learned that Belinda Leigh came out of her coma. Looks like she's going to make it."

Tears burned Rebecca's eyes, and she covered the emotion by taking a sip of the strong brew. "That's good news, I hope."

Recovery would be up to Belinda, Rebecca knew, and the woman might not appreciate the second chance she'd been given.

Darian wrinkled his nose. "On a less positive note, Albert Gilroy is on line one."

Rebecca glanced over at the flashing button, hate gripping her throat.

Following Robert Leigh's arrest, Gilroy had come out from where he'd been hiding, and did what he did best... made a total ass of himself.

"Is that the man who killed my son?"

"That's the man who killed your lawyer right in front of you," Rebecca responded instead, glancing over at the sheet-covered body Gilroy had sidestepped on his way to her.

"I want that madman in the electric chair," he sputtered, his face an alarming shade of red.

"Virginia abolished capital punishment in—"

He pointed a finger at her nose. "I'll bring it back!"

Wrapping her fist around the offending finger, Rebecca lowered it. "Please do. I have a feeling I know some people who can ride the lightning with him...if he goes to prison at all."

Gilroy yanked his finger from her grip but didn't stick it in her face again. "What do you mean? He's a murderer."

Rebecca felt all the life drain out of her eyes as she stared at him. She was so tired of this man and his pompous attitude.

"Right now, he's a mentally unstable individual who's raving about protecting his dead daughter from the people who got her killed. He's on the way to a mental health facility for evaluation."

"A hospital?" A blood vessel in Gilroy's forehead bulged. "I'll have your badge for this, young lady."

"Repetitive." She swiped a finger in the air. "Next."

A vein began to pulse in his right temple. "This is unbelievable. How—" He swayed.

As repulsive as he was to Rebecca, she jumped forward and caught his arm. "Paramedic!"

She was swarmed by two. The last she saw of Gilroy, he was being loaded in an ambulance.

"Sheriff?"

Rebecca glanced up to find Darian watching her closely. "Yes."

He frowned. "Gilroy's on line one."

Her cheeks heated. "Sorry. The man drives me to distraction."

Darian grinned, his straight, white teeth a stark contrast against his dark skin. "Understandable. I'll leave you to it."

When her door clicked shut, Rebecca groaned. Maybe if she made Gilroy wait long enough, he'd hang up. She snorted at the thought.

She snatched up the receiver and took a deep breath. "How can I be of service, Mr. Gilroy? I trust you're feeling better?"

"I demand to know the status of the investigation."

So charming.

She stepped straight into her standard response. "Robert Leigh lost his daughter a couple weeks ago. We caught her killer almost immediately. But Robert never recovered from that loss. I'm afraid he's gone mad. I also investigated his daughter's case, and I haven't found any connection between your son and Owen Miller."

Okay. Maybe that last line wasn't standard, but it was meant to get the bastard off her back. She didn't feel a bit bad about manipulating the facts.

"Who is Owen Miller? And what does he have to do with my son?"

"He's the man who seduced and then killed Robert's teenage daughter. As far as I can tell, he has nothing to do with your son, Jake Underwood, or Steven Campbell. And he sure as hell doesn't own a superyacht."

Several seconds ticked by before Gilroy spoke. "I could have told you that."

She pressed her fingers to her temple. "Anything else I can do for you today?"

"Considering how…reasonable you're being, I'll remove my candidate for consideration as sheriff." He presented the idea like a man selling used cars.

"That's good to hear."

And it was. Taking him and his cronies down would be much easier with the full weight of the sheriff's department and its resources at Rebecca's back.

32

"Here ya go! You two let me know if you need anything else." The waitress grinned as she placed a huge plate in front of Rebecca.

Before the young woman took two steps back, Rebecca picked up her burger and took a large bite. Her eyes rolled up in her head, and she would have moaned if her mouth wasn't full. The pickles were crisp, and so was the lettuce. The burger was juicy, and the slice of tomato was thick and tasted farm fresh.

"I told you they had good burgers." Hoyt laughed and set his beer can on the table. They were both off the clock, and he'd talked her into joining him for some much-deserved food.

Rebecca washed her burger down with a coffee stout.

Hoyt wrinkled his nose. "How can you drink one of those things while having a meal? It's basically a wheat field in a can."

"Like this!" Rebecca took another gulp, then followed it up with a bite of her burger, smaller this time so she could eat a sweet potato fry too. Swallowing it down, she flicked a disdainful finger at his can. "Better than that horse piss you're drinking."

"Filtered horse piss, thank you very much." He tapped his finger on the can. "They even put the horse right on the label."

Rebecca laughed. "I'll stick with mine. You should try it, though. Step out of your comfort zone a little."

Hoyt shook his head, picking up his burger. "I drink beer to *be comfortable.* What's the point of being uncomfortable while trying to get comfortable? It just doesn't make any sense to me."

Still munching on a fry, she had to agree with him. "That does make sense. I suppose. It just seems a shame not to try something new."

"You mean like telling a suspect to pretend he's insane in order to avoid charges?"

Rebecca nearly choked but managed to make it sound like a laugh. She covered her mouth with her hand, giving herself time to think. Hoyt couldn't have heard her talk privately to Robert Leigh. He must have been referring to what he did hear her say when talking the man down. "That's...not new. It's actually one of the oldest tricks in the book."

Halfway to his mouth, Hoyt froze with his burger in midair. He frowned. "What?"

Thinking quick, she lifted a shoulder. "You know we're allowed to lie to suspects, right?"

He nodded and took a bite. "Uh-huh."

"And tell them that the charges will be fewer if they cooperate?"

Hoyt swallowed. "But...you basically told him to pretend to be insane. Right?"

"I don't think he was pretending. Did you notice how white his hair is? His daughter died on the twelfth. I double-checked it when I got back to the office. Two weeks ago, he didn't have a spot of white in his hair. Now it's taking over like crabgrass in the spring."

Hoyt ran a hand through his graying strands. "Maybe he missed his hair appointment?"

Rebecca smiled at the deputy's attempt at humor. "Psychotic breaks are strange things. That's one sign that it could have happened, hair turning white due to a severe emotional shock. Either way, a trained professional would've been called in to evaluate him. Any attorney would insist on it. This beelined him to Southwestern. Besides, it worked. He stopped shooting and surrendered peacefully."

Rebecca wasn't sure why she was downplaying what she'd done. It wasn't that she distrusted Hoyt, but maybe she didn't fully trust him either. After all, she had trusted people close to her in the Bureau, and look how that had turned out.

She wasn't lying to Hoyt either, just not telling him the whole truth. Just like she hadn't told him that she planned to pump Robert Leigh for information moving forward.

"And the deal with taking him to the hospital for evaluation?"

Rebecca leaned in. "That was so he wouldn't have an 'accident' in jail. He killed three wealthy and well-connected people who aren't afraid to confront a couple of armed law enforcement officers in a parking garage."

Hoyt paled. "True."

"From what I've seen in the little time I've had to go over Wallace's files, Wallace did try to file charges a few times, but even a solid case would fall apart once it moved up the pipeline."

Hoyt wiped his mouth with a napkin. "That happened more than a few times. And I know we didn't screw anything up."

Rebecca ran a finger around the rim of her beer can. "I

agree, but once a case hits the courts, that's a different story. I'll need to dig into those court cases to see if they have anything in common."

"You're just going to look up the court records and... figure this all out?"

She wished it were that easy.

"It'll take time. I'll need to examine why some cases are tossed but not others. For example, if the same Assistant Commonwealth's Attorney always tosses our cases, then that ACA may have it out for us for some reason. If it's the same ACA, but he lets some go through and others not, then I need to see if it's the same officer that's on the paperwork, and on and on and on from there. Simple scientific method. To find out what's causing the unwanted result, you search for the variables in common."

Hoyt squeezed the bridge of his nose between his thumb and index finger. "I can tell you now, from what I remember, those cases didn't have a lot of people in common, and there's no way all of them had the same person involved each time."

"Then it's the facility we need to check, and we need to find out what links the people who were charged." She took another bite of her burger.

"That sounds like a lot of boring, mind-numbing, butt-flattening, tummy-fattening, overtime-sucking hours sitting at a desk." Hoyt lifted his chin, frowning at something over her shoulder.

She glanced behind her. "What's wrong?"

"Turn around. Check out the news."

Rebecca wiped her hands on her napkin and twisted in her seat until she could see the television on the wall.

The ticker along the bottom had city and county names running across the screen. It took her a second to realize that they were all nearby areas. And the title on the left-hand side read *Tropical Storm Boris Strengthening into Category One Hurricane.*

Rebecca turned to face Hoyt. "You said it was projected to hit the Carolinas first."

He held up his hands like she was pointing a gun. "Shit happens and storms turn."

"Turn that shit up, would ya?" someone in the restaurant called out.

Swiveling back to the screen, Rebecca strained to hear the weatherman.

"Tropical Storm Boris continues to build speed and is projected to be a category one hurricane by the time it makes landfall tomorrow afternoon." The weatherman motioned to another mass of clouds coming in from the west. *"Initial projections predicted Boris to hit in the Charleston area of South Carolina, but this storm system is pushing Boris farther up the coast."*

The camera shifted to a perky blond wearing a crimson blouse. *"Any ideas where Boris will make landfall?"*

The weatherman waved a hand over a huge chunk of the Atlantic coast.

Rebecca whirled back to Hoyt. "What the hell does that mean?"

He snorted. "That's weatherman speak for 'who the hell knows?'"

"You've got to be kidding me. Is there ever a dull moment on this island?"

Hoyt finished the beer and crushed the can in his fist.

"Not since you got here."

The End
To be continued...

Thank you for reading.

All of the *Shadow Island Series* books can be found on Amazon.

ACKNOWLEDGMENTS

How does one properly thank everyone involved in taking a dream and making it a reality? Here goes.

In addition to our families, whose unending support provided the foundation for us to find the time and energy to put these thoughts on paper, we want to thank the editors who polished our words and made them shine.

Many thanks to our publisher for risking taking on two newbies and giving us the confidence to become bona fide authors.

More than anyone, we want to thank you, our readers, for sharing your most important asset, your time, with this book. We hope with all our hearts we made it worthwhile.

Much love,

Mary & Lori

ABOUT THE AUTHOR

Mary Stone

Mary Stone lives among the majestic Blue Ridge Mountains of East Tennessee with her two dogs, four cats, a couple of energetic boys, and a very patient husband.

As a young girl, she would go to bed every night, wondering what type of creature might be lurking underneath. It wasn't until she was older that she learned that the creatures she needed to most fear were human.

Today, she creates vivid stories with courageous, strong heroines and dastardly villains. She invites you to enter her world of serial killers, FBI agents but never damsels in distress. Her female characters can handle themselves, going toe-to-toe with any male character, protagonist or antagonist.

Discover more about Mary Stone on her website.
www.authormarystone.com

Lori Rhodes

As a tiny girl, from the moment Lori Rhodes first dipped her toe into the surf on a barrier island of Virginia, she was in love. When she grew up and learned all the deep, dark secrets and horrible acts people could commit against each other, she couldn't stop the stories from coming out of the other end of her pen. Somehow, her magical island and the darkness got mixed together and ended up in her first novel. Now, she spends her days making sure the guests at her beach rental cottages are happy, and her nights dreaming up the characters who love her island as much as she does.

Connect with Mary Online

facebook.com/authormarystone

goodreads.com/AuthorMaryStone

bookbub.com/profile/3378576590

pinterest.com/MaryStoneAuthor

Made in the USA
Las Vegas, NV
03 February 2023

66770436R00151